"We're go[...]
as adults who are only interested in
our daughter's best interests?"

Megan nodded, hoping to reassure him.

"All right. Sounds like a plan." Grabbing his
glass in one hand and the decanter in the
other, Nic strode toward her. "Come on. Let's
go talk money."

Megan didn't get a chance to reply, or to
back away from the archway of the entry
to the dining room before he was on top
of her. Hanging on to her own glass so she
didn't do anything stupid like spill wine all
over herself, she glanced up at him and was
startled at what she saw in his golden-brown
gaze.

Surprise.

It flared in his eyes unmistakably, and with
a gasp of premonition, Megan knew what he
was going to do even before he took that last
step that closed the distance between them.

Before he brought his mouth down on hers.

Dear Reader,

New Orleans, Louisiana. Historic. Legendary. One of a kind. A city that has always been near and dear to my heart—and to the hearts of so many whose lives were touched by Hurricane Katrina.

In the years since Katrina, this magnificent city is reemerging stronger and more unique than ever through the efforts of brave citizens, generous benefactors and people who care enough to take an opportunity to make difficult changes for a greater good.

Change doesn't come easily. Opening our eyes to our flaws demands a great deal of courage and accountability. But it's through change that we grow. So in honor of New Orleans, *Then There Were Three* is a story all about growth and second chances. *Ordinary women. Extraordinary romance.* That's what Harlequin Superromance is all about.

I hope you enjoy Megan, Nic and Violet's story of how they grow into a unique family unit all their own. I love hearing from readers, so please visit me at www.jeanielondon.com.

Peace and blessings,

Jeanie London

Then There Were Three
Jeanie London

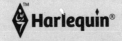

Harlequin®

TORONTO NEW YORK LONDON
AMSTERDAM PARIS SYDNEY HAMBURG
STOCKHOLM ATHENS TOKYO MILAN MADRID
PRAGUE WARSAW BUDAPEST AUCKLAND

ISBN-13: 978-0-373-71699-9

THEN THERE WERE THREE

Copyright © 2011 by Jeanie LeGendre

www.eHarlequin.com

Printed in U.S.A.

ABOUT THE AUTHOR

Jeanie London writes romances because she believes in happily-ever-afters. Not the "love conquers all" kind, but the "two people love each other, so they can conquer anything" kind. She lives in sunny Florida with her wonderful family—two beautiful daughters and her very own romance hero, who reads fantasy and watches football and doesn't mind eating the same meal three nights in a row while she's writing. And she loves to write! She has published twenty-five books in romance mass market, trade paperback and hard cover, winners of such industry awards as *RT Book Reviews* Reviewers' Choice, National Readers' Choice, Holt Medallion, Reader and Bookbuyers' Best, Venus Book Club and Waldenbooks' Most Romantic Moment. As far as Jeanie is concerned, she has the very best job in the world.

For everyone impacted by Hurricane Katrina.
All those who lost their lives. All those who lost
loved ones. All those who lost beloved pets,
treasured homes and much-needed jobs.
All those who were able to rebuild.
All those who weren't. All those who found
hope and all those who brought hope.
God bless you all.

And special thanks to Maryam H.
for your writer's eyes. You are talented and
creative and smart and generous
and such a delight to know!

CHAPTER ONE

"MOM WOULD KILL ME IF she knew where I was right now," Violet Bell whispered, though no one was around to hear her. The words bubbled out of her mouth anyway as she ran across the street to change her hiding place for the zillionth time. The alley was the best place to hide, but then she couldn't see the front of the building without being noticeable. She didn't want to be noticed.

Dashing into the alcove of a parking garage, she pressed against the wall and waited, straining to hear any sound from inside. The garage echoed like a cavern, so she'd hear an approaching car with lots of time to get out of the way before the door opened.

Violet knew the drill by now.

Daring a glance, she shifted her gaze from the locked doorway of the brick condo building across the street—she'd already tried to get in—to the garage entrance.

Nada. Not a soul in sight.

She swallowed a laugh. Hysteria, probably, because she felt really bad. She wouldn't lie. Mom and GigiMarie would be having total cows right now, not knowing for sure where Violet was. Mom was insane about that kind of stuff on a normal day. And GigiMarie, who called herself Violet's honorary grandmother, wasn't much better. They were on a whole different *continent* today, which was hardly normal.

Or maybe Violet was distracting herself from how

badly she needed to pee. She'd been stalking this building ever since the taxi had dropped her off around two o'clock this afternoon.

It was after ten now.

The only thing saving her was that she hadn't had anything to drink in forever. On purpose. Earlier there'd been places open with bathrooms. She'd found a bunch of art galleries and a kids' museum in one direction. But she couldn't get in without paying admission and she hated wasting Mom's money on something so stupid. Not on top of everything else she'd been spending.

The tire place a few blocks in the other direction had been perfect. She pretended to belong in the customers' waiting area. Someone's kid killing time in front of the TV while the car was serviced. That had worked until the tire place closed.

Violet hadn't taken one sip of water since. Of course, she'd barely been able to choke down the crumbled granola bars that had made up one very crappy dinner, but she'd been starving so, oh, well.

And now that *he'd* come home she wasn't moving from this spot. He'd been driving an unmarked police cruiser. She'd only caught a glimpse of him through the windshield—the only window that wasn't too darkly tinted to see through—before he'd turned, but she would have recognized him anywhere.

Her *dad*.

She'd searched him on the internet before leaving Chile and had found a few photos. The best had been on the New Orleans Police Department website, but there'd been others. The newspaper had published one with the mayor who'd appointed her dad as chief of police. Another had been an announcement that a brother who looked like her dad had accepted some fellowship at Charity Hospital.

Violet had an uncle, too. And he was a doctor.

Just the thought gave her a thrill. Who needed a drink or a bathroom? She'd hold it all night if she had to because now that her dad had come home, she wasn't leaving until he did. She didn't want to miss him.

Not that he was likely to be going anywhere at this time of night, but he was the chief of police. Cops got dragged out on calls all the time if she could believe *SVU* and *NCIS*.

Resting her head against the wall, Violet swallowed another laugh. She couldn't believe she was really here.

Of course that thought lasted about one second before she thought about Mom again.

Ugh.

It wasn't that she wanted Mom to get gray hair. But what was Violet supposed to do? Let Mom keep her from her dad? That wasn't fair. And Mom was usually pretty good about things like that. She always let Violet and GigiMarie decide what projects to accept with that nutty job of hers. Not that Violet didn't like traveling. She did. So did GigiMarie. But Mom's projects always lasted at least a year…who wanted to get stuck in a jungle somewhere for that long?

But this time Mom had turned down a project without ever even saying a word. And a project right here in New Orleans at that. They hadn't been in the States since Violet was eight, and this was the only place in the world they had any real family.

Okay, so Mom wasn't tight with the grandparents. Violet had only seen them, like, three times in her whole life. Something was up with that, but would it have really killed Mom to suck it up so Violet could see what being around family was like?

She didn't think that was asking too much. But Mom hadn't even asked what Violet thought about going to New Orleans, which was totally un-Mom. Instead, she'd shot back an email declining to even think about the project until some other time. Violet made it her life's quest to find out why.

And found *him*.

Which had been sheer brilliance, if she had to say so herself. Her birth certificate hadn't helped one bit.

Father unknown?

That was the stupidest thing she'd ever heard. Mom had to know. Violet thought about asking, but hadn't had to. One trip into Mom's locked fireproof box had given Violet a big head start.

A hiss echoed through the quiet. She frowned in the direction of the sound, gaze riveting to the front door of her dad's building as it swung wide and someone stepped outside.

OMG! Her *dad!*

Just the sight of him melted away all the bad. She was in New Orleans, the only place in the world she had any family. But now…she had a *real* family. A dad and a doctor uncle.

And there her dad was, walking quickly across the street, as if he knew exactly where he was going and wanted to get there fast. Her heart just came to a complete stop when he got close enough that she could actually see the expression on his face. Serious. Kind of like his photo on the website. His face was all hard lines and his hair was buzzed short.

Then he passed and her heart started beating again. He hadn't noticed her. Whew! Still, she didn't leave the shelter of the garage until he'd turned the corner of Magazine Street. Then she hauled butt after him.

Thank God the street was lined with cars to keep her out of sight. Her dad was a cop, so he noticed things. If he spotted her, she'd have to explain who she was. She wasn't ready to do that yet. Stupid, since she'd traveled all this way to see him, but... He didn't scare her. He looked okay, as far as dads went.

He was tall and rugged. Buff but not too buff, and he had her dark blond hair and tan skin. But she'd already known that from the photo. She was Italian. Who knew?

Violet shouldn't be surprised that he was fit. Mom was obsessed with fitness, always eating right and taking vitamins and getting enough exercise... She could hear the familiar litany streaming in her brain even on a different continent.

Her dad wasn't really dad material, she decided, the more she watched him. At least not like other dads she knew. Her friend Camille's father always joked about the doughnut around his middle, but that doughnut was more like the tire on a 4x4.

And Maddie's dad was even shorter than Maddie. That was saying something. Gabby's dad never came out of his shed so Violet couldn't be sure about him.

Esperanza's dad was about the only one who was remotely babe material, and he was gay. Of course, he'd only figured that out after marrying Esperanza's mom. But guilt worked big-time on Christmases and birthdays and whenever Esperanza needed the newest technology, so she didn't make it a big deal.

Nope, Violet's dad wasn't really dad material, after all. Totally not the kind of guy she could see Mom hooking up with. Violet shook off that thought fast. The idea of Mom *hooking up* made her twitch. *Puh-leeze.* Fortunately, her dad distracted her by crossing the street.

She could see better now and not worry so much that he'd hear her and turn around. If she'd have known she'd be doing the whole stalker thing, she'd have worn sneakers and not flip-flops that made stupid soft slapping sounds with every step she took. And she couldn't even change because all her clothes were still in the duffel bag she'd stored in a locker at the airport.

But her dad didn't notice. He seemed pretty focused actually, distracted. Violet wasn't sure. She tried to blend in, but there weren't many people around. She guessed tourists weren't in this part of town at night.

And it wasn't too, *too* dark, either. The almost-full moon still let her see the sky through the trees and the buildings. And the streetlamps helped her keep her dad in sight.

Her *dad*.

The cell phone in her pocket vibrated and she automatically slipped it out to see who was calling.

Mom.

For a second, Violet froze. Oh, man. The very last thing in the world she wanted to do right now was pick up. She'd been shooting Mom drive-by texts since leaving Chile, telling her not to worry. Of course, Violet hadn't told her where she was going. She'd left Mom to figure out that part on her own.

The vibrating stopped. The call had rolled to voice mail.

Mom would be in a panic, Violet knew and felt bad. She should shoot another text to keep Mom from having a total meltdown. But Violet couldn't. Not right now. Not when she was stalking her dad. If she took her eyes off him for a second, she might lose him.

The vibrating started again.

Mom would know that Violet's phone was on since it took so long to go to voice mail. She'd know Violet was ignoring the call. Or, knowing Mom, she'd think Violet was being held captive by some pervert and *couldn't* pick up the call. Or, even worse, that she was dead.

Argh.

She hit the talk button. "I'm alive, Mom."

The dead silence that greeted her from the other end of the phone swelled so loud that Violet felt guiltier than she'd ever felt in her life. She breathed a sigh that had nothing to do with how fast she was walking.

"Mom, I'm okay."

More silence. Now her dad was approaching a big intersection, so Violet had to hang for a sec to see what he did. And pay attention because there were lots of cars zipping up and down this street.

"Violet." Mom totally didn't sound like Mom.

"I'm perfectly okay, so please stop worrying."

"You're safe."

"Totally."

If one didn't count crossing a busy street against the light. But her dad was crossing when there was a break in the traffic—some chief of police!—so Violet had no choice.

"I know you're going to kill me." She cut right to the chase. "I'll probably be grounded forever, but please give me a chance to explain—"

"Violet, we can discuss everything when I get there," Mom shot back, suddenly sounding like Mom again. "Right now all I'm interested in is your safety and your location."

"I'm in New Orleans—"

"I know you're in New Orleans, and I'm glad you're okay. *Where* are you in New Orleans?"

Mom did not want coordinates. Oh, man. Here goes...

"With Dad." Violet watched the figure in the distance, still slipping in and out of the light from the streetlamps.

"You're with your father now?"

"Yes." Sort of, anyway.

"Okay." More silence. "You'll be safe until I get there?"

"You don't have to come—"

"Violet Nicole Bell, I'm not sure what part of this you think is acceptable, but—"

"Violet Nicole Bell *DiLeo*. You forgot—"

"I did not forget anything, young lady."

Whoa! Violet pulled the phone from her ear and glanced at it. She'd never heard *that* tone before.

"I would have explained if you'd given me the chance," Mom continued, her voice a raw whisper. "All you had to do was ask. You didn't have to put your safety at risk by *running away*."

"Really, Mom? Really?" The words were out of Violet's mouth before she could stop them. "Like I haven't traveled before."

"We'll discuss this in person. Now please put your father on. And don't vanish. I'll speak with you when we're through."

Violet didn't have a chance to respond because one second her dad was in front of her and the next he was gone. Oh, man. She was lagging because she wasn't paying attention. Did he turn the corner? She started to run.

"Dad can't talk right now. Can we call you back?"

"First give me the details about where you're staying, and a phone number, too—"

"Gotta go. Battery's dying." She tried not to sound winded, but she was starting to breath heavy. "I'll charge my phone and call you back, okay?"

"Violet, don't—"

Click.

Calling back wasn't okay. That much Violet knew, but she had to find her dad before she lost him completely.

"Don't worry, Mom," she whispered, even though Mom wasn't there to hear her.

CHAPTER TWO

MEGAN BELL SANK INTO the chair, relief sapping every drop of strength from her legs. She stared disbelieving at the BlackBerry as the display darkened.

Violet.

Then she let her eyes flutter shut, blocked out everything but the sound of her daughter's voice, impatient, irritable, *alive*... Okay, Violet was alive.

Start there, Megan, she warned herself. *Don't get too far ahead here. Violet's alive.*

Since this whole nightmare began, Megan had received three texts. She'd tracked credit card purchases to piece together a trajectory that had her daughter heading to New Orleans of all places, but until she'd heard Violet's voice...

"Take a deep breath, dear, and tell me what she said."

Megan did exactly that then forced herself to open her eyes to find Marie looking as relieved as Megan felt. As always, Marie's presence had a calming effect.

A slender, stately woman with bright white hair that fell in gentle waves around her face, Marie Gleason was an honorary grandmother to Violet and dearest friend in the world to Megan. She was such an important part of their lives, in fact, that after her husband had passed away nearly six years ago, she'd come to live with Megan and Violet, traveling to whatever part of the world Megan's job took them. As a project consultant for nonprofit organizations, she worked all over the world.

"I'm good." She forced the words out, as much to reassure Marie as to convince herself. "Violet's with... *him.*"

Too many years had passed for Megan to wrap her mouth around *his* name so easily. Years of mental preparation to explain the situation to Violet about why she'd chosen not to tell him about his daughter. But all Megan's careful preparation for an unavoidable conversation was wasted since she hadn't anticipated the impulsivity of a headstrong teenager.

Marie crossed the room and sat on the ottoman in front of Megan. "Well, you've known it was coming. I'm surprised Violet lasted this long. A girl's relationship with her father is so important. You know that."

"I know." Her own father had influenced so much in her life, rocky though their relationship had been for the past fifteen years.

Reaching forward, Marie slipped her hands around Megan's and gave a supportive squeeze. "It's going to be okay, dear. You can only control so much."

Megan nodded. She knew that, too.

Had it only been twenty-four hours since this nightmare had begun? Twenty-four hours since Violet hadn't returned from her friend's house, where she was supposed to have spent the night during their spring break from school. She'd been texting at all the appropriate times—at night before bed, in the morning when she awoke—so Megan had had no reason to suspect her daughter wasn't where she was supposed to be.

If she'd had any clue that Violet had unearthed the hidden past, Megan might have been able to address the situation before it had gotten out of control. The very thought made her struggle for another breath.

Out of control? This situation was a train wreck.

"If she had questions, why wouldn't she ask me, Marie? Why all this subterfuge and drama?"

"I'm as surprised by that as you are," Marie admitted. "By the subterfuge, anyway. Violet doesn't usually mince words. I'm not surprised much by the drama. She is fourteen."

Fair enough. Violet was an only child, used to exercising a fair amount of control over her life. While Megan took her parenting responsibilities seriously, she felt equally strongly that their daily lives should take everyone's needs into consideration. She liked to think of it as a democratic dictatorship, with the dictator part only surfacing if all attempts at negotiation failed.

She'd never wanted to shelter or control her daughter the way she'd been sheltered and controlled growing up. She wanted Violet to learn to explore and enjoy life, not live by someone else's narrow interpretation of right and wrong. To have balance and flexibility and accountability and appreciation for whatever life threw her way.

And, Megan supposed, she was getting a taste of her philosophy in action now. Violet clearly hadn't thought about the effect of her actions on anyone except herself. She hadn't even considered school, which would be back in session next week.

"We've been dismissing all her moodiness as hormonal." Megan groaned, feeling stupid and guilty and horribly powerless. "How could I have missed this?"

"You're not a mind reader, dear. If Violet had something brewing and wanted to keep it from you, then she would have."

"No argument there. This had to have been percolating for a while. How she even managed to find out who he was…" This was all Megan's fault. For trying to cover all the bases.

If she hadn't asked her attorney to add a clause in her will entrusting Marie, as Violet's guardian, to facilitate a meeting with Nic should Violet want to know her father…

If she hadn't kept that photograph, one of her only connections to the past, so Violet would have one keepsake of her parents together…

"And the trip. She hopped on a flight for another continent without even leaving a note."

Marie's eyes twinkled, and for the first time since this whole nightmare began, she looked amused. "Well, you reared her, after all. Did you really expect anything less than a competent and independent young lady?"

"*Competent? Independent?* Marie, she flat out *ran away.* From South America to New Orleans. And right when I've been angsting over whether or not to take a project there. The timing can't be coincidental. Oh, I honestly can't believe this."

Megan buried her face into her outstretched hands, unable to wrap her brain around Violet's journey. All the things that might happen to a young girl traveling alone— Another deep breath. Her beautiful daughter— Right now she was north of the equator while Megan was still south.

With *him.*

What part of this was okay?

"Come on, dear," Marie said softly. "You'll have nearly seventeen hours in the air to dwell on all the whys and why nots and what you might have dones.

Let me help you pack. We have to leave for the airport soon."

Deep breath. She looked up, ready to cope again. "Okay, thanks. I don't know what I'd do without you. You're always the calm in the storm."

"Then you should let me fix you a bite to eat, too. You haven't eaten anything."

"I'm fine. I had soup last night."

Marie had the advantage and ran with it. "I would hardly call hot water and a bouillon cube soup. You didn't even drink the whole thing."

"I'm having trouble swallowing." Stress had that effect.

Marie didn't approve, but didn't bother arguing. "I'm packing munchies in your carry-on. They'll be there if you start to feel faint."

"Thank you." Megan propelled herself into action, suddenly infused with purpose—mania most likely— but she'd take whatever she could get.

Striding across the living room of the rental that had been their home for over a year and a half, she headed into her closet and dragged out the bag that was never far away.

Marie was right. She'd have plenty of time on the flight to obsess about the mess she'd made of all their lives.

At least Violet was safe now. With *him*.

Megan might not have spoken with the man since the summer after her high school graduation, but she knew in her heart he would never hurt their daughter regardless of whether he'd known of her existence or not. Of course, finding out he even had a daughter would knock him back a few steps.

That thought overwhelmed her again, forced her to

grab the doorjamb to hang on. Squeezing her eyes shut, Megan tried to manage the sensation that things were impossibly out of control.

It wasn't only *him* or the idea of him being sandbagged by an unexpected daughter after so many years. As if that wasn't enough. She was also struggling with memories of a time in her life when she'd felt so powerless and alone, so betrayed.

But not by *him*. There'd never been any doubt he'd assume responsibility, none at all. She'd felt betrayed by her parents, by their refusal to accept that Megan didn't want to give up her daughter for adoption.

Nor had they prepared her for any life but the one they'd deemed acceptable. They'd sheltered her so completely that Megan didn't have the first clue about how to cope when an unplanned pregnancy had turned her life upside down.

She was a much stronger and better person for learning how to stand on her own, and for that she was truly grateful. But she'd tried to rear Violet differently, to embrace life to the fullest, to be responsible for her actions. She'd always wanted Violet to have the skills to cope with whatever came up, to roll with the punches and trust herself to make good choices.

This choice had not been good. Her daughter had been clever enough to track down her father, but she didn't know the whole story, wouldn't understand why Megan had chosen to keep her a secret.

A memory of the sweet little girl who'd loved to chatter about everything, always trusting her thoughts to her mom, suddenly brought tears to Megan's eyes. Those sturdy little arms would wrap around her neck and cling so tight.

Clearly, Violet didn't trust her thoughts to Megan anymore.

If she had only asked... Of course, she shouldn't have had to. Megan should have been honest, instead of choosing to wait until Violet asked, which would have signaled she was old enough to handle a truth that would rock her world. But there had been no perfect solution to the mess Megan had made. None.

There had only been damage control.

Throwing open the closet doors, she stared blindly at the neat row of clothing. Formal wear. Suits. Business casual. Casual casual. Purses and belts hanging from a unique hanger that Bonsom, their maintenance man in Ghana, had fashioned from akasa, a local wood. Shoes lined neatly on a three-tiered shoe rack for easy access. Orderly.

Exactly what her thoughts weren't right now.

Megan hoped with her whole heart and soul that *he* had handled the shock of finding out about his daughter well.

Violet had sounded okay, but Megan knew her daughter, and meeting her father must have been the most important thing in her world to prompt this titanic mutiny.

If things didn't turn out well, Violet would be so hurt. And *he* hadn't had a chance to prepare. He would have been blindsided by the news. Who knew what was going on in his personal life? She could only learn so much on the internet. What if Violet had to not only contend with her father's reaction, but the reactions of his loved ones? Given his position in the NOPD, what if an illegitimate daughter was not only a shocker, but an embarrassment?

Megan had almost placed Violet for adoption. She'd

learned all about the process. She knew children sought out birth parents all the time, but reunions didn't always yield fairy-tale endings.

If only they'd have had the one all-crucial conversation, they could have come up with a solution to deal with this mess together. A solution that would have prepared Violet and not left *him* unexpectedly facing a daughter who looked so much like him.

Megan's thoughts raced with a plea— *Please, please, please don't let Violet be heartbroken.*

Or...*Nic.*

There, she'd said his name. In her head at least.

CHAPTER THREE

"NOW WHAT IN HELL IS this problem you couldn't tell me about on the phone, Jurado?" Dominic DiLeo, newly installed Superintendent of the New Orleans Police Department, demanded when he caught up with the night's shift commander.

"It's a juvenile, Chief." Deputy Chief Emile Jurado cast a scowling glance around the operations center as if afraid half the duty shift might overhear them. "Picked her up last night in the Quarter for curfew infraction."

Nic stared at the short powerhouse of a man, clearly missing something. "What's the problem?"

Another glance around the room. "Not here."

"Let's go to my office." Nic led the way through the rank and file of New Orleans's finest, inclining his head in silent greeting whenever he made eye contact with any of his men.

Keeping the benign expression on his face proved to take some effort. He was in no mood to play twenty questions this morning. Not after a near-sleepless night spent dealing with his younger brother Damon's latest drama.

No one in the family was remotely unhappy Damon's girlfriend had dumped him and run. No one was even surprised—except by how long she'd hung around. If

Damon ever listened to anyone, he wouldn't have been shocked Roxy had vanished from the apartment they'd shared with no more than *Ciao* scribbled on a napkin and the contents of their joint checking account.

Nic was damned tired of cleaning up Damon's messes. And everyone else's for that matter. Nic had put his own life on hold after his father had died. As the oldest, it had been his responsibility to see everyone settled.

Vince's residency at Charity Hospital should have been the end of the line for Nic. He'd gotten his youngest brother through med school. Marc traveled as a bounty hunter. Anthony had a life with Tess and the twins. Damon was a train wreck, but Anthony had given him space for a dojo above the auto repair shop, so at least Damon could teach martial arts whenever he wasn't getting involved with the wrong kind of woman.

His baby sister, Francesca, had blown out of New Orleans the day after she'd graduated from high school, so there wasn't much he'd been able to do there. Except blast her for not keeping in touch. On voice mail, usually, since she didn't bother picking up his calls.

Everyone was as settled as they were going to be. But no sooner had Nic started looking forward to a life that didn't involve taking care of someone named DiLeo than he'd been derailed when the new mayor had appointed him as the new superintendent, a glorified title for the chief of police.

"We've got to clean up this department, Nic," the mayor had said. "We've got to earn the community's trust again. I don't care what the good old boys around here say. They're part of the problem. You're the right man for this job and the Feds agree."

What was Nic going to do except trade his title as commander for superintendent and postpone living a while longer?

In the corridor to his office, he reached for the door—

"Wait a sec, Chief. You don't want to go in yet."

Nic paused with his hand on the knob and glanced over his shoulder. "Why not?"

"She's in there."

Nic shook his head, unsure he'd heard correctly. "Let me get this straight. You picked up a minor in violation last night and she's not at the curfew center, but in my office?"

Jurado shrugged. "It seemed a good idea at the time."

"And why's that?"

"Because she refused to talk to anyone but you."

"Help me out here, Jurado. Where'd you pick her up?"

"Big Mike's place on Iberville."

That got Nic's attention. He'd taken a stroll to Big Mike's place on Iberville last night, and since he didn't believe in coincidences… "You want me to start guessing wildly?"

"Got the call after midnight. Ever since we received that anonymous tip Busybodies Massage Spa was a front for prostitution, we've been keeping an eye on the place."

"That much I already know." He'd still been Eighth District commander when Big Mike, proprietor of Insane, Ink, had leased space to Busybodies to keep his doors open in the down economy.

"Disturbance in the massage spa. Customer allegedly got handsy with one of the therapists," Jurado explained. "The owner called in because she thinks we're looking for some reason to shut her down. She was afraid this customer would cause trouble if he didn't get what he wanted."

"Let me guess…Dubos."

"Good wild guess."

Not so much. An informant from Nic's days as commander had tipped him that Busybodies was Judge Hugo Dubos's new massage joint of choice. Nic had been keyed up after a dinner with the mayor and U.S. attorney last night, so he'd hit the streets like in the old days, walking to take the edge off.

Might have worked, too, until Damon.

"Get anything?"

Jurado snorted. "Statements from the therapist and the owner. That's about it. Apparently, there was an argument. Dubos left before the duty officers got there. Couldn't get a statement out of Big Mike. Said he didn't see or hear anything. Details are in the incident report." He held up a lumpy folder.

No surprises here. Big Mike had been around long enough to be a French Quarter institution. He'd weathered Katrina when many businesses had gone under or relocated and wouldn't want attention given to the way he skirted legalities to make ends meet. His infractions were small potatoes in this city.

Until Hurricane Katrina.

When New Orleans had emptied out, the crime had gone with it. That's why the U.S. attorney and his federal buddies had come to town—to make sure the new mayor and police chief got a grip on the city as it filled back up. That would take some doing because they weren't only cleaning up the city but cleaning inside the department.

"This juvenile see something?" Nic asked.

"Told you, Chief. She won't talk to anyone but you."

Obviously, Nic wasn't going to get this on his own. He tightened his grip on the door handle, ready to end the suspense. "Anything else?"

"Good luck." Jurado handed him the file folder containing the incident report. With a sigh, he headed toward Operations. "You know where I'll be."

The instincts that had kept Nic alive for so long on the streets suddenly revved into gear. He didn't know what was on the opposite side of this wall, but Nic knew that whatever—*whoever* she was—would rock his day.

Not bothering to glance at the report, he opened the door to find a teenage girl dozing in his chair, sandaled feet with brightly polished toes propped on the corner of his desk.

She jerked awake at his entrance. Her head snapped back, and she glanced at him, blinking away sleep.

Nic had been with the NOPD for years. Before the new mayor of New Orleans had appointed him police chief, he'd been commander of the high-profile and highly pain-in-the-ass Eighth District, which included the French Quarter, Central Business District and Harrah's Casino. He'd seen it all. Nowadays it took something really good to surprise him.

The young girl staring at him through unfamiliar eyes surprised him. Probably because the only thing unfamiliar about her were the eyes. The rest of her, from the top of her tawny head to those brightly painted toenails, was pure DiLeo.

Nic blinked, but the girl was still there, staring up at him from a face all-too recognizable to deny a blood connection.

If the tawny hair and olive-skinned features didn't

give her away, the look in her eyes did—a mix of curiosity and attitude and a little too much pride.

This girl was a DiLeo, no question.

He wasn't going to catch a break, was he? And here he'd thought he was done cleaning up family messes.

With a mental sigh, Nic calculated her age, trying to guess which one of his brothers might be responsible.

Fourteen, he decided, early high school. She seemed to be poised right on the brink of becoming a real have-an-answer-for-everything, demand-the-car-keys teen. Nic knew the look. Knew it very well, in fact, as the oldest of six siblings. Which took his youngest brother, Vince, out of contention straightaway. Too young. That left Marc, Anthony or Damon.

Nic's money was on Damon. But to be fair, Marc could have done the deed. He would have been knee-deep in his rock-star phase about the time this young girl became more than a twinkle in her daddy's eye. Marc's band had practiced in the garage behind the family house and no matter how often Nic and his mother had patrolled the premises, the groupies marching through those practices rivaled a Mardi Gras parade.

Definitely not Anthony. His girlfriend of the time had spent more time at the DiLeo house than Anthony. Still did. No way could she have kept a pregnancy secret.

So Nic was going with Damon. Just because he was on Nic's shit list today.

"I didn't do anything wrong," the girl announced before he'd gathered his wits enough to begin the interrogation. "I didn't know about the curfew. And if that disgusting old pervert hadn't been yelling at those women, the police wouldn't have even come at all."

Nic noticed a few things straight off. Her accent for one. There, but distinctly not there. As if no one place had taken root, yet many had left an impression. For some reason he wanted to say European, but knew that wasn't right.

Then there were the glaring flaws in her reasoning. Namely, she would have still been breaking the curfew ordinance even if she hadn't been caught. So unless there was parent or guardian in possession of a notarized letter in the folder he held, that fresh piercing on her nose also contradicted the part about her not doing anything wrong, too.

Nic was back to his original question.

Opening the folder—no parents or guardians in here—he glanced down at the incident report and…a passport. A few more facts clicked as he snapped open the booklet one handed. The girl was a U.S. citizen, a traveler.

Croatia. Africa. Thailand. He'd been right about the accent. The most recent custom stamp came from Chile, South America.

Raking his gaze over a photo taken a few years ago, when she'd been ten maybe, he glanced at the name—

Violet Nicole Bell.

The hair on the back of his neck crawled, and for a blind instant, he could only stare as every shred of reason rebelled.

Violet Nicole Bell.

The name jolted him from the present and filled his head with a memory from long ago…a memory of the beautiful girl he'd once been involved with.

Megan Bell.

He might not have thought about her in years, hadn't seen her in even longer, but Nic didn't have to close his eyes to pull up a vision of her face. Heart-shaped with a delicately pointed chin. Porcelain skin and a full mouth, a kissing mouth if ever there had been one. A mass of silky chocolate hair and eyes so deeply blue they looked almost violet.

Violet Nicole Bell.

With a quick shake of his head, he tried to dispel the image of that face, tried to shock himself back to the present where a young girl was staring at him, a young girl who couldn't…*shouldn't* exist. Nic shook his head again, determined to get control of himself, of the memories and speculations and facts that were paralyzing him. He needed to get a grip, so he could figure out what to think, what to feel.

Fingers trembling over the remaining papers, he forced himself to focus on the documents—a visa, some sort of permission form, a photo.

He knew this photo before he could bring himself to look at the smiling young faces. He fingered the paper frame that had yellowed over time, cartoon gravestones and grim reapers with scythes, a keepsake from a French Quarter ghost tour.

Unable to stop himself, he glanced at the back of the photo at the inscription.

Always, Nic.

At the time, he'd meant it.

Now, he had to force himself to flip the photo over, to look at the image, to shock himself with the knowledge that *always* hadn't lasted a month after this photo had been taken.

And there they were. He and Megan sitting together on the curb, so close they might have been fused at the hips, his arm around her shoulders, her hand resting casually on his thigh. Their heads were pressed close. Their expressions revealing no clue of what would be in store for them. They were immortalized in a way that couldn't have been any more permanent than the young girl in front of him.

Nic was suddenly aware of her gaze, tense, expectant. She was waiting for something.

His reaction?

He didn't have one. Megan had disappeared shortly after this tour, though she hadn't intended to leave for her pricey private university until August. Nic had refused to believe she would walk away from him without a word, but Megan had never contacted him again. Not even to explain why she'd left so suddenly.

Nic's shock must have been all over him because suddenly the girl—*Violet*—laughed and said, "I know. Crazy, isn't it? I just found out myself."

Her laughter finally penetrated his shock. Megan's laugh. He hadn't even known he remembered.

It took every ounce of his not-inconsiderable willpower to keep a poker face as he lifted his gaze to face this beautiful young girl with unusual blue eyes.

One glimpse of the uncertainty she was trying so hard to hide, and he knew his reaction mattered. He could see it all over her. He could feel it in the tight knot in his gut.

Somewhere in the back of his brain, the gears started grinding, and the only thing Nic knew for sure right now was that he couldn't give over control of this situation.

It didn't matter that a levee had collapsed and the past flooded in. It didn't matter that his head was buzzing and long-ago memories and resentments were colliding inside. Not when Violet—*his daughter*—stared at him expectantly.

So Nic forced a smile. Then he said the only thing he could think to say, "Crazy works for me."

Her expression melted, all the expectation evaporating into relief. He could see amusement, too, uncertain amusement, true, but it was still there.

A place to start.

CHAPTER FOUR

"WE'RE BEGINNING OUR descent," the captain announced.

Thank God! Of all the flights Megan had taken over the years, forgettable and memorable, smooth and turbulent, these flights would hold the distinction of being the worst ever.

Nearly seventeen hours in the air, out of contact with Violet, angsting about everything from her daughter's physical and emotional well-being to what the future might hold for their family. Nearly seventeen hours of imagining scenarios of what the meeting between Violet and Nic had been like and stressing about the potential long-term consequences. Nearly seventeen hours of revisiting every decision she'd ever made regarding Violet and analyzing why she'd made it.

And gearing up to face this mess she'd made.

Once in the States, she'd sent Violet a text message:

Boarding in Atlanta. You have three choices. Pick up your phone. Text me your address. Or be at that gate when I arrive. I expect to see or hear from you. I trust you'll make a good decision. Love you very much. Relieved you're okay.

An understatement to say the least, but now the ball was in her daughter's court.

Would she be at the airport? Or would Megan have to track her down? No, Violet may be fiercely independent, which was a trait she'd had since she'd been old enough to form the words, "I do it." She may have gone berserk on this quest to find her father, but she was still an intelligent, good kid.

No, Megan wouldn't have to chase her.

But when Megan emerged from the gate with her carry-on over a shoulder, she didn't find Violet, but *him.*

She could have spotted him in the middle of the Rex Parade crowd on Fat Tuesday. He stood taller than most of the people, his light hair cropped close. The chiseled features were the same, yet different. Weathered by life. Damage had been done to the once-straight nose. A fight, most likely, as there was a small but deep scar she didn't remember marring his eyebrow.

She recognized the boy she'd been wildly in love with so many years ago.

Nic.

A man now. A stranger.

The uniform he wore only added to the impression. All sparkly brass and knife-creased edges.

Her daughter wasn't anywhere in sight, and her absence combined with Nic's presence rattled Megan. She didn't even realize she'd stopped until someone bumped into her.

"Excuse me." A man brushed past so fast all she saw was the back of him as she steadied her bag, which was suddenly swinging her off balance.

She hadn't realized she'd stopped breathing, either, until she tried to respond. Her mouth moved, but no sound came out because Nic had spotted her. His gaze swept over her in an assessing glance, taking in everything at once.

But giving nothing in return. Nothing to make her brace herself. Nothing to reassure her. Nothing but grim recognition on that still devastatingly handsome face.

Sucking in a deep breath, Megan propelled herself into motion. The burden of this meeting was all on her shoulders, and she wouldn't shirk it. Holding his gaze, she strode toward him, determined to deal with this mess head-on. She would not make a difficult situation any more difficult.

If that was even possible.

"Nic, I am so sorry." The words gushed out. "I don't even know what to say. Is she okay? She said she was, but—"

"Seems to be." He inclined his head curtly.

Megan tore her gaze from his, glanced around, suddenly needing to look anywhere but at him. "She didn't come with you?"

"She's with my mother. Thought it would be best if we talked alone first."

That made sense. A very good idea, in fact. She was glad someone was thinking, because despite her best intentions, she was overwhelmed: by the stranger he'd become, by the realization that fifteen years away from this man didn't make one bit of difference because they were still connected through their daughter.

"Do you have a suitcase?" he asked in that stranger's voice.

"I do." Spinning on her heel, she took off in the direction of baggage claim.

What was wrong with her? She'd known this day would come, but right now all her rationality, all her carefully planned explanations didn't seem so rational as she faced that guarded look in Nic's eyes.

Betrayal?

He had every right to feel however he felt. Every right. She'd made all the choices. And he hadn't known he should have had an equal say until their daughter had popped into his life out of the blue.

There was no way for Megan to sugarcoat her mistakes or the consequences, no way to miraculously avert this train wreck.

He was suddenly beside her, and she could practically feel him, a physical sensation. The feeling wasn't unfamiliar, either, which surprised her. Fifteen years hadn't diminished her awareness of him. It was ridiculous, the absolute last thing she needed to notice right now.

He was working hard to stay calm and controlled. It wasn't obvious in his expression or in the way he strode silently at her side, so she wasn't sure why she thought that. Maybe it was the silence. Heavy. Accusing. It didn't matter that there was an entire airport filled with people, noise and chatter filtering through the place in tidal bursts. The silence between them was deafening. Or maybe she was projecting her anxiety.

Megan was relieved when they arrived at baggage claim and her flight number flashed on the overhead sign. She moved to plunge into the crowd, but Nic caught her arm. Nothing more than a light touch, but a touch that stopped her in midstride.

"What does your bag look like?"

"Lime-green. Can't miss it." She stopped obediently, not surprised. Nic, the boy she'd once known, had been equally attentive to details.

As he moved closer to the conveyor belt, the crowds parted to let him through. It might have been the uniform, but more likely it was the imposing figure he cut in the uniform.

Very imposing. Solemn, almost.

Megan hoped it was the circumstances. She didn't like to think that the ultraresponsible teenager he'd once been had matured into a man who didn't look like he smiled much.

Nic didn't miss her bag. No one could miss a neon bag on the conveyor belt.

"We'll need to pick up Violet's before we leave, too," he said after wheeling her suitcase over.

"She stored it?"

He nodded. "I've got the key. Want to grab a cup of coffee first? There's a Starbucks."

"Of course."

Then Megan found herself on the concourse, standing on one side of a table facing Nic over two steaming cups of coffee. She could handle this. She'd known this day would come. And she wasn't eighteen anymore. She was a woman who'd made choices and couldn't take them back.

But as luck would have it the very first question Nic asked was one she hadn't expected.

"Why didn't you want our daughter to know me?"

CHAPTER FIVE

NIC HOPED LIKE HELL THE shock of the situation would wear off soon. Otherwise, he was in real trouble, because it didn't feel as though fifteen years had passed since he'd last seen Megan.

More like yesterday.

Every time he met her gaze, he felt punched in the gut. Even her turmoil tugged at him. It was all over her face, a face he shouldn't be so familiar with. Not after so long. Not after she'd blown out of his life without a glance back.

But he was aware, all right. Of every soft intake of breath. Of the way her lashes fluttered over her eyes as if she might block out everything for an instant. Of how her face had settled in with age, as if she'd grown into so much beauty, the blue, blue eyes, the full, soft mouth. Of the way her fingers tightened on the cup as if she were bracing herself.

He could relate to the feeling.

But when she lifted that magnificent gaze to him, she faced him squarely. "I didn't keep Violet from you because I didn't want her to know you. That never even crossed my mind. Not once in all these years."

He didn't have words. If she had wanted him to know his daughter, then she would have told him she was pregnant. That much seemed obvious.

"Why?" It was all he could manage, giving her a

chance to make sense of this for him. It didn't. None of it. Not the way she'd run away. Not the way she'd hidden her pregnancy.

She took another deep, shuddering breath, visibly steeling herself. He could see it all over her, in the tense set of her mouth, the rigid way she stood. She should have been a stranger by now. She wasn't.

"Quite honestly, Nic, I was completely unable to cope with the situation. I freaked. My parents freaked. I wasn't in any position to raise a child, and I knew you weren't, either. Abortion wasn't an option, but adoption seemed like a good one. My mother found a private agency that handled everything from the medical care to the legalities. She took a leave from the university and we went to one of their maternity centers." She paused briefly as if considering her next words. "At the last minute I couldn't go through with it. That's it. I know that doesn't even begin to explain—"

"No, it doesn't." The words were out of his mouth before he could stop them. "Last I heard there were laws that protected fathers from this sort of thing."

She flinched, but held his gaze steadily. "There are."

God, he was struggling. He'd promised himself not to feel anything until he had the facts, to treat this no differently than any case, buy himself some time to figure out how to feel.

The anger surprised him, and he was suddenly grateful they were standing in public, an external control that would help him keep the floodgates in check.

He was the one who'd been kept in the dark, who'd been sandbagged by the sudden appearance of a daughter he'd never known existed. He had every right to be pissed. For a hundred reasons. Every one of them valid.

"What did you do, Megan, lie?"

"Yes."

Simple. Factual. How could he attack an admission like that? The fact that he wanted to warned he'd better get a lid on his reactions before he found his face plastered all over the front page of the *Times-Picayune* with the headline: New Police Chief Creates Scene at Airport.

This was Damon's damned fault. If Nic had slept last night, he wouldn't be standing here, raw-edged and ready to explode. He might have had self-control on his side when he'd opened the door to his office and stepped into a minefield.

Megan wasn't helping. She waited, so stoic, as if she'd known she'd have to face the music and was determined to take whatever he dished out. As if she felt she deserved it.

And she did. Every damned bit.

"Did you think I wouldn't help?" He wanted an answer. "Or did you think I wasn't good enough for you?"

Good enough to sneak around with, but not good enough to stand beside when life got demanding.

"Neither, Nic. I wasn't thinking," she said simply. "Not for myself. That's the point. There was never any question you'd do the honorable thing, none at all. I knew you'd help in any way I needed you. I thought you might even suggest marriage."

Another sucker punch. "That wasn't good enough."

She shook her head, sending dark waves trailing over her shoulders. "What I wanted had nothing to do with it. You have every reason in the world not to believe me, but I'm being entirely honest when I say it wasn't about you at all. I was in love with you. I knew how hard you worked. I respected you for it. You made me feel spoiled and selfish by comparison. But I also knew how much you wanted a future, a chance to go to college. You didn't need another family to support."

"That wasn't your call to make."

"No, it wasn't. But I didn't realize that at first. I just reacted. You would have been able to handle the situation. I didn't know how. I relied on my parents to make the decisions like I always had. What they said made sense at the time. They had their reasons—"

"Don't bother telling me about your parents' reasons. I don't want to hear about how I was your dirty little secret."

She paled in response to that verbal punch, her grip tightening on the cup until he thought the lid might pop off.

He gave a harsh laugh. "I never even questioned why you didn't let me pick you up from your house. I suppose that should have been my first clue—"

"I'm so sorry, Nic." Her words spilled out, a broken whisper. She let her gaze slide from his, couldn't face him. "I am so, so sorry. If I could take everything back, I would. I never meant to hurt you."

He couldn't open his mouth. Simply didn't trust himself. The past might have happened years ago, but the anger poisoning him was all about right now, about wanting to deny he'd ever given her that much of him.

"I have no excuses." She shrugged, such a helpless gesture. "What I did was wrong on every level. I knew my parents didn't approve of you, but I wasn't strong enough to stand up to them, so I sneaked around behind their backs because I wanted to be with you. It's really that simple. I handled my pregnancy no different. I listened to what I was told and let it make sense."

She finally let go of the cup. When she faced him again, he saw resolve in her expression, and resignation.

"For the record," she said, "I don't blame my parents. Not for my choices. They did what they felt was right. Whether I understand or respect their reasoning doesn't take away the fact I was responsible. What I did was unfair to you and our daughter. If I'd have been thinking, I might have realized it. But I panicked. By the time I'd figured everything out, I'd made a huge mess and didn't know how to fix it."

Even the hurt he felt didn't touch the anger. And her apologies didn't take anything away, didn't explain why he was only finding out he had a daughter when she was nearly grown.

He brought the cup to his lips, more for something to do than the cooling coffee. At this stage of the game, caffeine wasn't going to do a damned thing except wind him even tighter.

Nic was so aware of her *standing* across from him, that ridiculous neon bag by her feet. He heard what she said, but nothing was processing. He didn't understand, was almost disbelieving that the girl who'd not only given him her virginity but who'd lain in his arms and claimed to love him would have handled things this way. God, it was like he was eighteen years old all over again.

That made him angry, too.

"Even if I wanted to believe you," he finally said, "how does any of that translate into now? Every day you woke up with our daughter, every time you took her on a plane and moved her from one country to another, you chose to keep her a secret."

"I did. And that was intentional, Nic, damage control, because the choices I made impacted Violet."

"I'd say so."

"If you'll give me a chance to explain, this part might actually make sense."

He sincerely doubted it, but nodded anyway.

"The minute Violet was born, I knew I couldn't go through with the adoption. Everyone tried to reason with me—my parents, the people at the maternity home. Everyone said it was a knee-jerk reaction to giving birth. But it wasn't. It was the first time in my entire life I actually thought for myself. I heard what everyone was saying, but I knew what I wanted. Strangers were not going to raise my daughter. That's about all I knew. I didn't have a clue how I was going to care for her.

"The agency is a reputable one. It's a religious notfor-profit that operates in several disadvantaged locations around the world, places with high mortality rates from poverty and disease. This agency places children with stable families wherever they can find them. The maternity homes are for mothers who've lost husbands or whose families can't afford to feed them. Sometimes these homes are the only chance an infant gets to survive. They really do a lot of good work."

Keeping him in the dark was good work?

"Your mother took you out of the country so you could circumvent the law about getting my permission for the adoption?" He wasn't sure why he asked when the answer was obvious. Maybe he simply needed to hold her accountable in some lame way, to feel the illusion of some control.

She nodded, that haunted look on her face not making

him feel any better. "Since the agency isn't based in the States, the legalities are easier to get around. But if I had admitted who Violet's father was, you'd have been contacted. That's the way it works to make adoption legal."

She didn't get a chance to continue when a woman with small kids passed, her stroller bumping Megan's bag. The table rocked and Nic grabbed his coffee.

"So sorry," the mother said, correcting the stroller one-handed while hanging on to a toddler with the other.

Megan smiled automatically, nudging her bag farther under the table with a foot. "No problem. You've got your hands full."

The mother rolled her eyes and swept past with a smile. Megan watched her vanish into the crowd, looking thoughtful. She lifted the cup to her lips and took her first sip.

"It took me a long time to get on my feet, Nic. I had no job, no way to support us. I needed to get through college so I had some employable skill."

"Your parents?"

She only shook her head. He didn't ask, although now that he thought about it, Violet had been his first clue all wasn't well in that quarter. She'd told him how she'd been stalking him at his condo before following him to Big Mike's tattoo place. If she'd had a relationship with the Bells, she probably wouldn't have been burning the night at Insane, Ink. She might have told Jurado to call them when she'd been picked up.

Nic wasn't sure what he thought about that, except to admit he was surprised. "How'd you manage?"

"The maternity home let me stay for the first few months. They weren't happy I reneged on my end of the deal, but they are in the business of helping people. They understand that things don't always work out as planned."

She sounded as if she was on more solid ground now. "My parents were waiting me out, convinced I would change my mind when the reality of being a single teenage parent set in. That wasn't going to happen. Not when every second I spent caring for Violet only strengthened my determination to keep her."

And yet she still hadn't contacted him, hadn't given him a chance to help her, or help take care of their daughter. She'd toughed out the situation on her own. He didn't understand why.

"What about your job? Violet said you travel. You made it through school?"

"Finally. Took forever, I won't lie. I took online classes in between taking care of Violet and working." She met his gaze and he thought she was putting on a brave face for his benefit.

"What did you do?"

"I was fortunate. I became friends with a couple at the maternity home. They were like angels. He worked for the consulting firm I'm with now. His wife was a volunteer who liked to travel with him. He hired me as his administrative assistant, and I learned the ropes of dealing with not-for-profits. By the time I finished school, I'd been with the company so long, I stepped into a permanent position as a consultant. I worked my way up from there."

Nic might not understand all the reasons for the choices she'd made, but he didn't doubt what she said— that she'd had a long time to consider the effects.

He'd had a couple of hours. No damned wonder he felt like the top of his head was about to blow off. "Did you know Violet was coming here? She's been side-stepping some of my questions, so I figured she wasn't telling me everything."

Megan shook her head as if still disbelieving. "Not a clue. As far as I knew she was at her friend's house spending the night. I'd spoken to the mom beforehand and Violet texted me at all the right times. Then she didn't come home…" Her voice trailed off, and he could see a suspicious glint in her eyes.

Nic knew this look. He'd seen it through the years in every frightened parent he'd ever had to face. Kids rebelling. Kids running away. Kids foolishly getting behind the wheel after partying in the Quarter. Sometimes kids guilty of nothing more than being in the wrong place at the wrong time and winding up as tragic statistics.

For the first time since seeing Megan in the crowd at the gate, Nic felt his anger dull, enough maybe even to think past it.

"I am so sorry about everything." Her voice hitched and she started again. "I never lied to Violet about you, and I was fully prepared to explain the situation when she was ready to hear it. She didn't give me the chance. I hope one day you'll be able to forgive me. But I respect however you feel, and how you choose to handle it."

She inhaled deeply, shrugged. "I'm not sure where we go from here, but I do hope we can work together to figure out something. I trust that regardless of how you feel about me you'll put our daughter's best interests first. If you don't believe anything else I've said, I hope you'll believe that."

Suddenly he could see how tired she looked, the bruised smudges beneath her eyes, the tightness around her mouth. She was running on adrenaline, and when

Nic thought about it, he could guess what the past few days must have been like for her.

The shock of discovering Violet had disappeared. The worry. The uncertainty. The fear. Toss in the fact that she was going to have to face him and a really long flight, and it was a wonder she was still upright.

Nic didn't know what to believe, wasn't going to take the time to figure it out. Not when someone needed to be thinking here. Megan may have gotten off that plane ready to face her past mistakes, but there'd been no way she could anticipate the mess Violet had unknowingly stepped into at a tattoo parlor in the Quarter. But Nic knew.

Their daughter was now an eyewitness to a crime involving a judge on the criminal bench. Being an eyewitness could make Violet vulnerable anywhere, but especially in this city, ranked top in the nation's criminal activity for a decade running. Nic knew all too well how eyewitnesses could run into trouble around here, which meant getting his head on straight, because he needed to resolve this situation fast.

As usual.

CHAPTER SIX

EVEN VIOLET WAS A LITTLE rattled by how fast her dad
unloaded her. He'd wheeled his unmarked car into a
handicap space in front of Angelina's Hair Salon. She
couldn't figure out why they were here, but was going
with the flow. Her hair was a wreck but, come on, even
though she hadn't taken a shower since leaving Chile,
it couldn't be *that* bad.

Jumping out of the car before her dad had a chance to
get her door, she followed him inside. The salon wasn't
very big—only four stations—but it was decorated nice
with big windows in the front. There was a lady cutting
hair at one station and another shampooing at the sinks
in the back.

But it was the woman behind the reception desk who
caught Violet's attention. She was an older lady, but
really pretty in an older lady sort of way. Makeup and
hair were perfect. Her shirt was summery and bright.
She even wore matching earrings and necklace. Very
put-together, Mom would have said.

She looked up as they entered, peering over her reading glasses, and said instantly, "Nic, what's wrong?"

Violet couldn't see her dad's face, but he stepped
aside, put his arm around her shoulders and drew her
next to him.

"This is my daughter." He blurted it out, drawing the

attention of everyone in the place. "Can she stay here for a while? I have to pick up her mother."

The woman behind the desk blinked. Everyone else was staring, too. Violet felt a little awkward, she wasn't going to lie.

Her dad didn't even wait for an answer. He looked at her and said, "This is your grandmother. You'll be okay here until I get back." Then he headed toward the door.

"She's not going to be Mary Sunshine, FYI," Violet called after him. Only fair to give him a heads-up. Mom was already steaming. Sending him to the airport hadn't been one of the options in her last text.

"Got it," he said before walking out.

Violet watched him hop in the car and speed off. "Good luck with that."

She turned to find the whole place filled with people staring at her. Swallowing hard, she looked at the woman behind the desk.

Her grandmother.

"So, what's your name, gorgeous?" her grandmother asked.

"Violet."

"That's beautiful. Matches your beautiful eyes. So you're my Nic's little girl?"

Violet nodded, still kind of embarrassed by the way she got dumped here. "I think I freaked him out when I told him Mom was about to land."

"Oh, I don't doubt that. Big-time, I'll bet."

Violet didn't think that was a bad thing because her grandmother was suddenly smiling. "He's picking your mother up…at the airport?"

Violet flipped open her phone to check the time. "A flight from Atlanta. She'll be landing in about ten minutes. Will he get there in time? It shouldn't be too traffic-y, do you think?"

Her grandmother shook her head, didn't seem to care that everyone was watching them. "He'll use his light and siren if he's in a hurry."

"Oh, that's right. He's the police chief. He can do that." Violet felt better already. If Mom got off that plane with no one to greet her… That hadn't been an option, either.

"So you're from Atlanta?" her grandmother asked.

"No, Chile. There's a layover in Atlanta."

Her grandmother looked surprised. "Well, that must be a long flight. And your mother is…?"

"Megan."

For a moment her grandmother stared, then if possible, her smile grew even bigger. "Megan Bell."

It wasn't a question, but Violet nodded anyway.

"Imagine that." She laughed, a really happy sound. "Well, there's definitely a story here, Violet, and I want to hear every word." Popping up from behind the counter, she addressed their audience. "I say we head to the house for lunch, ladies. I'll whip something up. What do you think?"

She must be a really good cook because everyone liked that idea. The lady at the shampoo bowl said, "I'll finish here and lock up."

"Perfect. Lunch will be on the table in thirty minutes. Give or take." Her grandmother glanced at the hairstylist who stood behind the chair with the scissors still poised over her client's wet head and said, "Corinne, will you swing by Mauricio's and pick up some bread?"

"Will do." Corinne never took her eyes off Violet's reflection in the mirror. "Want me to cancel your appointments for the rest of the day?"

"You're a doll," her grandmother said while circling the desk.

She was a teeny-tiny woman, Violet realized. Even with heels on her sandals, she was barely eye-level with Violet, who wasn't all that tall herself.

"Are you hungry, gorgeous?"

"Starving," she admitted.

"Perfect." Looping their arms together, her grandmother led Violet through the salon. Not toward the front door, but into the back. "I need to let Anthony and Damon know I'm cooking. I'll never hear the end of it if I don't, and one of them needs to give us a ride home."

Violet had no idea who Anthony and Damon were and honestly didn't care. She had a chief dad, a doctor uncle and a really, really cool grandmother.

Did it get any better?

MEGAN WATCHED NIC TOSS his empty cup in the trash, recognizing their interview was over.

"Ready to get Violet?" he asked.

A no-brainer, but Megan nodded, determined to keep things moving as smoothly as possible. "I appreciate you picking me up and giving us a chance to talk privately."

He inclined his head and led her in the direction of the airport lockers. "We've got a lot to discuss."

She managed a smile at the understatement. "Once I collect Violet, I'll start making arrangements for a place to stay while we're in town."

"Your parents?"

"No, a hotel, I think." Her plate was brimming at the moment without heaping her parents on. She'd visit, of course, wouldn't feel right about being in town and not seeing them. But only after she got things settled with Violet and Nic. So much was up in the air right now, and she didn't have a clue what sort of working situation they'd come up with, couldn't even begin to formulate a plan until she got a hold of her runaway. "Someplace central so it's convenient to get around."

Violet would want to see and do everything, and that would likely start with spending time with her father. Megan wondered how much time Nic would make for her.

"How long can you stay?" he asked.

"As long as it takes," she answered honestly. "I'm afraid I don't have a clue what Violet has in mind. And it's only fair to give you a chance to wrap your brain around this and figure out what you want, too."

He inclined his head, so solemn. "What about work and school?"

"School won't be too much of a problem. Violet takes several online classes, so they won't be an issue. I'll talk to the school about the rest. Her teachers will make her work available so she can keep up. And the timing isn't so bad for work, either. I'm on the tail end of a project, so everyone's trained and functioning independently. If anything comes up, I should be able to solve any problems long distance."

"Violet said you consulted for nonprofit organizations. She didn't seem too clear on the details."

"Pretty much what it sounds like—I set up their organizational structures and help them get established and operational."

He fished a key from his pocket as they arrived at the lockers. Scanning the rows, he found what he was looking for on the bottom.

Good girl, Megan thought. Violet had remembered

to store her bag on the floor rather than at eye level or overhead where thieves were more inclined to break in. Nice to know her daughter paid attention sometimes.

Nic opened the locker and slid out a duffel bag in a familiar shade of neon-green. "I thought you must have gotten a helluva deal on that suitcase, but I guess not. You actually chose this color."

"Custom made. We paid a fortune," she admitted. "But we travel so much it makes life easier at baggage claim." She reached for her own bag. "I can take—"

Their fingers brushed as Nic reached for the handle at the same time. His warm fingertips connected with hers, a physical sensation. He jerked back as if shocked.

"Sure. Go ahead. I'll get this one."

He headed toward the terminal exit, leaving Megan flush with the knowledge that he was as whacked about being together as she was. He had seemed like a stranger with his law enforcement poker face that concealed so much more than it revealed. But now she knew.

Seeing her was rattling him.

And she felt bad. Nic hadn't caused this awkwardness. The last choice he'd had any control over had been when Violet had been conceived. The rest was on her head.

Following him in silence, she reasoned that the only thing she could do to ease the tension was buy this man some time to come to terms with all these changes.

He led her to an unmarked cruiser, stowed the gear in the backseat. Ever the gentleman, he held the door. Megan slipped in, and the silence stretched as he wheeled onto I-10 and headed toward town.

"I left Violet with my mother at her shop," Nic finally said, as if the silence had been getting to him, too.

"She's still doing hair?"

He nodded. "At her own place. Not the house."

"Good for her," she said. "She make out okay with Katrina?"

He shrugged. "Better than some—the damage was mostly on the lower level. We managed to keep her out of a FEMA trailer while we repaired the house. She had fun redecorating. What about your parents? Are they still in town?"

"Yes, thanks. They made out okay." She gazed out the window at the passing city. Another stranger. "I was almost afraid to see what everything looked like. It's totally different, but some things haven't changed at all."

"Looks a lot better than it did," Nic agreed.

Megan could definitely see the changes. Lots of new construction in long-established neighborhoods. Easements with no landscaping. Vacant lots with weeds and not much else. But her hometown had character, and though there were still boarded-up windows on shop fronts, other places showed the strength of people determined to rebuild.

"We were living in Hat Yai at the time," she said. "We didn't get a lot of news coverage. But what we saw was so horrible. Took me days to track down my parents to make sure they'd gotten out okay."

Of course, the real culprit hadn't been spotty cell reception, but that her parents had changed cell carriers and Megan hadn't had their new numbers. She didn't share that information with Nic. Not when it was such a sad commentary on the health of that relationship.

By comparison, Nic's family had seemed to have grown closer in the years since Megan had left, judging by the sign above the parking lot Nic drove into.

The large commercial property that housed Anthony

DiLeo Automotive also was home to Angelina's Salon and International Studio of Martial Arts, Damon DiLeo, sensei, on the upper story.

Nic was already scowling as he pulled right up in the handicap space, close enough to read a sign on the door that read Be Back Soon.

"Not good?" she asked.

"My mother must have closed the shop and taken Violet with her."

Megan reached for her purse. "I can call—"

"They're probably at the house."

Without another word, he eased into traffic and took her to the house he'd grown up in. The DiLeo's modest two-story was in a residential neighborhood in the Lower Garden District. The house and yard were well cared for with a colorful array of springtime blooms dripping over the fence. Cars crammed the driveway and overflowed onto the street, and while the house looked barely large enough to raise a family with six kids, it had a lived-in look and a friendly feel that still felt welcoming.

"Damn it." Nic drove up on the curb without preamble and made a spot to park on the front lawn. "What is she doing? Throwing a block party?"

Megan didn't know what was taking place inside that house and didn't care as long as her daughter was among the guests. Megan had weathered the storm and now finally, *finally,* all the uncertainty of this nightmare, all the fear, all the guilt of facing her actions and putting on a good face for Nic came crashing in on her. Violet would be inside, and the most important part of this nightmare would be over. The rest she could handle, as long as her daughter was okay.

"You ready?" Nic asked.

She nodded. And then they were on their way inside

a place that had been a forgotten memory. The decor may have changed, but the impression of Nic's home remained the same.

A home filled with love and laughter.

A sort of numb disbelief took hold as Megan walked beside him. She knew exactly where he was heading—the kitchen at the rear of the house. They passed through the hall then the living room and…there she was.

Seated at the head of the table, Violet held court, alive and in one piece and not looking any worse for the trip.

She glanced up as if it was the most natural thing in the world to find Megan standing there. "Hey, Mom."

As casual as if she'd arrived home from a friend's house. As if the past few days had never been and she belonged in the family home of the father she hadn't known existed in the entire time she'd been alive.

She hopped up with that long-legged grace Megan knew by heart. No longer her beautiful little girl, but an independent young woman, her own person, who thought for herself and knew what she wanted and wasn't afraid to do what it took to get it.

Even if it meant running from one continent to another.

But none of that mattered right now. They were mother and daughter and came together as naturally as breathing. Violet slipped her arms around Megan's waist and rested a cheek on her shoulder in a familiar hello.

And Megan held on.

No matter what had passed between them, the decisions, the mistakes, the tiny betrayals, love won out over all of them. Violet was as relieved to see her mom as Megan was to see her. She could feel it in those slender arms that held her close, hear it in the sweet voice that asked, "You okay, Mom?"

They were together and that was all that mattered. Now wasn't the time for recriminations or accusations or anything but the only thing that was really important.

Violet was okay.

Megan pressed a kiss into her daughter's hair. "I am now."

CHAPTER SEVEN

NIC CAME TO A STOP IN the doorway. His life had suddenly become a YouTube video, loading jerkily into his brain, streaming only long enough to *almost* make sense of what he saw.

Violet. *His* daughter. She sat in the middle of *his* family. Anthony and his wife, Tess, each with a twin on their lap. Vince, still in dress pants and shirt, which meant he'd come straight from the hospital.

Damon was in the thick of things as usual, looking like a rebel with his long hair pulled in a ponytail, laughing it up as if he hadn't kept everyone awake last night with his nonsense. Mom's stylists were there, and a mechanic from Anthony's garage, too.

The usual crew.

Marc wasn't in town right now; his job as a bounty hunter was keeping him on the road more and more lately. A few other familiar faces were missing as well, but then, it was the middle of a workday when normal people worked.

When had this family ever been normal?

Violet had made herself at home, facing everyone with a blinding smile and fast laughter until she looked up and saw Megan.

Nic must have blinked, because the next thing he knew Megan and Violet were standing in the middle of the kitchen.

Somehow he knew Megan was thinking about every horrible thing that might have happened to Violet on a solo trip from South America, every tragedy she'd ever read about in the paper or seen on the news. He didn't need to see her face to recognize the relief melting her slim body as she wrapped her arms around Violet, a motion as natural as breathing.

He could see Violet, though. She was barely taller than Megan, the perfect height to rest her face on her mother's shoulder. From where he was standing, she looked like a young girl who had nestled into the safest place in her world.

Every image of a mother and child Nic had ever seen flashed in his head. Memories from his family. Scenes from television. This was what a mother and daughter were supposed to look like. He didn't see examples often enough in his line of work.

He tried to grasp onto the fact that this was *his* daughter with the woman he'd once loved so much it had hurt, but Violet raised her head, took a step back and asked, "You're not going to melt down about my nose, are you?"

"Saving the meltdown for later." Megan's return was deadpan. "It's coming, though. Be forewarned."

Violet narrowed her gaze in a look that was all surly teen and lightning-fast mood swing. Megan turned enough so he saw her narrow her gaze and scowl right back, giving as good as she got.

Everyone watching the exchange had the sense to keep their mouths shut—even Damon—as Violet flounced to her seat of honor at the head of the table.

A miracle for this family.

Violet motioned Megan forward. "Come on, Mom.

Sit down. Do you know everybody? If you don't, I'll introduce you."

She demonstrated such a curious mix of youth and maturity that Nic suspected was a function of her unusual upbringing. And being an only child. He'd heard that made a difference, too.

Damon was the one to rise and drag over a chair, making some crack about butt space for the chief's baby mama. Nic didn't get a chance to respond because little Rocco made a play for the serving fork in the lasagna pan and Anthony intercepted with a loud, "I don't think so, buddy."

Then the moment passed and, looking somewhat shell-shocked, Megan sat—she didn't really have a choice—while Nic stood his ground in the doorway, envisioning the headline: Chief of Police Arrested on Alleged Murder Charge.

Only there wouldn't be anything alleged because he was going to kill Damon one of these days. Guaranteed.

The only thing saving him right now was paralysis from watching Megan and Violet together...a family of two.

Except he was here. Standing in his mother's kitchen surrounded by his family with his daughter and Megan.

What in hell did he do with this?

Suddenly, his mother appeared beside him. "How are you holding up?"

He shook his head. He didn't have an answer for that, either. She knew better than anyone how much Violet had sandbagged him. Was probably the only one on the planet who'd been privy to the intensity of his relationship with Megan all those years ago, his confusion over the way she'd dropped out of his life so suddenly and completely.

"How could she not tell me?" That was all he could manage to say.

Glancing at the table, his mother frowned. "I don't know, Nic, but give it time. This is a big shock for all of you."

"All of us?"

"Violet told me she found you on her own. Megan had no idea she was coming here."

That much he already knew. "I'm not interested in how Megan feels right now. And you're about to be down one son if Damon doesn't get some manners."

His mother rolled her eyes. "Finding out you're a father is not your brother's fault."

"No, but it is his fault I didn't get any sleep last night. A few hours and all this might not feel so shitty."

She arched an eyebrow in a skeptical expression. "You think?"

Dragging his fingers through his hair, Nic wondered if there was any possible way he could bow out of here. Claim he had to get back to work, which wouldn't be a lie. He was the damned police chief and he'd waltzed out of the station and not looked back. Hell, he couldn't even remember his schedule for the day. Did he have appointments? He always had appointments. And crises. Hadn't he given up this family drama? He was sure he had.

"Give it some time, Nic," his mother said. "I know you haven't asked for my opinion, but if you've never listened to anything I said before—which you haven't—do yourself a favor and listen to me now. What's happening is important. Violet and Megan are your family whether you were aware or not. You'll want to make sure you react in ways that count."

He wanted to argue that Megan wasn't anything but someone who hadn't had the courtesy to share some essential facts, but technically, his mother was right.

Whether or not he'd known he'd fathered a child. Whether or not he'd seen Megan yesterday, six months or fifteen years ago, if a DNA test proved he'd fathered Violet, then the law considered him and Megan intimate partners.

He didn't need a DNA test, or his name on a birth certificate for that matter, to know he'd fathered Violet.

His mother reached up and patted his cheek. "Do you have any idea how long they're staying?"

"Megan said as long as it takes. Whatever that means. She's planning to get a hotel—"

"Her parents aren't in town anymore?"

"She said they are." He shrugged. "I don't have a clue what's up with that. She said they'd get a hotel."

"No. They'll stay here."

"Excuse me?"

"They'll stay with me." His mother nodded decidedly. "Bring their stuff upstairs, will you please? Put Violet in Damon and Vince's old room. Megan in yours."

Arguing would be a waste of time. Nic might have even considered saving Megan from publicly going head-to-head with his mother had it not been for his concern about Violet. He still had to get her down to the station to give a statement.

He needed Megan to do that.

Violet was a minor. Megan was her legal guardian. Fathers who weren't on birth certificates had no authority. In this case, though, the only difference that made were the potential ethical questions.

Jurado had taken one look at Violet and known she was a DiLeo. All sorts of questions could arise if and when someone found out Violet belonged to him. The press had been having a field day looking for any damned thing they could find to question his appointment. An illegitimate daughter would sell a lot of papers.

Until Nic got a grip on whatever was going down with the judge, he wasn't comfortable with Violet staying at some random hotel. Big Mike might not be talking, but that didn't mean he didn't have anything to say. Violet had seen a kid passing off an envelope to the judge. Add that envelope to the equation, and Nic had a little mystery on his hands. One that stank of graft. One the U.S. attorney would want to know about.

Judge Hugo Dubos was a remnant from an embarrassing past, an era when public corruption ran as rampant as the criminals on these streets. No one had evidence to convict him of anything, but he was a weak link in the judicial chain, part of an ugly cycle that undermined the police department's best efforts to clean up this town. Nic wouldn't be surprised, and didn't think anyone else would be either, to learn Dubos was on the take.

If they could build a case against him, Nic's department would be doing its job and a public service. New Orleans would have one less burned-out, corrupt or plain bad public servant who couldn't easily be removed from the bench.

The NOPD could arrest criminals, but when judges like Hugo Dubos consistently set obscenely low bails, witnesses and victims who'd agreed to cooperate changed their minds. They knew the criminals would end up back on the streets, wanting retribution from the people who'd turned them in. When no one was willing to talk, the district attorney's office would wind up dropping the charges. It was precisely this sort of thing that had undermined the department with the public for too long.

Megan might be getting worked up about the ring on Violet's nose, but that was only because she hadn't heard about the real trouble yet. Their daughter had been picked up by the NOPD and potentially witnessed a crime.

That should go over well. Megan would think she'd reproduced with an idiot. Nic wasn't sure why he cared. He couldn't have known he had a daughter when walking out the door last night since he wasn't a mind reader, but he damn sure should have known he had a tail.

No, until he got a lid on what was going down, Violet—and Megan by default—needed to stay someplace safe. Nic knew who he could trust in the department and who not to turn his back on. The officers he'd assigned to this beat knew his mother's house and kept their eyes on it. Family was important to the good guys on the payroll.

He doubted Violet had gotten around to filling Megan in on the details of her ride to the station in a cruiser, so he would probably get to break the news. Irony at its finest. He and Megan hadn't had a thing to do with each other for fifteen years and now all they needed to do was talk.

"Yo, Daddy, you ever joining the party?" Damon's annoying voice broke into Nic's thoughts. "Save us from giving your life history to my beautiful niece."

"Looks like congratulations are in order, big bro," Vince said. At least Nic had one brother who wasn't such an asshole.

"What's with this family? Doesn't anyone work?" Nic hissed under his breath as he glared at his mother. "You pick today for a freaking family reunion. Thank you."

"I wanted Violet to feel welcomed, and I thought you could use backup." His mother headed into the kitchen to run interference, probably scared she would be down more than one son with Nic in his current mood.

"Knock it off, you two," she admonished. "Nic and Megan haven't eaten yet. Let me grab some plates."

Tess started to rise, but his mother motioned her to stay seated. "Thanks but no thanks, honey. You've got your hands full. Come on, Violet. It's time for a tour."

"You're Italian." Anthony winked. "Kitchens are going to be a big part of your life from now on."

Violet hopped up, so clearly eager.

"Tell me you've been raising my niece right." Damon wrapped an arm around Megan's shoulder and gave her a squeeze. "She does know what a cannoli is, right? *Aglio Et Olio?*"

Megan smiled cordially. "We traveled through Abruzzo on our way to Rome while we were living in Croatia. Does that count?"

"Yeah, and it was so great we went back to hike in Majella on holiday." Violet stood on tiptoe to grab the good plates that were in a cabinet above his mother's reach.

"Abruzzo?" Damon asked in mock horror.

"We're from the wine country in western Sicily," Anthony explained. "Your grandfather was from Ravenna, but we don't like to talk about that."

"Don't let them worry either of you." Tess bounced Annabelle on her lap. "The closest I've ever been to

Italy is a neighborhood in New York, and I make out fine around here."

"Don't know how we ever got along without her." His mother blew a kiss to Tess. "She helps me keep these boys in line."

"And they are a handful," Tess added. "Trust me."

With a laugh, Violet set a plate down in front of Megan, and Damon did the honors of serving. Megan's eyes widened as he heaped enough pasta on her plate to feed a small country.

"Just a taste, please."

"When was the last time you ate Mama's food?" Damon asked.

"Honestly, so long ago I don't remember."

Nic remembered, though. The last time he'd brought her to the house for Sunday dinner, a time-honored DiLeo tradition. She'd been quiet even then, over-whelmed by all the noisy chaos of his big family, of the family and friends coming and going at all hours.

Now she didn't look so much overwhelmed as de-termined to hold her own in the midst of a lot of strong personalities. A protective mother, maybe. Or unsure of her reception. Nic couldn't figure it out.

"Trust me then." Damon drizzled olive oil over the plate. "You'll want seconds. Parmesan or Romano?"

Nic didn't hear her reply because Violet appeared and asked politely, "Where would you like to sit?"

He could see the uncertain excitement in her expres-sion, the waiting. His mother was right. He needed to be careful with whatever he said and did right now.

"Next to Anthony, thanks." Wouldn't hurt to keep the table between him and Damon in his present frame of mind.

"Budge up," he told his brother then slid another chair to the crowded table and sat.

Violet set the plate in front of him then returned to artfully arrange a place setting in front of him as if it mattered. She didn't seem to notice everyone watching her. Megan looked as if she was barely holding it together.

He wasn't sure why he noticed.

"Thanks. Looks great." He wasn't sure what else to say, but he did want her to know he appreciated her effort.

"Would you like something to drink?"

He wanted coffee, but as she'd set a glass in front of him, he said, "Water, please."

Off she went back to the counter to grab the pitcher, and he half expected someone—Damon most likely—to make a crack about her eagerness to serve him, but even his idiot brother kept his mouth shut this time.

Normally, every damned one of them would have thrown him under the bus, but today they cut him slack, seeming to understand the importance of this first family gathering, the fact that he and Megan—and Violet for that matter—hadn't figured out how to handle the situation yet.

Or deal with the shock, in his case.

So they kept Violet talking about school and living abroad and her hobbies, getting to know the new family addition, while Megan pushed food around her plate, answering questions whenever they were directed her way. Talk finally circled to how long they intended to stay in New Orleans.

"Megan, you mentioned going to a hotel." Nic braced himself to meet that blue gaze across the table. "But my mother invited you and Violet to stay here. You good with that?"

Surprise flashed in her eyes, and he knew he was putting her on the spot. But she might as well get used to being part of the family. She said she wanted to work something out, and at the very least that meant they'd be running into each other on important occasions for the rest of their lives.

Graduations. Weddings. Baptisms.

They were Violet's parents. They were in this together, forever.

He started pushing food around his plate, too.

"That's very nice of you to offer," Megan began.

"I insist," his mother said, going straight for the throat. "I absolutely insist. I've got this big empty house and Violet said you've been living in South America. Who knows when I'll see you again?"

Guilt. Another glance at Megan's stricken expression and Nic knew it was working. Then his mother zeroed in on Violet, pulling out the big guns. "Wouldn't you like getting to know your dad? I've got pictures and home movies—"

"A trip down memory lane." Anthony grimaced. "Call me when you're through. I won't be over till then."

Tess punched his arm. "You be nice."

"Cut him a break, green eyes," Damon said. "Who in hell wants to revisit thirty-plus years of chief tyrant here when we're dealing with the real thing every damned day?" He turned to Violet. "Cover your ears, niece girl."

"Come on, Mom, please," Violet said. "Why can't we stay here? It'll be great."

Nic winced when he thought about the sheer amount of memorabilia his mother had stored in the attic. He had been the first. His every breath immortalized. Home movies recording his milestones. First tooth. First steps. First T-ball game. Then there was school stuff. Science fair ribbons. Lined paper filled with paragraphs of grade-school wisdom. School photos depicting the evolution of childhood in all his goofy glory.

Katrina had destroyed the house nearly to the roof but hadn't swept any of that stuff away. No such luck.

"Megan?" his mother asked. "What do you say?"

She'd been outvoted, so there really wasn't any gracious way to decline. Megan knew it, so she simply said, "Thank you. You're very kind."

Violet whooped and Damon raised a fist and said, "Pound it. I want you to save an afternoon for me. You can come to the dojo. I'm going to teach you to defend yourself."

"Really?"

"Really." He shifted his gaze between Megan and Nic. "If it's okay with your mom and *dad,* of course. She's a beauty, you guys. You definitely want me to teach her some moves."

"*Mo-om?* I can, can't I?"

"That sounds like a very good idea," Megan said. Nic, being a nonparent and all, didn't bother weighing in.

"Now that's all settled." His mother grabbed an apron off the baker's rack and tied it around her waist. "Nic, I told you where to bring their bags. Get Vince to help if you need him." She added as an afterthought, "What are your plans for today? Will you be heading back to work?"

That was the one question he could answer without much thought. "I am. In fact, Violet's coming with me to give a statement." He threw the napkin on his plate and shoved the chair from the table. "Megan, as legal guard-ian, you'll need to be there, too. I don't want any ques-tions coming up about circumventing due process."

She glanced at him, surprised. "I don't like the sound of this at all."

Nic looked at Violet, suddenly feeling every inch a father. "You want to break the news to your mother or shall I?"

CHAPTER EIGHT

MEGAN STARED UP AT THE fortress that was the police station, the very last place in the world she'd ever imagined visiting with her daughter.

"Back again," Nic said to Violet, reinforcing Megan's anxiety as he ushered them inside.

Megan followed, but she stepped aside to allow Violet to walk beside her dad. All the mental preparation she'd done to face the consequences of her choices hadn't prepared her for being with Nic again.

Not even remotely.

She distracted herself with the reminder that she was on the same continent as Violet, who was alive and well if in possession of a new piercing. And Nic hadn't dropped dead of a heart attack when Violet had arrived on his doorstep, either.

Things were turning out better than she'd had a right to hope. Even more unexpected had been Nic's family. They'd been entirely gracious given the circumstances, courteous, avoiding opinions and recriminations to focus on what was most important—welcoming Violet to the family.

They'd accepted the situation in a loving way, and she couldn't help remembering the first few times Nic had brought her around, how much she'd liked his family. How different they had been from her own, and how much their obvious love for each other had influenced her while rearing Violet.

Their acceptance now meant the world. Violet was no longer a child, as she'd so clearly demonstrated. Whatever arrangement Megan and Nic worked out would involve traveling to the States. That was going to be difficult enough without worrying about whether or not Violet would be well cared for.

Megan felt reassured.

That said, she'd also learned that her daughter had been picked up by the police at a tattoo parlor in the Quarter in the middle of the night. She didn't have the details yet and was trying not to jump to conclusions, but it looked as if Violet had been lying through her teeth about a few more things.

"Where are you in New Orleans?" Megan had asked.

"With Dad."

Yeah, right.

Megan warned herself to tackle one thing at a time. As long as Violet was okay, they could figure out everything else.

She and Violet followed Nic through the station, coming to a stop every time an officer demanded his attention on the way to his office.

"He's so great, Mom," Violet whispered while awaiting Nic, who spoke with the duty sergeant. "I can't believe you kept him a secret all this time. See how much everyone likes him?"

Which translated into: *See how much I like him?*

Megan kept her reply mild when she said, "We'll talk as soon as we can get a few minutes alone."

Which didn't look like it would be happening anytime soon given that they'd be staying with Nic's mother.

But the last thing she needed was for Violet to shut

down, which happened all too often of late. No, Megan needed to keep the communication open to understand what was going on in Violet's head, so she could deal with it constructively.

The only thing Megan knew right now was that Violet had a plan that extended beyond the "Hi! I'm your daughter!" part of this situation.

Megan needed to get a bead on what it was.

They eventually made it to Nic's office, a functional, somewhat nondescript place that noticeably lacked any personal touches. Or a woman's touch. Which didn't mean he didn't have one, but there weren't any family photos or knickknacks. Just a wall filled with diplomas and awards.

"Come on in," he said. "Get comfortable. I'll make it as quick as I can. I know it's been a long day."

For him, too, no doubt.

"NP." Violet dropped down in the chair behind the desk.

No problem? Maybe not for Violet, but this whole situation was taking a toll on Megan, who'd never even contemplated disobeying rules until she'd met Nic. She may be all grown-up now and have an arsenal of coping skills, but the impressionable young girl was still inside, cringing at the idea of breaking the law and hoping to avoid conflict of any kind.

Megan scowled at her daughter, who'd hijacked her father's chair. Violet smiled, and Nic didn't seem to mind.

Grabbing a file from a stack, he half sat on the edge of his desk and said, "I'm going to look over this incident report then ask you a few questions. Sound good?"

Violet nodded eagerly then leaned back, politely settling in for the wait.

He lifted that dark gaze to Megan. "As soon as I'm through, I'm going to call in my deputy chief to witness the statement. Are you good with that or would you prefer a female officer?"

"Your deputy chief is fine," Megan assured him.

Nic told her to sit, but she declined, still not over her experience of flying seventeen hours in coach. Instead, she occupied herself with the neatly framed documents to learn something about the imposing man who'd once been a boy she knew.

Nic had studied criminal justice, earned an associate's degree at the community college then his bachelor's and master's at Loyola University. That surprised her since both her parents were tenured professors there.

Nic had certainly known her mother was dean of the Department of Languages and Cultures and her father of History. Had her parents known that Nic had been a student there? If so, they'd never mentioned him. The very thought of them having Nic in a class, knowing about the existence of their grandchild, sent a brittle chill through Megan.

That she'd put everyone in such a situation… Obviously her parents hadn't betrayed her secret. She couldn't imagine why they would have when they'd so wholeheartedly disapproved of Nic and had been so disappointed in her for getting involved with a boy they considered so unsuitable.

Megan glanced over her shoulder at Violet and Nic sitting close, such an impossible sight. They looked so alike. The way they leaned slightly forward, relaxed. The way they both tilted their heads to the side—Nic to read his report and Violet to watch her dad. Female and male. Youthful and mature.

The sight of them wrenched Megan hard. She wanted

some miraculous way to erase all the bad decisions, all the lost time, wanted to figure out how to work out something that would meet everyone's needs so they wouldn't waste any more days. In that moment she felt like such an outsider.

The woman who'd kept them apart.

She'd lived with the guilt for a long time. Ever since struggling to become independent, to think for herself and trust her abilities, only then did she recognize what a mess she'd made of the situation. She felt so much more than guilt now.

Practicality had buffered her from the shame, she realized. She hadn't allowed herself the luxury of unburdening her guilty conscience, didn't deserve to be relieved of the endless guilt of her lies. But she'd suffered instead, determined to consider the impact of her own moral failure on Violet, how it might affect her emotionally.

She'd wanted to present the truth to Violet as smoothly as she could. Nic, too. She'd wanted to ease the transition between them, knew the truth would change both their lives forever. They'd be forced to deal with each other, forced to live with the consequences of *her* actions. No matter what happened between them. Even if they chose never to see each other again, they'd both know the other was there. They'd have to make the decision, know there was no happily-ever-after.

Megan had told herself she was only being responsible. She'd told Nic that, too. She hadn't unburdened her guilt to start the journey toward redemption. If redemption was even possible. If she couldn't forgive herself, how could she expect Violet or Nic to?

No, Megan had reconciled herself to the situation and placed her daughter's needs above her own. That's what good parents did. And she'd spent her entire adult life trying to be a good parent.

But had she been lying to herself? Had she suffered the guilt so she wouldn't have to deal with the shame of knowing how much she'd failed the people she loved the most?

Seeing Violet and Nic together, all the hard-won independence, all the confidence she'd gained through the years felt like nothing. She felt small and so utterly failed.

"Violet." Nic glanced up from the folder. "You ready?"

Their daughter nodded, so heart-wrenchingly eager. Megan wondered if he realized how much his approval meant to his daughter, how much Violet wanted him to care.

That was Megan's fault, too.

Nic spoke into the intercom, and the spit-polished deputy chief arrived, the formal witness to a statement Megan prayed Violet would never have to make in a courtroom.

Nic conducted the introductions, and Megan got the chance to thank the deputy chief for taking care of her daughter.

Then they got down to business.

"Violet, I want you to start from the beginning and tell me exactly what happened."

Violet sat up in the leather chair, suddenly at attention. "I saw you walking by the tattoo parlor before that hot rod picked you up, so I thought I'd check it out in case you were on official business and got called away."

Violet sounded as if she were reciting lines from a television cop show. But there was nothing amusing about this situation. Not her daughter running away to wander the French Quarter streets at night. Not her eagerness to find and help the father she'd been kept from all her life.

"Okay, good." Nic inclined his head. "But can you start back a little further so I'm clear on all the details? Tell me about when you left South America."

Violet shot Megan an uncomfortable look, clearly not wanting to rehash all this now. Not with Megan or a strange police officer in the room. Megan turned toward the wall, making herself as invisible as possible. She watched Nic in her periphery. He looked all business, but she had the sense he was starting from the beginning for his benefit and hers.

Or maybe so that if any ethical questions arose, the fact that he hadn't known about his daughter would be well-documented.

"I took a radio taxi to the airport from my friend's house then a flight to the States," Violet began.

"What airport?"

"Santiago. It's the capital."

"Is that where you live?"

"No. We live in Los Andes. It's north. In the mountains."

"Who's we? You and your mother?"

"And GigiMarie."

"Is that your stepfather?" he asked.

Violet gave a snort of pure disbelief. "Mom is *not* married. GigiMarie lives with us. She's like a grandmother."

With a few fast motions, Violet whipped out the cell phone from her pocket and started pressing buttons.

Megan's heart stepped up its pace. Why wouldn't Nic be interested in whether or not there was another man rearing his daughter? Hadn't she researched him online, trying to find out whether or not he was married? It wasn't as if they'd done a lot of catching up since her arrival. Nothing so simple.

Violet held her phone to Nic. "That's GigiMarie in the middle."

"Is that a penguin?" Nic asked incredulously, and Megan knew what photos Violet was showing him. "Where are you?"

"Chile. Didn't know there are penguins there, did you?"

"No clue," he admitted.

Deputy Chief Jurado hid a laugh behind a cough.

"Yeah, the south is really close to Antarctica," Violet explained. "We visit the parks in the Lake District on weekends. Pack a picnic and the bikes and go say hi to the fuzzies." She turned the phone back toward her and glanced at the photo with a half grin.

"Sounds like fun. Have you lived there long?"

"'Bout a year and a half. Be time to relocate soon. We never stay anywhere longer than two years. Right, Mom?"

"Right." Megan tore her gaze from a recent award from Cops for Kids, which appeared to be a youth program sponsored by a number of city departments. Nic had been honored for contributions that had gone above and beyond the call of duty.

"Project's almost over, another month or two at the most."

"Then where are you headed?" he asked.

Megan opened her mouth to reply, but Violet cut her off at the pass. "You know, that's a good question. You'll have to ask Mom because I don't have a clue. She usually asks us where we want to live, but for some reason she didn't this time."

That drew Megan around, where she found her daughter glaring at her. "I assume you're referring to New Orleans."

"Um, yeah."

"I suppose that's one part of the mystery solved." Megan folded her arms across her chest. Of course the timing hadn't been coincidental. "Would you mind sharing how you found out?"

Violet slipped the phone into her pocket one-handed, didn't look the least repentant. "You left your email open."

"Why didn't you ask me about it, Violet? If I left my email open, I obviously wasn't trying to hide anything."

Megan could feel Nic's gaze on her, but the man had sense enough not to comment. Deputy Chief Jurado tried to vanish into a corner himself.

"Right." Violet accused. "You turned down the project. You never even asked us if we wanted to go stateside. GigiMarie hasn't seen her sister in a long time."

Translated: *Violet wanted to be around family.*

They might not be all that close to Megan's parents, but they were still the only family Violet had known she had.

"So that's what started all this." Not a question. "Well, FYI, young lady, I didn't turn the project down. I simply postponed making a decision. Helping Hands is having trouble with a grant, so I had a window before I had to commit. If you had asked me instead of making assumptions, I'd have explained that. I wanted time to think things through before discussing the situation with you." She glanced pointedly at Nic. "I don't think I need to explain why."

Violet rocked in the chair with a huff. Folding her arms over her chest, she clamped her mouth shut tight.

So much for keeping the lines of communication open.

"Pup, we can talk more about this later, okay?"

Silence was her only reply.

After a few moments, Nic intervened. "Ready to get back to the statement, ladies?"

Deputy Chief Jurado eased toward the desk, and Megan decided she liked Nic's second in command right there. The man was quite gentlemanly.

"I didn't know about the curfew. I swear," Violet said, eager to talk with her father though she'd shut down on Megan. "I wouldn't have been out walking around if I had, but when you left, I wanted to see where you went."

"So you followed me from my place?"

Violet flashed a quirky half grin. "I was stalking you."

Nic clearly wasn't thrilled. Because his teenage daughter was walking the streets at night or because the deputy chief looked amused at Nic's expense, Megan couldn't say.

Megan wasn't thrilled, either. For any number of reasons, not the least of which was the reality of shared parenting. Violet had figured out how to bump one parent for the other rather quickly.

"When exactly did you arrive in New Orleans?"

"Yesterday. Landed around one and got to your place a little before two."

Nic made a notation on a notepad. "Okay, then what?"

"I followed you until that hot rod picked you up. I didn't have anything to do then, but since you were so interested in that tattoo place, I figured I'd check it out. Are you thinking about getting a tattoo? Or a piercing?" She absently prodded the ring on her nose with a fingertip.

"Neither. Doesn't fit with the uniform," he admitted. "So you went inside Insane, Ink, after I left?"

"Mmm-hmm. I've wanted a piercing forever, and I did have a permission form."

The deputy chief was openly smiling now as Nic fished through the folder, then pulled out the form that had disappeared from Megan's fireproof box.

"For the record," Nic informed her. "Your mother would have needed to accompany this form in person for that piercing to be legal in Louisiana. You took this from home?"

Violet looked crestfallen. One thing to rebel against her mother. Another to admit stealing to a police chief father. If Nic didn't already think his runaway daughter was a problem, he was probably becoming fast convinced she was a full-fledged delinquent. Megan didn't even want to speculate about the impression the deputy chief was formulating about Violet.

"Let's talk about what happened while you were there." Nic rearranged some papers inside the folder. "I've got statements from the owner and a massage therapist. But nothing from you."

"Got my nose pierced. Looks cool, don't you think?" She didn't give him a chance to reply. "Then I was hanging out, you know, killing time looking at the jewelry and stuff. That's when people started yelling on the other side of the shop."

"Could you see them from where you were?"

Violet shook her head. "No. But in the mirrors I could see a lady haul butt from behind the counter. There was more yelling and she came back to the counter to use the phone. That's when the pervert showed up. He was still running his mouth. Then he saw the guy who'd come into the tattoo parlor and shut up fast."

"This was the guy you mentioned earlier?"

"Yep. The really cute one." She gave a breathy little sigh that made Nic scowl.

"What did this really cute guy do?"

"Gave the pervert an envelope."

The deputy chief visibly perked up at this revelation, and he exchanged a glance with Nic, who made another notation on his notepad before glancing inside the folder again.

"Where was the guy who gave you that ring during all this?"

"Keeping his eyes on me, but pretending like he wasn't." She smiled. "Probably thought I was going to rip him off."

"Is it possible he didn't see the guy with the envelope?"

Tilting her head to the side, she considered that. "I don't think so. He kept moving around. In and out of the chairs. Behind the counter. But he never really took his eyes off me. And he stayed up front once the door opened and the cute guy came in. He couldn't have missed it because the door had those chime-y bells."

"So he was still up front when the guy gave the envelope to the pervert?"

She nodded. "He was pretty manic. Pacing and swearing under his breath about cops and how he never should have rented space to a bunch of...*foreigners*."

Violet scowled, and Megan suspected that wasn't

exactly what the guy had said, but her daughter was too polite to repeat what she'd heard. Megan wanted to understand what Nic was looking for. He was gathering information, but sharing nothing. She knew from the glances he exchanged with the deputy chief that he was looking for something specific.

"Describe the guy who gave the pervert the envelope."

"Curly black hair. Big brown eyes. Gauges."

Dark hair and eyes were nondescript, Megan knew, but oversize holes in a kid's earlobes should help narrow the suspects, shouldn't it?

"Anything else, Violet?" Nic asked. "That description could match half the males in New Orleans. What was he wearing?"

She hesitated, thinking. "T-shirt with Buddha on it. Jeans. Gray Converse high-tops."

Not much to work with there.

"How old?"

"Not too much older than me. A junior or senior maybe."

"Okay. Now I want you to close your eyes and try to picture him." Nic paused, let a few quiet moments pass. "Anything standing out in your memory? Any piercings?"

"No, but he had a tattoo. I didn't notice it at first because it was in a weird spot."

"Where?"

Lifting her left arm, Violet motioned to the underside of her bicep. "I didn't see it until he handed the pervert the envelope. His sleeve sort of covered it."

"Any idea what it was?"

"The Great Eye."

"You're sure? Even with the sleeve?"

"It was the Great Eye," she repeated.

Another beat of silence. "And what's that exactly?"

Violet's eyes popped open, and she looked at her father as if he'd sprouted a second head. "Sauron, you know. Mordor."

Megan bit back a smile. She knew without a doubt Nic hated admitting he still didn't have a clue what his daughter was talking about.

"Come on, Chief," Deputy Chief Jurado said. "Even I know this one."

Violet shot the man an approving grin and saved Nic the trouble of asking. Cupping her hands in the shape of an O, she held it up and said dramatically, "The lord of Mordor sees all. His gaze pierces cloud, shadow, earth and flesh. A great eye, lidless, wreathed in flame."

"A movie?"

Deputy Chief Jurado gave a snort of laughter.

"OMG. Tell me you've heard of the *Lord of the Rings.*"

Nic looked relieved. "I have."

Violet looked relieved, too, as if she'd been considering heading back to South America with her big bad mother rather than admit to being the spawn of someone who hadn't heard of her favorite movie in the world.

"Okay, so Great Eye guy gave the pervert an envelope. Then what did he do?"

"Left with the pervert. Only they didn't go in the same direction. Great Eye guy took off the same way you went."

"Okay, good," Nic said, making a few more notations. "That'll do it for now. But if you remember anything else, anything at all, I want you to tell me, okay? It's important."

Violet nodded. "Okay."

Nic closed the folder, and Megan couldn't keep her mouth closed another second. "What happens now?"

He met her gaze levelly. "I write up a report then we start looking for Great Eye guy so Violet can ID him."

Megan didn't say another word. She didn't have to. She saw everything she needed to in his brown gaze, his stoic expression. She suddenly knew why Nic insisted they stay with his mother rather than in a hotel. He was worried.

About Violet's safety.

CHAPTER NINE

NIC FINALLY LEFT THE precinct and headed to his mother's house, relieved the sun hadn't set yet. He didn't want to look like he was avoiding the situation, but he had to work. Violet's sudden appearance had derailed him from a normal busy day—and yes, he'd had appointments. After standing up the mayor, Nic's assistant had cancelled the rest of them.

Now he had to get moving with the investigation into Judge Dubos. That took precedence right now. He needed to find the runner—Great Eye guy—Violet had seen passing an envelope to Dubos and find out who the kid worked for. That would start with a personal visit to Big Mike.

Nic had detectives who could do the deed, and he should probably let them. It wasn't that Nic didn't have men he trusted in his department. He did. But just because he'd stepped up a rung on the ladder didn't mean he wasn't still paying close attention to what was happening on the streets—especially in his former district. That was the message he'd been conveying to this town.

And precisely why he'd taken a stroll last night.

Big Mike wasn't going to get off talking to two beat cops, not this time, not when the trouble had to do with Violet. Both she and Megan had returned to his mother's house to get settled hours ago. He hadn't heard a word since and had no clue what his mother had cooked up for her guests. He supposed his first official act as father and intimate partner should be getting his daughter's and her mother's cell phone numbers.

He half expected a repeat performance of the impromptu family reunion his mother had hosted earlier, but the house was quiet when Nic let himself in. He slid out of his jacket and tossed it on the bench in the foyer. He could hear the low hum of the TV and headed toward the family room. Sure enough, the TV was on, but no one appeared to be watching it. Both Megan and Violet were curled up on the couch fast asleep. And the unexpected sight rooted him to the spot.

Megan had nestled into the corner of the big leather couch, legs drawn up beneath her, her arm around Violet, who was propped against her, head on a hip, legs stretched out across the couch, an afghan covering her.

They were curled up together in a position that looked as if they'd had years to perfect. A lifetime, in fact. Violet's. A lifetime of settling in to watch movies. Kid movies at first, he guessed. Like those Anthony's goddaughter loved. Nic tried to imagine Violet as a child, nestling against Megan with a bowl of popcorn. Or maybe a slumber party with a bunch of girlfriends all spread out on blankets in front of the TV.

He couldn't. All he knew about his daughter was that she liked *Lord of the Rings*. And piercings.

Nic realized the sound from the TV was looping, and a glance at the screen revealed the menu from the movie they'd been watching. *Star Trek*. The new one with the guy from *Heroes*.

He knew this movie, liked it even, having grown up on the various versions of the franchise. Not that he had much time to watch movies. He didn't, but some crazy part of him was relieved that he had something to share, some common ground. If Violet had been watching the movie, she must like it. Right? And what about Megan?

He stomped that thought fast. He wasn't interested in what Megan thought.

"They fell asleep about halfway through," his mother whispered. "I left it playing. I was afraid to wake them. They were both exhausted."

He glanced at her, saw the worry in her expression. For him. But there was something else, too. When she glanced at Megan and Violet, her features went all soft, thoughtful.

He could practically hear what she was thinking and took evasive maneuvers.

"Don't even look at me like that," he said. "I don't have the energy tonight."

"You never do."

"I don't want to hear it."

"I haven't said one word."

He retreated into the hall so as not to disturb their guests. *His* family. "You don't have to."

She shrugged. "Forgive me if I find the situation a little ironic, and very amusing."

Amusing? He didn't consider missing his daughter's entire life remotely entertaining. But he was *not* having this conversation. Spinning on his heels, he headed into the kitchen to raid the fridge.

"Sausage and peppers?" She arrived in his wake. "Corinne brought bread from Mauricio's. I'll make you a sandwich."

"Thanks."

She motioned him away from the refrigerator, fiercely protective of what she considered her turf.

"What can I do to help?" he asked.

"Stop living everyone else's lives and start living your own," she replied without missing a beat.

"Damn it, Mom." He sank into a chair. "Not tonight. I mean it."

"Okay. But know that'll be a big help. For you and the rest of us."

Dropping his face into his hands, he massaged his temples. He had a life—or as much of one as he'd been able to squeeze in through the years around work and school and this family. He had buddies. He dated. Maybe not since he'd taken on this appointment, but Nic would settle into a rhythm in time, and when he did, he'd pay attention to that part of his life again.

Who knew? He might actually meet someone he was interested in. It had been known to happen on occasion.

"Would you like your sandwich hot or cold?"

"Cold."

"You're sure?" She surfaced from the refrigerator with two plastic storage containers. "That'll only save you the time it will take me to heat everything, and it's not as if you can leave. Unless you're planning to abandon your family."

"Abandonment's not my issue."

"This much is true."

She would keep sucking him in until she had her say. He knew it. She knew it. And she was right. He couldn't even leave until he dealt with *his* family in the living room.

"Hot then. With Tabasco."

She smiled, clearly satisfied.

"Go ahead," he said. "I'm listening."

"That would be a first." Grabbing a ladle from above the baker's rack, she aimed it at him. "I've been telling you to stop worrying about everyone else and get a life for yourself. But you don't listen. Now a ready-made family drops into your lap. That's what I meant earlier. This is important."

"Jeez, Mom. I *know* it's important."

"I don't think you do. You're a very lucky man, Nic. Much luckier than you deserve. Your father's watching out for you from up there." She pointed the ladle skyward and not, Nic knew, toward the second story of this house.

"He had a wonderful family that he loved more than anything, and he didn't even get the time to see his kids grow up. He doesn't want you to let your life pass you by without living it." She ladled peppers into a bowl then speared a sausage with a knife before popping everything into the microwave. "I know you always felt it was your place to look out for everyone—"

"It was my place."

"Was, Nic. *Was*. And your job was *helping* this family. No differently than it was Marc's and Anthony's and everyone else's. You just had the distinction of being oldest, so you got a head start. It was never your job to replace your father."

"I know that." No one could have replaced his dad.

"I don't think you do, Nic. Everyone's all grown-up and living their lives. Everyone but you." She glanced over her shoulder at him and grimaced. "You've done right by every one of your brothers. Your sister, too, for as much as she'd let you. You should feel good about that. Not as if this family is your personal cross to bear."

"I don't."

"No? You sure act like it." She held his gaze steadily, seeing too much with all-seeing, all-knowing mother's sight.

As much as Nic didn't want to admit she was right, she was right. He'd been waiting for the day he could stop funneling every spare dime into Vince's education. That had been his yardstick. His chance to start paying attention to what he wanted. The mayor's request had delayed his new beginning.

But if that was the case, then did that mean the arrival of a daughter he'd never known about would delay his new beginning even more?

It sure felt that way.

But he couldn't deal with this today, too, not after the day he'd had, not with all the surprises he'd faced, not with his family, his *own* family, asleep in the living room.

Since he couldn't deny her claim, he said, "That it?"

"If you promise me you'll think about what I've said."

"I promise."

Her frown suggested she wasn't hopeful, but, true to her word, she dropped the subject. She cut bread, made a sandwich, handed him the bottle of Tabasco sauce.

"Thank you." He took the plate. "For dinner and for caring."

Her smile told him he'd appeased her nurturing Italian mother's soul. He ate while she went to check on their guests.

Nic was finishing when he sensed a presence. He didn't need to turn around to know he'd find Megan standing there. And that felt like the most natural thing in the world. He had no idea what that meant. Didn't want to know because he couldn't handle anything else tonight. Not when he was so busy noticing the way she looked.

He'd never been with her like this before, still drowsy from sleep. Sleeping together in the true sense of the word hadn't been part of their repertoire. They'd always stolen their moments together, rushing to get dressed so they wouldn't be caught. They'd never had the luxury of falling asleep in each other's arms, of waking up together.

Nic thought he would have liked falling asleep with her. At least with the Megan he'd known long ago.

She wasn't the same woman now, he reminded himself, forcing his gaze to pick out the differences, an effort at distraction. Her hair was shorter. Not really short, but shorter than she'd worn it all those years ago. That was new.

And the secret she'd kept. That, too.

"Can we talk?" she asked.

"Have a seat."

"Actually, I'd like to walk, if that's okay with you. If I sit down, I'll fall asleep again. The flight did me in."

"Yeah, sure." He wasn't exactly dressed the part, but he'd make do since he had things to say, too. He needed to get an investigation underway, and as Violet's legal guardian, he needed Megan's help to do that.

He didn't know where his mother had disappeared to, but Violet was still fast asleep on the couch as they passed the family room and exited through the front door into fading daylight.

"Any particular way?" Megan asked.

"Your call."

She stepped lightly down the porch stairs and headed

in the direction of St. Charles Avenue. Nic walked silently beside her, two of her brisk strides making up one of his own. She wasn't dressed for walking any more than he was, with her long flowy skirt and low heels that didn't look much more comfortable than his own dress shoes, but she moved so gracefully, clearly happy to be outdoors.

He should open his mouth and get straight to the point, keep things business between them. But Nic found himself unwilling to break the companionable silence, remnants of how easy he'd once found being around this woman.

They'd walked all over this city, absorbed in each other's company, talking about everything that mattered to two kids trying to figure out life. He was still trying to figure it out. Every time he thought he had a bead, life threw him another curve. He wondered about Megan. Didn't ask.

He could hear the St. Charles line rattling down the street a few blocks away. The neighborhood he'd grown up in was now known as the Lower Garden District. Much had been parceled off to become the nearby Arts and Warehouse Districts, but to Nic these residential streets were simply home. Some houses were better cared for than others as residents aged or moved away, but all in all, folks around here kept their eyes on each other, helped out each other.

That had been tested in the wake of Katrina, when the hurricane had brought life as they'd all known it to a screeching halt. The media played up the chaos, but for every horror story there'd been an unprinted account of someone rescuing a neighbor's kid or salvaging a devastated home or caring for stranded animals. People helping each other survive.

Nic knew firsthand because he'd been on those streets.

People from all over the country had poured into New Orleans with the floodwaters. Parades of utility trucks from Florida, Texas, Oklahoma and so many other states had arrived, driven by normal working people with the skills and desire to help. Those convoys resembled krewes on Mardi Gras parade routes, proving to the people around here that they hadn't been cut off by the storm. Those convoys had brought help and hope.

But about the last thing Nic wanted to think about was hope. Not when he didn't feel much, didn't have a clue how he was going to reconcile what he felt for the woman beside him. Megan. He still hadn't wrapped his brain around the fact that she was back.

"Listen," he said. "I can't lend you my cruiser, but Anthony's going to drop off a car in the morning so you'll have something to drive while you're in town. I thought you might have people you want to see."

"Oh, Nic. That's so thoughtful, but I'll rent a car. I don't want to be any trouble." She gave a soft laugh. "Well, any more trouble than I've already been."

"It's not trouble. Anthony keeps loaners at the garage. They're for customers." He exhaled heavily. "I'm trying to do the right thing here. But I haven't exactly had time to figure out what that is yet, so I'm playing things by ear."

She nodded, smile fading. "I hear that. You'd think I'd be prepared, but I'm afraid I'm not, either. I only know we can't afford to alienate each other for Violet's sake."

He had no clue what to say. What came next? Did he demand visitation? Would he even be able to afford a plane ticket from whatever remote corner of the world they were living in after he paid back child support?

"What about a document of parentage?" he asked. "Are you planning to add me on her birth certificate while you're here?"

Her eyes widened. "Oh, I hadn't thought that far ahead. I can. Do you want to give some thought to—"

"What's to think about? She's my daughter, isn't she?" Way too much emotion showing. So much more than he wanted to feel.

"Yes, Nic. She's your daughter. If you'd like proof, we can have blood drawn—"

"Megan, I have eyes in my head."

She took a deep breath, clearly determined to weather this storm productively. "If you're worried about financial arrangements, please don't be. I make a decent living and get a housing allowance. We live pretty simply. We've never wanted for anything at all. Not even in the beginning."

Nic wished he was feeling half as productive. "I want to be a part of my daughter's life. I expect responsibility to come along with being a father."

There weren't too many places for her to go with that, and they lapsed into silence again. It didn't take long for Nic to decide he didn't like the silence much either, so he headed to the place he was most comfortable.

Work.

"We need to talk about what happened with Violet last night."

"Is she in trouble because of that piercing and breaking the curfew?"

Her voice was a whisper in the summer twilight, no longer day, but not yet night. The fading sky layered in the pinks and golds of sunset, the traffic quieting but still there, the sounds of the city.

"I wish it was that simple. The piercing isn't an issue. The curfew isn't a big deal either since it's only a first offense. In any other circumstances her parent would have been called to pick her up." *Parent*, singular in this case. "But Violet saw something important."

"The boy with the Great Eye tattoo."

Nic nodded. "And she had quite a few people witness that she saw it."

Megan shook her head as if to clear it. "What does that mean, Nic? Just tell me what's going on. I need to know."

He didn't want to worry her, but he suspected that what was going on inside Megan's head right now might be harder to handle than the truth. The Megan he'd known hadn't sharpened her worrying skills into a science. He wondered if single motherhood was to blame.

"You heard Violet's statement. You heard what she said about the man who was causing trouble in the massage parlor, the man Great Eye guy passed off an envelope."

Megan nodded.

"I know the man and believe what Violet witnessed was a payoff."

"Who is he, Nic?"

"I can't give you specifics, but suffice to say he's someone high up on the city food chain."

"Oh, no."

Nic nodded. "And we got a few too many witnesses who know what Violet saw. If it was a payoff—and I'd bet money it was—we've got the man himself, Great

Eye guy and the tattoo parlor owner who all saw what went down and know Violet did, too."

"Oh, please tell me she's not in any danger." Not a question, more of a pleading demand.

Nic wished he could oblige, but before he could voice his concerns another thought apparently occurred to her.

"What about the women in the massage parlor?"

"That much is in our favor," he assured her. "From what I can tell from their statements, they're only interested in what happened inside their shop."

"You believe them?"

"I do. They're worried about protecting their license. They don't want trouble with the police. If they were scared of this man, they wouldn't have made the call in the first place."

Megan nodded, accepting his logic.

"I've got to get the investigation going," he said. "So I can get to the bottom of what's going on and extricate our daughter. I'll need your written consent to photograph her."

"Of course, but why?"

"Like I said, I want her out of the situation, but she's the only one talking. The tattoo parlor owner denies seeing anything, and I don't know who Great Eye guy is. I'm going to use Violet's piercing to put some pressure on the tattoo parlor owner to give a statement. It's lame, no question, but it's all I have right now. I don't want to have to rely on Violet's account."

"You are worried about her." Not exactly an accusation, but he could tell she was trying to pull the pieces together, to decide how worried she should be. He could hear it in the soft intake of breath, see it in her expression as she turned to him. "That's why you want us at your mother's."

"I wouldn't risk Violet's safety, Megan. And I don't think there's a threat. Yet. But I don't know all the players, either. The ones I do know about I wouldn't trust as far as I can throw, so until I figure out what's going on, I want you someplace where I've got trustworthy men keeping their eyes on you. And no, I don't want to put a teenage witness on the stand. Not in this particular case."

Dubos had been around a long time. Nic didn't know who he'd have in his pocket, and it would take time to find out. He wouldn't place his daughter at risk in the process. No one could officially connect Violet to him yet but, like with Jurado, one look at her and there'd be no missing the fact that she was a DiLeo.

Their connection only complicated things. Nic didn't doubt for one second that Dubos would try to strong-arm Nic by threatening his daughter. It was exactly the sort of tactic to expect from the man, the kind of rampant corruption Nic was determined to drive out of the department. He wasn't going to explain these particular details to Megan.

He didn't have to. She'd grown up here. She knew the history. Public corruption was never pretty. Particularly when it involved violent crimes perpetrated by the guys who were supposed to be upholding the law.

"I read about your appointment," she said. "You're working with the new mayor and the government to clean things up."

Nodding, he told himself that she only wanted to know about him to be practical. With their daughter traveling halfway around the world to introduce herself, Megan would want to know what Violet would find when she got here. What *she* would find, since this whole situation had blown up in her face.

He wasn't sure he believed himself.

"This is my fault." He might as well toss that out. Anything to distract him from thinking about Megan. "Violet wouldn't have known about that tattoo parlor if she hadn't followed me there."

"You didn't even know Violet existed, let alone *stalked* you."

"I had a fourteen-year-old tail."

"That's what your deputy chief thought was so funny, wasn't it?"

Nic scowled, the only answer she was going to get.

"Well, I suppose when you put it like that, I understand how you might feel that way, but don't take everything on yourself, Nic. Violet's clever. Trust me. She managed to find you and run off to a different continent under my nose."

"You're not a cop."

"No, but I'm a mother, and one who pays attention."

He snorted in disgust. Why in hell was Megan reassuring him? To make him feel better? This whole situation was a bad joke. It wasn't enough that memories from a forgotten past had been ambushing him ever since he'd discovered Violet in his office with her new nose ring and old photograph.

Now he had to contend with Megan trying to rationalize his stupidity. No, he hadn't had any reason to suspect anyone would be following him and, no, he wasn't a mind reader. But that didn't wipe away his guilt because Violet had come to town to find him and had stepped in quicksand as a result. He'd led her straight to Big Mike's. And if that wasn't bad enough, he'd left her alone on the street when he'd taken off with Anthony. Now the very fact that she was his daughter could make her a target.

"Nic, I know you don't know our daughter yet, but trust me when I tell you she's got a mind of her own. She's wanted a piercing for a while now. Whether or not she followed you, she was going to make it inside a piercing place eventually."

Our daughter.

There it was. The intimate part of intimate partners.

"Would you have taken that job?" The words were out of his mouth before he could talk himself out of asking. He shouldn't care. Her answer shouldn't matter.

But it did.

She didn't reply right away, just kept walking, gaze fixed ahead.

"I wish I could say yes," she finally admitted. "But to be honest, I can only say I think so. I've been going back and forth for weeks trying to figure out the best thing to do. Like I told you, I decided a long time ago to tell Violet when it became important to her. While she hasn't actually asked about you, she has been talking about family a lot. The timing seemed to be six of one, half a dozen of another."

"Why?"

"Well, I was worried about dropping out of nowhere into your life. I'm not sure the reality of the situation could live up to Violet's expectations. On the other hand, I liked the idea of being in town to parent her through the process. She doesn't actually do a lot of listening at the moment, but she does talk when something's on her mind. I try to pay attention so I don't miss those opportunities."

Nic didn't want to understand, but he saw good and

bad parents every day in his line of work—often the extremes of good and bad. Megan was trying to be one of the good parents.

"There are so many other things to consider, too."

"Like what?"

"Like getting myself out of the way mostly. Coming home to New Orleans means dealing with my parents. Violet doesn't know them well, but she wants to, and I'm not sure what to expect from them. She's young, Nic. Emotionally, she's all over the place, and I can't help thinking that a little more maturity wouldn't hurt her when she's dealing with the situation. Then again, I can't help but think the opportunity to return home wouldn't have happened unless now was the right time." She gave a wry smile. "I guess what I'm really trying to say is I would have made the decision when I convinced myself it was the best thing for her."

Which Nic interpreted to mean when she convinced herself that *he* was the best thing.

CHAPTER TEN

NIC WAS FINALLY HOME. He stared into the kitchen
cabinet, where he'd installed a wine rack shortly after
moving into his condo on Julia Street a few years ago.
He knew every bottle by name but pulled each out to
glance at the label, considering. Going through the process somehow helped ground him after this eternally
long day.

He'd started the morning dog-tired thanks to Damon,
but not in his wildest dreams did he imagine he'd reach
nightfall as a father.

He knew the instant his fingers touched the bottle
that tonight was the night for the 1986 *Cos d'Estournel*.
Since acquiring it, he'd known this particular Bordeaux
was destined for something special, though he'd had no
clue what that "something special" would be.

He'd considered opening it a few times already. To
celebrate his move into this condo.

During Vince's residency celebration.

The birth of Rocco and Annabelle had been a serious
contender, but when it came down to actually opening
the bottle, Nic had realized the "something special"
actually belonged to Anthony and Tess. But when they'd
asked him to be Annabelle's godfather, he'd opened a
1982 *d'Issan, Margaux* to commemorate the baptism,
a bit lighter and more suited to Tess's taste.

Tonight was *his* something special.

Setting the bottle on the counter, he reached inside another cabinet for a decanter, telling himself that opening this bottle wasn't a total waste although there was no way he'd come close to finishing it. A glass or two at most. He hated drinking alone, but what the hell. Sleep was nowhere in sight—yet again—even though he was tired, so damned tired.

This whole situation seemed as ironic. People usually celebrated fatherhood by gathering outside a hospital delivery room or inside church for a baptism. The occasion always filled with well-wishers.

Not Nic's fatherhood though.

Just he, himself and him in his quiet condo tonight. His newly acquired family was at his mother's place.

Definitely the *Cos d'Estournel*.

Whatever was left of the bottle would be in fate's hands. The wine would hold up for a day or so though never come close to tasting the way it would tonight. Didn't matter how he stored it. But his need to drink probably wouldn't go away by tomorrow. The thought made him feel better about opening the bottle.

Reaching into the drawer for a corkscrew, he heard a sound coming from the dining room. The front door. Someone was coming in, and as very few people had the key to his place, he wasn't surprised when he peered into the dining room to find Anthony walking in with Vince in tow.

Nic hadn't realized how damned quiet his place was until his brothers shouted out greetings, apparently unaware it was almost midnight.

"Normal people sleep at night." The sound of his voice made him feel so much better now that he wouldn't have to worry about wasting half a bottle of good wine.

Anthony spotted the opener and pointedly peered

through the archway into the kitchen. "No way. Forget all about *that*. We got an occasion happening here."

Sidestepping Nic, he marched right into the kitchen, pulled the cabinet open and set the bottle back on the rack.

"Babies are usually seven or eight pounds, Nic," Vince said. "I think you might have set a record."

"You learn that in med school, brainiac?"

"Sure as hell did." Vince grinned, holding up a brown paper bag with great ceremony and sliding a bottle from inside.

Wild Turkey 101.

"Time to celebrate."

The next thing Nic knew, he was seated at his dining room table, toasting fatherhood with a shot glass.

"So what in hell prompted this visit?" he asked, then tossed back a shot that burned so good all the way down. "And don't tell me you were bored."

"Vince wanted to drink. I wanted to whip your ass." Anthony produced a deck of cards.

"You wish." Sliding the shot glass toward Vince, Nic suddenly remembered that there was more to family than one problem after another. "You *so* wish."

And there might be an end in sight to this day, after all.

VIOLET WISHED THEY WOULD wrap up this photo shoot so she could eat breakfast in peace. She was barely awake yet, but Dad insisted on taking these photos even though Grandmama had the coffee brewing and the whole kitchen smelled good. Too many days of airplane food and granola bars had caught up with her. One good night's sleep and she was back to normal and starving.

"Smile pretty," Mom said, and Violet rolled her eyes.

Puh-leeze. Like anyone would even see her face. Not with Dad taking the photos. He was zooming in on her nose so no one could identify her. He said he wanted to use them in his investigation, but he was being so cryptic about the whole thing that she couldn't even figure out why he bothered.

He didn't know it yet, but she planned to make one of these photos her profile pic on Facebook. They were going to be really stupid and she wanted to post one just for laughs. And to show off her new piercing. Esperanza would be so jealous. Even a gay dad hadn't gotten her one of those.

After snapping off a few more shots, her dad checked them in the display. "Got what I need. Megan, did you sign those forms yet?"

"Yes." Mom grabbed an envelope off the table and handed it to him.

"Did you have any questions?" Dad asked. Violet hadn't realized how much taller than Mom he was. Mom wasn't exactly short, average maybe. It was just weird seeing them together.

"No. Everything looked very straightforward."

He nodded. "How about those cell numbers then?"

"Oh, that's right." Mom seemed flustered. "Violet, grab your phone."

She slid it from her pocket and handed it to Mom, who started playing musical phones with Dad to program each other's numbers into their contacts.

"Okay, we're all set," Dad said. "If you run into anything this morning, call. We'll figure it out."

"Okay, will do," Mom said.

Mom and Dad. Seeing these two together was hard to process. It had been her and Mom for so long. And

GigiMarie. But Violet wasn't complaining. Here she was thinking she'd be grounded for the rest of her life, but she hadn't counted on the worry factor. Mom was so relieved that she hadn't even brought up the consequences conversation yet. Or made Violet take out her nose ring. Fingers crossed she'd decide not to bother. Violet knew better than to think she'd forget.

Then again, maybe the being-around-Dad-again thing had thrown Mom off course. Her dad might always be this keep-his-distance proper. Violet didn't know, but she knew Mom wasn't. Mom did everything a lot. She laughed a lot. Worried a lot. Worked a lot. Had fun a lot. Any kind of *a lot* Violet could think of. Even kept secrets a lot.

That part sucked, but she wasn't ready to deal with it.

Neither was Mom. She was all, like, "let's play nice and work things out." Please. It was kind of pathetic, really. The real reason old people shouldn't hook up. They didn't know how to do it. Or maybe they were so old they forgot. Either way, watching these two together was painful.

Thankfully, Grandmama was taking her to the hair salon this morning so Mom could take care of stuff while Dad went to work. Violet was going to see Uncle Anthony's garage and Uncle Damon's dojo because they were all in the same building. Then she was going to lunch with Dad. No time for *the* conversation in there.

"I want to go by Bell-DiLeo, with a hyphen, okay?" Violet announced to give everyone something else to think about.

Both Mom and Dad stared at her, making her feel totally self-conscious.

"I thought you said you were going to that place this

morning to do the paperwork and add Dad? You said it wasn't a big deal."

Mom nodded. "It isn't."

"If they're making new copies of my birth certificate, you should be able to change my name, right?"

Mom looked at Dad for approval. "Nic?"

Oh, Mom wasn't worried about the paperwork. She was worried about Dad. God, this was *weird*. Violet couldn't even tell if her dad was cool with this. He had that whole police-officer-stare thing down cold.

"Still pretty shocked?" she asked matter-of-factly.

"Looks that way," he admitted. "Thought some sleep would take the edge off."

"Not so much?"

He smiled. Sort of. "Might have if I'd gotten some."

"Not so much?"

"Not so much."

"Good shock?" She tried to sound cool, as if it didn't matter. "I looked online, but couldn't find anything about, you know, like, a family or anything. Grandmama said you didn't have any except for a bunch of pain-in-the-ass siblings—"

"Violet," Mom warned.

"And a daughter," Dad added.

"So you've never been married. Ever?"

He shook his head again. Mom snatched her cup from the table and headed to the coffeepot. Violet knew she was hiding because she was embarrassed.

"That's cool." And interesting, too. Two parents. Neither ever married. What was up with that? "I didn't want to cause any trouble. Mom was worried."

Well, Violet was the one worried, but Mom always said if she should find herself in a situation that made her uncomfortable she could always use Mom as an excuse. Of course, she'd been talking about being out with friends who started doing stuff they weren't supposed to be doing, like drinking or drugs, but Violet was uncomfortable.

"You're no trouble, Violet," Dad said.

"So, can I go by Bell-DiLeo?" she asked. "It's okay if you don't want me to."

Then her dad smiled for real. It made a big difference, too. He all of a sudden looked friendly. Like Uncle Anthony.

"You can go by Bell-DiLeo if that's what you want. With a hyphen."

"I'll take care of it then," Mom said.

"Cool. I'll update my account info on Facebook. Does Grandmama have Wi-Fi at the salon?"

Her dad nodded as the front door opened and a voice rang out, "Car delivery service."

She could hear someone moving down the hall, then Uncle Anthony appeared in the doorway. He was wearing a work shirt with his name on it. "Got the best loaner in the house. Oh-eight Jeep Liberty. Last year of the old body style. The best in my opinion. Can't imagine what idiot thought we needed to go bigger with gas prices what they are." He looked right at her. "Of course, this one really wanted to borrow my Firebird."

"Is that the car you picked up Dad in the other night?" she asked.

"That's exactly what I picked up *Dad* in."

"You'd let me drive it?"

He crossed the room in a couple of fast steps and held out his hand for Violet to shake. "Make you a deal. When you're old enough, I'll teach you to drive in it. I taught everyone to drive around here. Even *Dad*."

"Isn't he older than you?"

"But I'm the best driver."

Dad snorted. "Better not let your wife hear you say that or you'll be driving her purple Gremlin. And by the way, he's also full of it, Violet. I even taught him to drive his Harley."

She turned to stare wide-eyed. "You have a Harley?"

Uncle Anthony winked. "Bright red chopper."

"I want to learn to drive *that*."

Uncle Anthony didn't get to answer because Mom said, "Not this week, young lady. You've quite used up your quota of rebellion, thank you very much."

Yeah, well, Violet couldn't exactly argue that. Luckily, she didn't have to because Uncle Anthony glanced at the clock on the wall and said, "Nic, you'll take me to the garage?"

"Yeah, I've got to head out now, too." He grabbed the camera and the envelope from the table. "Megan, my mother's not down yet. Will you drop her and Violet off at the shop?"

"Of course." She took the keys from Uncle Anthony and said, "Thanks so much. This is really nice of you."

Uncle Anthony kissed her cheek. "You're part of the family, and DiLeos take care of each other. Remember that."

Mom nodded, looking all blush-y. Totally lame.

Uncle Anthony kissed Violet's cheek on the way out, too, whispering, "We've got time to change her mind."

Violet winked at him. A pact. But she didn't get a chance to say anything because her dad was suddenly eyeballing her as if he wasn't sure what to do or how to say goodbye.

But Violet knew.

Hopping up from her chair, she went to him, stretched up on tiptoes and kissed his cheek. "See ya later, Dad."

For a second, he looked so surprised that Violet felt like laughing. Uncle Anthony did.

"Come on, *Dad*. Get a move on. I got full bays, a sick mechanic and about four hours of AutoTexCare paperwork on my desk."

"Yeah, right." Dad looked at her and smiled. Another one of the real ones. "See you for lunch."

"See you for lunch."

Then he and Uncle Anthony headed down the hall, filling up the narrow space with their broad shoulders. They looked so alike it was funny. The only way to tell them apart from behind was their uniforms. Dad was all official in his dress blues with the brass buttons and polished shoes. Uncle Anthony's uniform didn't even look like one from behind. And his hair was longer than her dad's, too.

"Megan's going to drop you and Violet off at the shop," her dad yelled up the stairs. "Anthony and I are heading out."

"You boys have a good day," Grandmama called back.

"You, too," Uncle Anthony said, then the front door closed behind them and it sounded as if a herd of buffalo were clomping down the porch stairs.

Violet reached for her glass on the table and took a swig of orange juice, happy. Uncle Anthony was right. They were part of the family now, which meant she was going to have to convince Mom to take the New Orleans project. She had to be around to learn to drive the chopper.

BELLS CHIMED WHEN NIC pushed open the front door of Insane, Ink. The place had only opened for business twenty minutes ago, and was dead empty. He waited patiently, guessing Big Mike was in the back and would make his way up front eventually to see who'd dropped by. The place might be open to catch the daytime tourists, but the real moneymaking traffic wouldn't start until after sundown.

Swinging doors that separated the public front of the shop from the private back creaked open.

Big Mike was called *big* for a good, if unimaginative reason. He was. Very. Six-five if he was an inch. That was a lot of hairy inked skin. In a muscle shirt and with pillow marks still on one cheek. Nice.

He planted himself behind the glass counter that housed a jewelry display, plunked down a take-out coffee cup and growled in a voice as big as the rest of him, "Well, well, well. Look who's here. Should I bow or something?"

"Nice to see you again, too, Mike." Nic withdrew an envelope from his inner jacket pocket. "Hate to interrupt your morning cup of joe, but I've got a few questions for you."

"About what?"

"About the incident that took place here two nights ago."

"I don't have any idea what incident you might be talking about, commander—" Big Mike broke off with a scowl. "*Chief.* Excuse the hell out of me. Can't friggin' keep up with you."

Nic waved the envelope and flashed a smile. Big Mike did not want to screw around today. Not when Nic was operating on two hours of sleep for the second night in a row and a hangover from too much excitement and bourbon. "Didn't think you would, so I brought along something to refresh your memory."

Big Mike issued a throaty roar. "I already told the beat cops I didn't see anything."

Nic always appreciated the way people volunteered information when they got nervous or put on the spot. Made his job so much easier.

"And I already read the incident report."

"Then what do you want from me? Maybe you should be talking to the massage ladies," he suggested, inclining his head in the direction of Busybodies. "They're all over there brewing tea or whatever they do this time of morning."

Nic narrowed his gaze at Big Mike. "I've already read their statements, too."

"Then you know I didn't see a friggin' thing. *Nada*. Heard raised voices, but by the time I got here all the excitement was over." Shrugging brawny shoulders, he set the hippy Hula dancer on his bicep into action.

Nic slid a 5x7 photo from the envelop, a zoomed-in shot of Violet's nose ring, flashed it in front of Big Mike's face and announced, "I'm here about this."

"Yeah, so it's a piercing. What's it got to do with me?"

"I'd like to see the notarized parental consent form that accompanied this particular piercing, please."

Big Mike opened his mouth then shut it again, seemed to be struggling for an appropriate response. "What in hell makes you think that's my work?"

"Cops picked the kid up here, Mike. Something about a curfew infraction and all that."

"Oh, that kid. It's around here somewhere."

Nic waited patiently while the man went through the motions of locating the document.

Finally, Mike confessed, "You know, Chief. I can't seem to find it. Must have misplaced it or maybe it got thrown away in all the excitement the other night."

"You mean the excitement you missed?"

Big Mike spread his hands wide and went the playing-stupid route. "The cops did show up. I'm talking about *that* excitement. They were taking statements from the massage ladies. And asking questions. I didn't know the kid went with the cops. Thought she might have slipped out when the lights started flashing. She looked pretty shifty."

"Did she now? What about the person she came in with? The legal adult who signed the paperwork? Did you see that person leave by any chance?"

Silence. Big Mike was busted. He had two choices—fabricate an adult who'd come in with Violet to make the piercing legal or admit he'd pierced a minor without regard to state law.

Nic was betting on the latter. Big Mike might like bending laws like pretzels to suit his needs, but he wasn't stupid.

Sure enough, a beefy fist came down on the counter making the glass rattle in the case. "Come on, chief. With all the shit going on in this town, since when do you have time to start trolling the streets looking for misdemeanors?"

Nic's turn to shrug. "The parents were pretty upset by what you did to their precious little angel. They were already talking court when they picked the kid up from the curfew center. That's where this photo came from. Evidence for the judge. Wouldn't be at all surprised if they've secured their attorney by now."

Big Mike's mouth opened and shut a few more times, reminding Nic distinctly of a gasping fish.

"You're going to bust my chops about a piercing?"

"A minor, Mike. You know the rules."

The rule today: Nic wanted answers about the judge.

And the ruddy flush creeping into the man's bristly cheeks told Nic he did know the rules and didn't like them one bit.

"She's no one, Chief."

Beep. Wrong answer. Nic whipped out a citation pad from another pocket. "Now that's where you're wrong, Mike. She's the minor who's costing you one significant chunk of change."

"You. Are. Shitting. Me."

Nic checked off boxes and scratched out his name. He handed Big Mike a citation for the max allowable fine. "No shitting today. But about that *other* incident, Mike, and all the excitement you missed—if it turns out you remember anything, anything at all, give me a call. You know where to find me."

Nic tucked the citation pad in his pocket with the envelope and photo. He smiled and said, "Have a nice day, Mike."

And headed out the door.

CHAPTER ELEVEN

TAKING A DEEP BREATH, Megan willed herself to calm down. She glanced at the clock on the display of her loaner car, a car that had proven surprisingly fun to drive—or would have been in any other circumstances.

Ten forty-eight.

She was meeting Nic inside at eleven. She'd already spent the past few hours standing in lines and getting information about legally changing her two-person family into a three-person family. Somehow the paperwork she held was driving home the situation in a way nothing else had until now.

STATE OF LOUISIANA
ACKNOWLEDGMENT OF
PATERNITY AFFIDAVIT
CHILD BORN OUTSIDE OF MARRIAGE

NOTICE: You must read all three pages and initial the third page of this form before you sign the affidavit.

This is a legal document. Complete in ink and do not alter.

Do not alter? Did someone have a sick sense of humor? Completing this paperwork would alter her life forever. While there might not be much time left for shared parental responsibilities, Nic would still be a part of Violet's life, which meant by default he'd be a part of Megan's. She might run into him on holidays. Certainly at Violet's milestone occasions. At the very least Megan would hear about him from Violet, about the part he was playing in her life.

All well and good. Nic should be a part of his daughter's life, no question, but Megan hadn't counted on her reaction to him, as if fifteen years and a lot of bad decisions had never happened. Why couldn't the man have gone on with his life and gotten married like someone normal?

If she'd have shown up in New Orleans to meet Violet's stepmother and six half siblings, she wouldn't be so aware of the man. External circumstances would have tempered her reaction. But she'd waltzed right through his mother's front door and sat at the dinner table as if she'd only run to the corner market to pick up a gallon of milk.

Ten forty-nine.

She had time.

Retrieving her cell phone from her purse, she depressed number three on the speed dial. The call connected quickly.

"Hello, dear," Marie said.

Megan rested her head against the steering wheel, eyes shuttering against the bright Louisiana sun for the briefest of instants as she said, "SOS."

Save Our Sanity.

A chuckle on the other end. "I will if I can. Tell me what's going on. But first tell me how you found Violet. I assume she's in one piece. Your text messages didn't say much."

"One piece and quite pleased with both her new father and her new nose ring."

A gasp. "She didn't."

"Oh, she did."

"Well, look at the bright side. At least the piercing will close up when she gets tired of it. Not like a tattoo."

Megan couldn't suppress a shiver. "You're right. I should stay focused on the positives."

Tattoos and body piercings. When had her life dissolved into using such a yardstick?

"You should," Marie agreed. "So Violet's pleased, but I'm not hearing the same from you."

Preliminaries over, Megan exploded. "Oh, Marie. I'm caught up. Just like I used to get. Just like *that*. I didn't even remember I felt this way until I started feeling this way."

"Slow down, dear. Take a deep breath."

"I have been. I've been taking so many I'm about to hyperventilate. It's not helping."

"Tell me what's going on."

Megan launched into the series of events that began with Nic's appearance at the airport and ending with the fact that she was sitting in front of a notary's office getting ready to meet him to legally include him in Violet's life.

Do not alter.

Altered irrevocably and forever.

Which Megan pointed out without stopping to draw air, so she was breathless and dizzy by the time she finished. Marie remained silent, and Megan could almost see her shaking her head to clear it, trying to find some sense in that verbal tirade.

"Let me get this straight," she finally said. "You and Violet are staying with his mother?"

"Yes."

"You're driving his brother's car?"

"Yes."

"And you're adding his name to Violet's birth certificate and legally changing her last name?"

"Yes and yes."

Another beat of silence then, "Oh, dear. Well, you are caught up."

Megan stared out the windshield at the people strolling through their mornings, tourists exploring the French Quarter, business people heading to appointments, city employees going about the variety of tasks that made life in New Orleans more convenient and pleasant for the folks who lived here. Most of these people were probably exhibiting much better coping skills than Megan was right now. What had happened to her? Between South America and the U.S. she'd transformed from a sane, independent woman into a panicked, confused wreck.

"I can't think around him, Marie," she admitted the truth in a whisper. "I never could. Even way back when I knew if I told him I was pregnant, he'd probably suggest getting married and I'd never be able to say no."

"Did you want to marry him?"

"I don't know," Megan said with a disgusted sigh. "I wasn't thinking about what I wanted. I was only hearing what my parents said and they were telling me all the reasons why marriage would never work."

If you care at all for Nic, you wouldn't want to saddle him the responsibility of a wife and child, or at the very least eighteen years of child support payments he can't afford.

Guilt, guilt and more guilt. Megan hadn't wanted to be a burden—the way she felt with her parents, as if a lifetime of accomplishment had been wiped away by her actions.

Would she have wanted to marry Nic?

She'd loved him enough to stand up to her parents in the only way she'd known how to be with him.

Yes.

"I think this is one of the reasons why I've been going back and forth so much on taking this project, Marie."

"It's not an easy decision with all the personal issues attached to it, but I know how much you want this project. Helping Hands is headquartering in New Orleans to help your home. You've got a chance to pitch in. Just because you've been gone a long time doesn't mean you care any less. You grew up loving the place. Your family is there, your friends, your memories."

"I know. I know. And the office environment will have such unique challenges because it's outreaching into so many areas that other not-for-profits have been working since almost right after Katrina. A lot of opportunities to work in conjunction with these other groups to get even more accomplished."

"That's why Robert wants you, dear. You know that as well as I do. It's a tough project. He needs your expertise, and he knows how much you like challenges."

Megan remembered Violet's accusation when they'd been in Nic's office and knew her daughter was right. Marie did want to spend some time closer to her sister. Megan knew right then that Marie wouldn't come directly out and say it because she didn't want to influence Megan either way. "And I haven't been stateside in such a long time."

Silence on the other end. "That's true as well, but your family is involved with this decision. You take the time you need to make the decision and it'll be the right one. For everyone."

Megan felt a tiny smile tugging at her mouth. "Have I told you lately how much I appreciate you?"

"In a thousand different ways every day."

"Good, because I do."

"Then trust me on this."

The smile faded. "Oh, I do, Marie. You know that, but it's *him*. I think that deep down I knew the minute I was around him again it would be all over."

"What would be over exactly?"

"My sanity."

"What precisely does that mean, dear?"

Oh, God, the woman had infinite patience. Why she'd chosen to remain friends all these years... "It means I get caught up in *him*, Marie. I managed to forget until I saw him in the airport. Or, I don't know, maybe I thought I'd outgrown it. I'm not eighteen years old anymore. I'm a single mother with a teenage daughter. I'm a businesswoman. A well-respected businesswoman."

"You don't have to convince me. I agree with all of the above. Add good mother and dear friend to the list."

Ten fifty-three.

"You're an angel." Megan had never meant anything more in her life.

"No, I'm your friend. And I want you to feel better."

"Thank you so much for always being here when I need you."

"The pleasure is mine. You know that. Just like it's yours whenever I need you. We're a good team."

"I don't think you ever need me as much as I need you."

"Ha!" Marie said. "Our needs are different, that's all. I can't imagine how lonely the past few years would have been if you hadn't allowed me to crash your family party."

Marie's only son had died tragically young, leaving behind a wife and child who'd gone on with their lives but weren't all that great about including Marie.

"I thank God every day you crashed when you did."

"Ditto, dear. Ditto. But I'm still not clear on this 'getting caught up' thing. What you're describing sounds no different than what I used to feel with Ed. The man could talk me into anything, I swear. Even traveling to Haiti to volunteer my time at the maternity house when I had a lovely home, an active church and a coveted position in the garden club."

She referred, of course, to St. Gianna's Maternity Home for young mothers, which was where she'd first met Megan and Violet. Megan couldn't help smiling at the memory, feeling nominally better.

"But Ed was your husband, Marie. I have no right to be getting caught up in Nic. Not now. Not especially after keeping his daughter a secret from him."

"Megan." Marie's usually soft voice shifted into a warning tone. "That's guilt talking. You made the choices you felt were best at the time. And you have to consider that while you were very young when you got involved with this man, you never really had a chance to end things properly. You're bound to have some unresolved feelings that don't involve guilt. You made a beautiful daughter with him. You obviously cared a great deal."

"That makes sense." She heaved a sigh. More in control. "What do I need to do to get things back in perspective? Will coming up with a game plan for Violet help resolve things?"

A beat of silence. "I don't honestly know."

"What do you mean?" Now that came as a surprise. Marie was a veritable font of worldly wisdom.

"It means that I never stopped feeling that way about Ed. I'm sure if he popped down from heaven right now and asked me to head back with him, I wouldn't be able to say no."

"Well, I'm sure that's because you two were committed, married people. I just need to remember I'm an independent woman who thinks for myself, not a teenager in love." She glanced at the clock again.

Ten fifty-seven.

Just then a familiar unmarked cruiser parked about a half a block ahead. Sure enough, the door whipped open and Nic stepped out, bristling with no-nonsense energy, so incredibly handsome with the sun bleaching out his features as he crossed the sidewalk.

"Heaven help me, there he is." She was *so* aware of him. Even on a street busy with people, she noticed him right away. Responsible Nic, right on time, always someone to count on.

How long had he waited for her at Audubon Park that day so long ago when she'd promised to meet him? He'd called her house and spoken to her father. And had found out she'd kept him a secret for his trouble. He'd told her that much.

She wondered what he thought today. That she wouldn't show up as she'd promised?

"Deep breaths, dear. Really deep. Promise me."

"Okay." Megan barely squeaked the word out past the sudden tightness in her throat. She had no right whatsoever to feel anything for Nic. Contrition, she'd earned. Anything else, she'd given up rights to the minute she'd decided to keep her pregnancy a secret.

But right now, with her throat tight and her heart suddenly pounding too hard, Megan could remember exactly why she'd rebelled against everything she'd known, why she'd thrown caution to the wind to be with him.

"I've got to go."

"Promise you'll call the second you can. Promise me."

"Okay. Love you."

"Love you, too, dear. Kiss Violet for me."

"Will do. Bye."

Megan disconnected the call and glanced again at the clock.

Ten fifty-eight.

She'd be on time today, too.

CHAPTER TWELVE

A FEW STROKES OF A MEDIUM-TIP black ballpoint and the stamp of a notary legitimized Nic, and a new identity was born.

Violet Nicole Bell-DiLeo.

Now he, Megan and their daughter were connected in the eyes of the state. Maybe not in the traditional sense, but they were a family of three, nevertheless. He and Megan were legally bound together as parents, intimate partners according to the law.

Seemed like something momentous should mark the occasion, but there were only signatures, copies and fees.

As it was the state would only process the affidavits and issue new documentation. Violet had never been a recipient of any kind of aid so there was no reason for Nic to be investigated for payment of back child support.

The state had enough to do chasing dads whose kids were on the government's payroll to worry about him. But Nic fully intended to contribute. He'd talk to Megan before she took off then get with his financial advisor to figure something out. One thing he did know—teens only got more expensive, not less. Cars. Insurance. Gas. Proms. Senior pictures. Class trips. College. Dorms. Meal plans. He knew the drill and intended to be a part of Violet's life from now on to make up for lost time.

With that same few strokes of the pen, all record of Megan's secret vanished. Violet's original birth certificate would be sealed in an envelope and filed in the vital records registry archives. That envelope would only be opened pursuant to an order of the civil district court for good cause. He couldn't imagine what might come up to constitute that good cause, so that was it. The past was over as far as the state of Louisiana was concerned.

He didn't think Megan felt that way, though. And he definitely didn't, but anger didn't fit his mood right now, either. Not when they'd taken this significant step.

"You should come to lunch with me and Violet," he said as they left the notary's office.

Megan glanced up at him, clearly surprised. "I appreciate that, Nic, but you don't have to include me. I've got the car. I can entertain myself."

"I know I don't have to. It just feels like we should do something together to make this special for her. I don't know—a parade. Throwing beads to the crowds. *Something.*"

A soft smile touched her lips. "You're right."

"So what does she like to eat?"

"She's pretty adventurous. Not much she won't try."

Nic supposed culinary flexibility came with traveling internationally. He had no real frame of reference. Most of the traveling he did was for work. Banquet rubber chicken didn't qualify as adventurous no matter what he thought when he ate it.

When he'd been younger, he hadn't had the money for vacations. There'd been college tuition to pay for— his and everyone else's. Damon's years of martial arts training hadn't come cheaply either. And then there was always something with the house. New roof, sewer line, hot water heater…

"She'd probably enjoy someplace local to give her the flavor of the area," Megan said. "I get the sense she considers New Orleans her hometown because she has family here."

Nic pushed open the door for Megan and glanced at his watch to distract himself from the lingering scent of her shampoo that wafted right under his nose. Something tropical. Coconut, maybe.

"Okay, then. We can still catch breakfast at Brennan's or there's the jazz brunch at the Court of Two Sisters." He let the door swing shut behind them and stepped down onto the street. "The wait might not be so long there."

"If you need to get back to work, she'll understand. We can grab muffalettas in the French Market and then hit Café Du Monde. Doesn't have to be anything fancy. She'll just like being together and soaking in the atmosphere."

Nic considered that. He felt rushed to make up for lost time with his daughter. As much as he wanted to go big and impressive with the impromptu celebration, he'd lost half the morning with this trip to the notary. Not to mention the visit to his mother's house earlier. The pit stop at the garage to drop off Anthony. The trip to see Big Mike.

"All right, why don't we do this?" he suggested. "We'll pick up Violet and do lunch in the French Market. A minicelebration. Then we'll decide where we want dinner, and I'll make reservations. Someplace decent. Antoine's or Commander's Palace maybe. How does that sound?"

Megan flashed a smile, the very same high-beam smile that had once punched him in the gut with its blinding intensity. "Sounds like the perfect plan."

"Okay, then leave the Jeep and we'll take my car. I'll bring you back."

He was about to unlock the car when his cell phone vibrated. Sliding it from his belt, he glanced at the display.

"What—weird. I never get these." He fumbled with the buttons, his fingers too big to work the keypad easily, but finally got the thing to open to read the text message.

From: Violet
Are you coming to get me for lunch or should I text Mom and have her bring me to you?

For a second, Nic stared at the display, surprised. Then it dawned on him. Megan had been running interference in his daughter's life since the beginning, had been making all the choices. Now that he knew about Violet, was officially acknowledged as a parent, it was time for him to establish a place for himself in her life.

Teenagers liked to text, and his daughter was a teenager, after all. He read the message and scanned the display. After depressing the reply button, he typed back: We're on the way.

Granted, he had a few misfires because his fingers were too big, but all in all he was pleased with himself when he pressed the send button.

He'd just shut the phone when it vibrated again.

Another text message: You and Mom?

He hit Reply again and typed: Yes.

This time he didn't bother closing the phone and, sure enough, within seconds she'd fired back another text: Kk. C U ;-)

"Everything all right?" Megan asked from where she was still standing on the curb, waiting for him to unlock the car.

"Oh, yeah, sorry. My first text from Violet. She wanted to know if I was picking her up."

Megan nodded, didn't seem surprised, which added another piece to the puzzle. Texting must be a normal form of communication for them.

Unlocking the car, he opened the door for her. She slid in, a lean, smooth motion he should not be noticing.

"You two text a lot?" he asked as a distraction.

"It's convenient. A lot of times we can text when we might not be able to take a phone call. Like when I'm in a meeting or she's in class. I like having that sort of instant access to her. Saves me from getting gray hair."

Nic might not text and his niece and nephew might not be old enough to have their own cell phones yet, but he did read. He knew all about the technology-savvy teens nowadays. Couldn't count the number he'd brought in during his years on the streets. Confiscating a cell phone was the equivalent of chopping off an arm. Handy little devices, too, for investigations. Cell phone records didn't lie.

"Speaking of gray hair…is that how Violet contacted you when she was on her way here? Just curious."

Megan scowled. "She was three texts away from a police escort picking her up at the airport. I'm serious."

He snorted. No question. "I didn't even know my phone could get text messages."

"If you don't have a text plan, you should let Violet know. You'll spend a small fortune at a quarter a message. She's a maniac. Averages upward of two thousand texts a month."

"Are you kidding?" he asked, stunned. "What does *that* cost?"

Megan grinned. "Eleven ninety-five for unlimited."

"Guess I will have to look into getting a plan."

"Probably a good idea."

They fell silent as he battled traffic the few blocks to the shop. "I'm guessing Violet was busy running around here this morning."

"That is one big building." Megan stared through the window. "So when did all this take place? Must be convenient for everyone to work together."

"Especially since my mother doesn't drive."

"Still?"

Nic nodded. "Forces everyone to chauffeur her around."

"Got it."

Anthony's compound was a huge commercial property that occupied a lot with great exposure. His garage took up most of the lower floor. The salon was around back with separate parking, and a staircase leading to Damon's dojo.

"I thought my brother was crazy to go so big his first time in business. Thought he should start smaller and grow, but he knew what he was doing. He and his father-in-law are like car kings. And this compound gave my mother and Damon opportunities that would have been difficult otherwise." He nodded in approval. "Anthony's got a good head on his shoulders for business."

"Must be much more comfortable for your mother. Wasn't she doing hair in the house way back when?"

"For years, until we converted the garage."

The very mention of the garage made silence fall between them like fog off the lake.

There were memories in the apartment above the garage. The garage where his dad had worked on cars when Nic had been little. After his dad had died, they'd used some of the insurance money to renovate the upstairs into an apartment, which they rented to make ends meet. But after a particularly difficult situation with renters, his mother had refused to rent it again.

That's when it had become sort of a clubhouse for each of the kids in turn. Marc had rehearsed with his band. Anthony had followed in their father's footsteps and reworked old cars. Damon had tried to become Bruce Lee. Vince had housed strays until he could find homes for them. Frankie had holed up there because it was the only quiet place she could find to hear her muse while she was writing. Nic had been the least imaginative of the crew—it had been the private place where he'd brought his girlfriend, the place where Violet had been conceived.

Was Megan remembering, too?

But he refused to even glance her way, didn't want to see recognition on her face, not shock, not sentiment. The silence was a good buffer between them, and he had no intention of disturbing it.

He didn't have to because just then Violet burst through the door, as if she'd been waiting and watching for them to arrive. Circling the car, she swung the back door wide and slid in saying, "OMG! This place is totally amazing. I got to see all Uncle Anthony's cars and the Harley, too. And Uncle Damon's dojo is so cool."

"Sounds like you had a good morning."

"The best." Violet rested her head back and closed her eyes, blissful. "I've been invited back whenever I want, too. Grandmama's going to teach me how to shampoo and Uncle Anthony is going to teach me how to change a tire, jump a battery and do an oil change. And Uncle Damon's going to teach me to defend myself so I don't get raped."

His mother was definitely going to be down a son as soon as Nic got a hold of Damon. The idiot.

Violet grinned. "Thought you'd like that, Mom."

Megan didn't miss a beat. "Knowing how to defend yourself is a very good thing."

Suddenly, Violet leaned through the open divider, straining against the seat belt. "Do you have a copy? Can I see it?"

Megan shook her head. "Snail mail. Four to six weeks."

Violet slumped, clearly horror-stricken. "Four to six *weeks?* That's so lame."

"We listed your father's address, so he can send us a copy as soon as it arrives."

Nic was about to offer an express service to be helpful, but never got the chance. One glance in the rearview mirror and he knew Megan had said exactly the wrong thing no matter how conciliatory she'd hoped to be. Violet huffed and stared out the window with an expression that Nic recognized as pure rebellion.

He may have only been a father for little more than twenty-four hours, but he knew teens, having assisted his mother in rearing quite a few.

"We're heading into the Quarter for lunch to celebrate your new name," Nic said, hoping to deflect the oncoming mood.

"I thought *we* were having lunch."

Megan frowned, clearly not missing the implication.

"We are," he said, a diversionary tactic. "In the French Market. All kinds of good stuff to eat there."

The short duration of his official father status seemed to have earned him a grace period because Violet smiled and said, "Cool. I'm starving."

He didn't think for one second that she didn't know what he was up to, but she'd decided to play along. Goodwill that obviously didn't extend to her mother at the moment.

"I don't want to go home until I get my new birth certificate," she informed her mother matter-of-factly.

Had one of his brothers made that kind of demand of their mother, Nic would have had something to say. But Megan rallied fast, all the hurt hidden away behind a sudden warning expression. And there was no question it was hidden. It hadn't vanished. Not a chance.

"I understand you're disappointed, Violet," Megan calmly acknowledged Violet's feelings. "But give this some thought. Do you really think this is the best way to address the subject? Or the appropriate time for that matter?"

"Whatever." Folding her arms across her chest, Violet stared out the window again. "Just thought you'd want to know."

"We'll make time to address the issue later."

Didn't take an experienced parent—or a rocket scientist, for that matter—to figure out that as far as Violet was concerned, the subject wasn't up for discussion.

But Violet didn't say another word, and as luck would have it, they arrived.

"Here we are, ladies," Nic said.

Violet seemed to have shaken off her mood. Toward him, anyway. She walked between him and Megan, chatting happily as they made their way toward Central Grocery, firing off questions about the places they passed.

St. Louis Cathedral…

"Are you Catholic like we are? Do you go to church?"

Steamboat Natchez…

"River cruises and bayou cruises? Is that something you like to do or is it only for tourists?"

Café Du Monde…

"Do you go there when you want coffee or Starbucks?"

Central Grocery…

"What's a muffuletta?"

"It's your lunch," he explained. "And it's pronounced—*muff-u-lotta*." He stretched each syllable slowly. "*Muff-u-lotta*. Try it."

"Muff-u-lotta."

"That's it. You got it. Can't have you sounding like a tourist. Bad for the family image." Since she was obviously hanging on to his every word, he took it a step further. "Wouldn't do for the chief's daughter to be walking around saying, *New Or-lee-ans*."

Even Megan winced at that.

"How do you say it right?" Violet asked eagerly.

"It's all in the drawl," Nic explained. "N'awlins."

"N'awlins."

"Wow. You're really good at this. How are you at speaking foreign languages?"

She feigned a yawn. "*Puh-leeze*. Couldn't live in some of the places we've lived if I didn't pick up the language fast."

Nic wasn't surprised. Megan had always had a knack for languages, too. They'd met when she'd been assigned as his Spanish tutor. Since he'd waited until the last minute to fulfill his language requirement, failing even one semester meant he wouldn't walk with his class.

"What is a muffuletta?" she asked, pronouncing it perfectly. "Am I going to like it?"

"You're a DiLeo, so you definitely will." Nic laughed. "It's a sandwich, a *Sicilian* sandwich. The guy who opened Central Grocery a million years ago made it to feed the truck drivers. Now it's famous all over the world."

"We're Sicilian!"

He nodded. "Good memory. That's a DiLeo thing."

She beamed, clearly liking mention of family connections.

Megan didn't say much as they strolled along, obviously recognizing that silence was the better part of valor right now. When they arrived at Central Grocery, he held the door for them. They gave Violet a chance to glance at the menu, but she just said, "Muffuletta, please. And water."

"They're pretty big, Violet. Do you want to split one with me, so we'll have room for beignets at Café Du Monde?"

Violet nodded, still giving Megan the silent treatment, and Nic placed their order. She stayed with him as they waited, but Megan wandered off, entertaining herself by looking around the grocery.

After they got their order and found a free table, he expected Megan to rejoin them. When she didn't, he glanced around and found her thumbing through Central Grocery's cookbook.

"She's looking at a cookbook," he said to Violet.

"No surprise there," she replied, dropping into a chair.

"She cooks?"

Violet nodded, grabbing stuff off the tray and starting to arrange the table.

"I didn't know that," Nic said more to himself than Violet, who was clearly uninterested in anything having to do with her mother. Back in the day, Megan's interests ran to more academic and charitable arenas. Tutoring at school. Youth group activities with church. Honor Society. Service Club.

"I hear you like to cook," he said when he reached Megan.

She smiled benignly. "Who knew? I had no clue until I actually had to learn. Now I try out local recipes from wherever we live, and by the time we move on, we've decided what we like and I've mastered them. Violet and Marie are my guinea pigs."

And she obviously knew her audience because the muffuletta was a hit with Violet. So were the beignets. And by the time the newly established Bell-DiLeos sat at Café Du Monde, sipping hot coffee and brushing powdered sugar off themselves and every surrounding surface, Nic finally felt as if he might finally be moving past the shock that had mentally paralyzed him since walking through his office door yesterday morning.

But if he was finally regaining his senses, then he also had to ask himself why he was sitting here as his daughter lobbied to learn to drive Anthony's chopper—an event that wouldn't be possible for another year and was solely prompted by the Harley shop next door—unable to stop wondering how Megan felt.

Obviously Megan and Violet were close, really close from what he'd witnessed. He understood that the relationship between mothers and daughters could get volatile during these teenage years. His mother and baby sister, Frankie, had been living proof. Still, there was a part of him that felt the urge to ease the tension between them, which was entirely stupid. Even if he had a clue about what he might do—which he didn't—it simply wasn't his place.

They might be connected, but they weren't a real family in any sense. While they were playing nice to work things out right now, as soon as Megan took off, Nic would be flying solo in the parenting department.

Not that much parenting was left to do. Megan had kept that part all for herself. No, he needed to establish himself as Violet's father. That was the only realistic thing he could do. But it was his impulse to fix things, probably because he'd been doing it for so long with his own family.

Still, as he sat at the patio table, roasting his ass off in his dress blues in the Louisiana spring, he couldn't deny that it bothered him seeing Megan this way, excluded and hurt. She didn't show it outright, but he apparently still knew her well enough to know she was. And there wasn't a doubt in his mind that Violet knew she was hurting her mother. Retribution for the secrets, maybe.

Megan handled the situation gracefully, a caring adult, not guilting Violet or bullying her. No, Megan seemed to have stepped back, recognized that she wasn't going to accomplish anything by engaging their daughter. Yet, she'd been quick to establish boundaries and hadn't let Violet abuse her. She'd simply tabled the topic of dissension and forced Violet to go along.

Nic respected that process, liked that Megan seemed

to give Violet the opportunity to make choices about her actions, holding her accountable in a constructive way.

But he also knew that he shouldn't be so impacted by the sight of her so quiet and withdrawn right now, by his own need to set things right between these two.

He must be ambushed by memories.

Yes, that had to be it.

CHAPTER THIRTEEN

MEGAN UNLOCKED THE FRONT door to Nic's family home and quickly crossed the foyer to input the security code to shut off the system. She tried not to think about how she was suddenly privy to intimate DiLeo family details, such as this security code, deemed trustworthy by Nic's mother even though she hadn't done a thing to demonstrate she deserved such consideration.

Except for giving birth to Nic's daughter.

Forgiveness. Second chances. Redemption. These were all concepts she'd learned during an active upbringing in church. These were all concepts she'd made a career of working with nonprofit organizations. Funny how a few days and a loving family could turn concepts into realities.

And that's exactly what they were. No longer concepts but action. Fifteen years after the fact, without any explanation whatsoever, she'd been accepted by Nic's family. They weren't holding her past decisions against her even if they didn't understand them. They seemed to trust that she and Nic would figure things out. Violet was Nic's daughter. Megan was Violet's mother. They were part of the family. It was that simple.

For a moment, she was struck by an image of a foyer very similar to this one, filled with antiques rather than baseball gear, baby accoutrements like a double-wide umbrella stroller and push-pedal sports cars in hot-pink and boy's blue. A foyer that was a showcase to be admired with the sun slanting through the windows illuminating dust motes rather than a place where a family passed through on their way to living.

She hadn't experienced this kind of acceptance with her own parents. Whom she had to call soon. She really couldn't stall much longer. Not only was guilt eating away at her, but she was setting a terrible example for Violet. Very much like the poor example she was setting by avoiding the overdue conversation they needed to have.

"We can't put off talking any longer," she said when Violet appeared in the kitchen doorway, ready to bolt for the stairs, to where there was a computer. No doubt she wanted to check Facebook for her friends' reactions to a nose ring and a new last name.

Eventful few days, no question.

Keeping her voice casual, she said, "We've got time until your grandmother gets home from work."

Violet bristled and looked at her through the eyes of a stranger. "What's there to talk about? How you lied? How mad you are that I ran away?"

Megan swallowed a sigh. There would be no dragging Violet from this mood, no way to engage her in constructive conversation. The best she could hope for was to glean some idea of the underlying issues and come up with a way to address them. She hadn't wanted to have a one-sided conversation, to deliver a soliloquy as it were, but things needed to be said.

"I wasn't so much mad that you ran away as I was worried, and surprised and disappointed," Megan admitted. "I expected more caution from you. You know better than most how dangerous traveling internationally can be."

"I'm alive."

"And I'm relieved about that." Megan forced a smile and tried distraction. "So is Marie. She wanted me to send you a kiss, by the way."

Violet only nodded, not mellowing one bit. She'd rather be anywhere in the world right now. That much was obvious.

Leaning back against the counter, she faced her daughter.

"So you read my email and thought I'd turned down the New Orleans project."

"That's what the email said."

"Declining to make a decision," Megan clarified. "That's what I told them. I didn't have to commit to the project until Helping Hands had a confirmation on their headquarters' location. It was simply a way for me to buy time so I could figure out what would be best for all of us in a very difficult situation. Your father included."

"Telling the truth might have worked."

Megan inclined her head, conceding the point. "Yes, it might have. And if I had the situation to do all over again, I would certainly handle it differently. I'm not making excuses for my behavior, Violet, but I want you to understand why I made the choices I did."

"Who cares about *why?*" she snapped. "It doesn't change that I had to find my own dad. That I didn't get to meet him until I'm all grown-up."

Megan let that one pass. Violet was talking, which was a good thing. She was a beautiful young girl on the brink of adulthood, testing the limits of her relationships and forming her own opinions and beliefs.

She had every right to feel angry, and Megan braced herself, telling herself they would weather this storm the way they'd weathered everything else in life. Together. The anger would only be temporary.

But deep down she also knew that once she'd loved her parents with the same youthful trust, had felt solid and secure in their love. Until she'd started testing her own limits. They hadn't accepted her independence, and she'd felt betrayed. That betrayal had dictated their lives ever since.

Violet felt betrayed now.

"I'm afraid my choices did mean you didn't get to meet your dad," Megan acknowledged. "And I'm sorry about that. I wanted to make the best of a bad situation. I didn't talk with my parents the way you and I talk, Violet. My upbringing was different."

"What, did Grandpa and Grandma Bell tape your mouth shut or something?"

In any other circumstance, Megan would have tabled the conversation right there. Violet's sarcasm was degenerating to nastiness, and that wasn't acceptable—for either of them.

But there was never going to be a good time for Violet to learn her mother was human, so Megan forced a calm into her voice that she didn't feel and said, "No. They did not tape my mouth shut. They were just…*different* than we are. That's not right or wrong. That's not a judgment. They believed the way they did things was the only way to do things."

Violet didn't say a word, which was the only invitation Megan was going to get. She knew it, and ran with it.

"I wasn't much older than you are now. I met your father and…my whole world changed. I couldn't think about anything else except spending time with him, doing things young people that age do. We were seniors so he asked me to the prom. I shopped with my friends to find the perfect dress and spent hours imagining how wonderful the night was going to be. I was seventeen and the whole world revolved around how I felt."

Those days had been filled with naive magic. She'd been head over heels in love and so blissfully unaware of anything else. She chose her next words carefully.

"Turns out that when I told your grandparents they weren't all that thrilled. They were strict, very protective and very involved in my life. I was only allowed to date boys from our circle of friends, so they knew the parents. They didn't know anything about your father."

Violet leaned against the table, not sitting because she didn't want give the impression that she was interested when she was actually hanging on to Megan's every word.

"Your grandparents loved me and wanted the best for me. They tried to make that happen the only way they knew how. I should have let them know how much going to the prom with your father meant to me, but I never gave them the chance to help me figure things out. I don't know if they would have. That's something we'll never know. I just made up my mind to handle things my way and did."

Very much in the same way that Violet had when she'd learned about Nic.

"I made a lot of choices that felt right at the time, but I was young and so was your father. We were making adult choices and got in over our heads."

"None of that explains why you didn't tell Dad about me." An accusation.

"No, it doesn't. But I hope you'll understand that I was trying to make the best choices I could for all of us. I was a pregnant teenager, Violet. I couldn't go off to college with a baby to care for. I didn't have a career to support us. Your father was in a similar position, only he was working all kinds of odd jobs to help out your grandmother. I didn't want us to be a burden to anyone—not your dad or his family or my family, either. I loved you too much."

Megan inhaled deeply, braced herself for the most difficult truth of all.

"It wasn't a good choice. It wasn't even my choice to make. Your father had every right to know about you. Just like you had the right to know about him. Unfortunately, by the time I realized that, I'd done a lot of damage. It wasn't as easy as calling your father and saying, 'Oh, and by the way, we have a beautiful daughter.' We've talked about this before, about how difficult it can be to fix the consequences of poor choices."

About how, sometimes, the damage wasn't fixable at all.

"I honestly did the best I could with what I had to work with, pup. I hope you'll believe that. That's why I've always been such a fanatic about giving you the skills you needed to make better choices. I didn't have them and a lot of people are suffering because it took me so long to learn. There are no excuses. What I did was wrong and I'm so sorry."

The urge to wrap her arms around her daughter almost overwhelmed her, to reach out and soothe away the anger, the confusion, the betrayal that seemed to roll off her daughter in a physical wave.

Megan wanted to explain that forgiveness was a one-step process, an essential one. That Violet would be the only person who would suffer if she didn't forgive, that she would feel her anger and betrayal bleeding into everything she felt, every word she spoke, every thought she thought.

It didn't matter about the effect on the person being forgiven, whether they were sorry or not sorry, whether they cared or didn't care, whether they remained involved or vanished forever. Forgiveness most mattered to the person doing the forgiving, the rest was only a bonus.

Megan knew because she'd been grappling with forgiving herself for so, so long.

But now wasn't the time for that explanation. Not yet.

Not while Violet was in the heat of anger and righteousness because she felt so hurt and betrayed. She would need time to process, to sort through all these truths.

Megan knew it the instant she met her daughter's gaze.

"I'm not going home," she announced, making sure she got her time. "I don't have to. I'm old enough to choose where I want to live, and I want to live with my family."

For an instant, Megan could only stare into that beautiful face, masked by such passionate emotions.

A part of her recoiled, braced to defend herself against words that felt like a physical blow, to remind Violet that her father would have to agree to the arrangement and she shouldn't be so certain a single man would want the full-time responsibility of a teenager. But the impulse died as quickly. Megan knew her daughter, knew Violet only lashed out to gain some control over the hurt.

Hurt that *she'd* caused.

Megan also knew enough about Nic to know that he'd assume the responsibility without batting an eye if that's what the situation called for.

And Megan's family would go on without her.

It took every ounce of strength she possessed to keep her expression from collapsing when every muscle in her face tugged in the wrong direction. It took every ounce of self-control not to give heartache an upper hand.

The only thing that mattered right now was Violet, how upset she was. Megan had earned her hurt and would bear it like the responsible adult she was.

It took every shred of energy she had to face her daughter and say, "I'm so, so sorry."

An apology. *So* worthless in the face of so much pain.

The words hung in the air between them, heavy and useless, before they sank in and had an effect.

Violet recoiled, physically pulled back. She exhaled sharply and took off without another word, without even glancing back before she disappeared from the kitchen.

Her footsteps resounded as she flew up the stairs. A door slammed. Then...nothing.

Megan stood there, a few frozen minutes, a lifetime, she didn't know. She couldn't seem to move or to think. Just felt as if she was being crushed beneath the weight of Violet's hurt, beneath the emotions colliding inside her, tugging at her.

She'd always known this moment would come.

And it was finally here.

Tears were swelling inside, trying to win this battle of wills, and Megan spun around, gripping the counter as if she might still push them back by sheer strength. But she could see through the kitchen window over the sink, saw through to the backyard, to the garage apartment outside.

The breath seemed to seize in her chest, the memories

crashing in on her, stolen moments with Nic, a time when she'd been so naively happy, the last place where she could claim to have known a sense of peace because once she'd left New Orleans she hadn't known peace since. She couldn't sort through the frantic jumble in her head except for one blinding thought that was like a lighthouse through the fog.

She had to get out of here.

If she didn't get out of here, she would literally crawl out of her skin.

Before Megan recognized what was happening, she found herself in that foyer again, but the sight of the stairs jolted her into some awareness.

She couldn't leave Violet alone.

Nic. The investigation. The whole point of staying here so someone could keep an eye on her.

Megan stood rooted to the spot, awareness blasting through her, leaving her no choice but to remain paralyzed by the need to run as reason and impulse collided.

A sound broke into her awareness. She couldn't make sense of it at first, not until the door opened and a woman stepped through, a dark-haired woman, juggling keys and kids.

For a blind instant, Megan stared...

Tess. Anthony's wife.

"Oh, hi—" Tess broke off suddenly in the process of letting the twins slide from her hips, their little feet stretching toward the floor. "Megan, are you all right?"

"Are you going to be here for a bit?"

The twins hit the floor ready to run, but were stopped short by the death grip Tess had on each of their hands. "Until Mama gets home."

"Do you mind if I go? Nic's on his way. I don't want to leave Violet alone until he gets here. She's upstairs."

Tess smiled, a kind smile. A knowing smile. "Go. I'm here. She'll be fine."

The tears were pushing hard, swelling against Megan's throat so all she could do was mouth the words, "Thank you."

She thought about calling upstairs, but couldn't force any words out. Violet didn't want to hear her voice right now anyway. Maybe not ever again.

Bolting through the door, she sailed down the stairs and onto the sidewalk, feet carrying her instinctively when her mind wasn't clear on what she was doing or where she was going, when she could only give in to the need to move, to get away, to run.

She thought about calling Marie, knew she'd talk Megan down from this place, where every thought in her head jumbled with the emotions coiling inside. But she had no words, couldn't imagine trying to find any. She knew Marie's voice would be like a cooling summer rain on the turmoil blazing inside her, but she couldn't even summon the energy to reach for her cell phone.

She needed to walk, just walk.

She barely noticed when lived-in houses of the residential neighborhood yielded to the stretched-out lawns with pristine fences and impeccably kept homes along St. Charles Avenue. She quickly crossed the street to avoid the streetcar rattling in her direction then kept moving, the sidewalk unfolding before her, dictating her path.

She barely noticed when the poise of this ageless neighborhood yielded to the stillness of the streets surrounding the university campus. Megan kept her head slightly bowed and forged ahead, awareness limited to her periphery.

And kept walking.

She was home. It didn't matter that she hadn't been here in fifteen years. It didn't matter that Hurricane Katrina had nearly blown the city off the map. The years of different locales and cultures and new people didn't change the fact that she knew New Orleans by heart.

When she finally slowed, the heat of the late afternoon wilting some of the urgency, Megan was on a familiar street.

She blinked to focus on Mrs. Bryson's butterfly bushes in full bloom, a crazy array of blue and violet and white reaching almost to the roof of her double gallery house.

Slowing her pace, Megan looked up and actually took in her surroundings… And the wrought-iron fence was still painted black beneath the climbing roses. The corabells still crept rebelliously beneath the fence line onto the sidewalk.

Another few steps and she could see the big rose-colored blooms of the dogwood tree in the front yard, the tree outside her bedroom window… Her own house with the side-gabled roof and gallery running the entire front of the house. Set back from the street, the bungalow-style house was still butter-yellow. The lacy Victorian ornamentation bright white.

Megan remembered the last time she'd seen the home she'd grown up in, in the darkness of predawn while hurrying from the house to catch a crack-of-dawn flight, the night concealing her shameful departure from the prying eyes of neighbors.

She'd left in such a rush, in such a state of emotional turmoil that it had never even dawned on her she wouldn't return, that her life as she'd known it had been over.

The gate was shut tight. There were no cars in the driveway. Given the time of day, her parents could easily have been teaching classes at the university a block away.

She looked at the empty driveway and suddenly remembered the red Toyota Camry they had bought her at the beginning of her senior year. Back then all three of their cars had lined up like little soldiers. Very inconvenient when one of them wanted out. Her dad had threatened to take away half of Mom's garden to have a circular driveway put in.

But he hadn't. There had been no need. Megan had left and hadn't come back. She wondered what they'd done with the Camry, had never occurred to her to ask.

She glanced at the smaller gate that led to the walkway, noticed more rust than she'd remembered being acceptable to her father, who'd been a naval jelly and steel wool fanatic.

"It's our home, Meggie. Our special place in the world. How we care for it reflects how we feel about ourselves, and how others see us."

She'd taken that lesson into adulthood. She and Violet always devoted a solid week after relocating to pulling their new home together.

They never shipped anything but personal items—far too costly for things like furniture. So they took that first week in their new home to find everything they needed. Made an adventure out of long days spent searching for exactly the right pieces, eating at the local eateries, meeting people and getting to know their new town.

Long nights spent endlessly arranging and rearranging, hanging curtains, sometimes even painting walls. Whatever it took to get their new home started. Each home reflected a new mood, and they often joked that by the time they finally got a place perfect, it was time to leave.

"I'm not going home." Violet's voice echoed in memory.

Would they ever create another new home together?

Or was that part of their lives, that beautiful, blessed part of their lives over, too?

The sound of tires slowing to a stop on the street dragged her from her thoughts and, somehow, she wasn't surprised when she heard her father's surprised voice. "Meggie?"

CHAPTER FOURTEEN

"ARE THERE A LOT MORE of these books?" Violet tried not to sound miserable. She didn't want her dad to think that she didn't want to spend time with him at work.

It was kind of neat being inside the police station as the chief's daughter, which was way better than making the trip in the back of a cruiser. But she was going to become cross-eyed if she didn't get a break from looking at photo after photo after photo of faces. There were, like, rows and rows of them on every page. And each book was fatter than the last *Harry Potter*.

She was looking for Great Eye guy, but she kept scanning those faces and hadn't seen him yet. Which was a total bummer because she didn't want to disappoint her dad.

But she was sorry she'd ever gone inside that tattoo place. Except that if she didn't have to look for Great Eye guy, Mom would probably have tried to take her home already.

Violet flopped back in the chair and grabbed the can of Mountain Dew that one of the officers had brought her. The can had sweat all over her dad's desk, so she used a sleeve to wipe the water away before it stained. Taking a deep swig, she wished it was a Red Bull. Mom didn't let her drink those, but Maddie brought them to school all the time. No big deal.

Everything was a big deal to Mom. It was so unfair.

All Violet wanted to do was get to know her dad. How was *that* wrong? He'd been right here in New Orleans her whole life, but she hadn't known about him. Because of Mom.

Taking another swig, she glanced around for some tissues or something to use as a coaster before she ruined her dad's desk. She settled on a folded-up piece of paper from the trash. The last thing she needed was both parents pissed off.

Mom hadn't made a big deal out of Violet saying she wanted to live with Dad. Mom hadn't even been home when Dad came to get her, but Violet knew better than to think Mom didn't care. The only time Mom didn't jump in with all her Mary Sunshine let's-fix-it crap was when she didn't have a clue what to do.

Good. She deserved to feel crappy. As crappy as she'd made everyone else feel. This situation sucked.

The door opened and her dad came in. "How's it going? Any luck?"

She hated disappointing him. "I still have a couple of books to look through. Maybe in there."

"Fingers crossed." He started digging through a pile of folders on his desk. "Listen, I know we talked about doing that dinner cruise tomorrow night, but Tess called—" He looked up with a stupid grin. "Your *aunt* Tess called. Her uncle is a race car driver who'll be competing at Dixie Downs. She wanted to know if you'd like to go with them. She can get an extra pass. Ever been to a race?"

Violet shook her head. "It sounds really cool."

"It is. Aunt Tess's uncle is the Exterminator, one of the nation's top-ranked drivers. It's good luck that he's in town when you are. Interested?"

"Can we do the cruise a different night?"

He set aside a pile of folders, obviously not finding what he was looking for. "Sure."

"Okay, then I'd like to go to the race."

"I'll call Tess back and let her know. You'll take care of letting your mom know?"

"I'll text her." She had no clue what Mom was up to right now or tomorrow. Hadn't bothered asking. "I was wondering…"

Her dad stopped what he was doing. "What?"

"Did I get the guy who pierced my nose in trouble?"

He shrugged. "Not too much. A hefty fine. But don't feel too bad. He wouldn't have even gotten fined if he'd have told us who Great Eye guy is."

"You think he knows?"

Her dad settled in with a hip against the desk. "Before I became chief of police, I was commander of the Eighth District, which is where that tattoo parlor is. The guy who owns it—the guy who gave you that piercing—knows everything that goes on in his place, which is why he's still in business. He just needs some convincing to cooperate. Hitting him in the cash register usually works."

God, this was so cool. Talking to her dad was just like an episode of *SVU*. She loved *SVU!* She and Camille would stay awake all night, watching episode after episode on the computer.

"But it didn't work this time?"

"Not yet. Not even when I threatened that your parents would press charges."

"You're going to press charges because I got a nose ring?" Violet wasn't sure how to feel about that.

"No. Never make it before a judge. I only told him

that so he knows we mean business. Try to convince him it'll be easier if he cooperates."

"Oh, I get it."

"It's weak, but the only thing I can do is inconvenience him at this point. I need to find out who Great Eye guy is so I can ask who he was delivering the envelope for."

"I promise if he's in here, I'll find him."

"I know." He went back to searching his piles. "Remember that I wouldn't even have this information if you hadn't been paying attention that night. That's been a big help already."

She liked that and was glad he didn't think she was some sort of creeper because she'd been stalking him. "You know, the longer your investigation goes on, the longer I stay in town."

"That's true." He looked over again, seemed to think what she said was significant. "You know that your mother and I will work out something so we can see each other, right? In fact, since you're going to the race tomorrow night, maybe I'll suggest she and I get together to discuss it. Sound good?"

It sounded ridiculous. She knew he was trying to be all reassuring, but he was totally treating her as if she was a little kid. She was way old enough to go before a judge and tell him where she wanted to live. She'd already checked online and there were lots of cases where people her age got to decide which parent they wanted to live with.

But Violet didn't tell her dad that. Not until she got to feel him out some more, not until she knew if he'd let her live with him.

"You know, my name is officially DiLeo." Wasn't she sorry she kept Bell now? "Well, it will be when all the paperwork comes. I could, like, live here and we could see each other all the time."

He tipped his head to the side and got this funny sort of smile. "Yeah, you could. We'd have to see what your mother has in mind, though."

Violet frowned, not sure what to say, but very sure *that* wasn't what she'd wanted to hear from her brand-new dad.

There was a knock at the door and some official-looking dude with a name badge and briefcase came in.

"Violet," her dad said. "I'd like you to meet U.S. Attorney Andy Fielder. Andy, my daughter, Violet."

"Pleased to meet you, young lady." Mr. U.S. Attorney shook her hand then turned to her dad. "Is now still a good time to talk?"

"Yeah, come on," her dad said. "Violet, you keep looking. I'll be back."

She smiled and watched them go, thinking that maybe her plan to move to New Orleans wasn't so hopeless, after all. Not if Dad was introducing her to his work buddies.

That had to be good, right?

NIC LED ANDY FROM HIS office and down the hall to a conference room. "Hope you don't mind if we talk in here. Easier than relocating her with all those suspect books."

"Looked like she was trying to be thorough for her new dad."

"Yeah. That she is. *Very* thorough. It's slow going."

Andy laughed. "I'll bet. She looks just like you, Nic. I can't believe you didn't know about her until a few days ago."

"Yeah, me, either."

Nic had shared his sordid little tale during the phone call that prompted this meeting. Andy was a family man himself, relocating his wife and sons from Washington, D.C., to take this gig in New Orleans. Nic was counting on him to understand the concerns about Violet's safety.

"Have a seat." He motioned to the conference table then pulled the door shut behind them.

Andy shrugged off his suit jacket and sat. "Any luck with the tattoo parlor owner?"

Nic sank into a chair opposite. "Planted the seed and made a few bucks for the department. That's about it. I'd like to say that he'll think twice before piercing any minors without adhering to the law, but I'm not holding my breath."

"So what's the next move?"

"That's why you're here, Andy. I'm debating my options. I want to make sure I cover all the bases since impeaching a judge is tricky business. I don't want to miss anything."

"That's the truth." Reaching into his briefcase, he withdrew a folder and set it open on the table. He leafed through the documents inside. "I pulled what I could get on Judge Dubos, and I'm not at peace with what I'm seeing. He's long established on the bench. A lot of powerful connections, which translates into a lot potential to take a wrong turn somewhere along the way."

No surprises there. Said something when even a newcomer to New Orleans could see signs spelling trouble. On the other hand, that was Andy's whole reason for being here.

"Judicial bribery and conspiracy is nasty business, Nic. You're going to have to make sure you cross every *t* and dot every *i*," Andy cautioned. "We're talking Congress and impeachment inquiries and hearings to insure constitutional rights. It's a mess. You know what I'm talking about."

"I read all about the last one you were involved with."

Andy scowled. "Classic kickback scheme. Pretty simple really, but nearly a hundred inmates were released over a five-year period. It was obscene."

"You won't get any argument from me," Nic said. "I've got too many criminal defendants waiting to get before a judge. A dishonest one only makes my wait longer. I assigned some men to comb through the judge's cases. One by one. That's the only way to see if there's anything there."

"Good start, but that's going to take time. What are these options you're talking about?"

"I'm trying to get the tattoo parlor owner talking, so I can ID the runner."

"You need to bring them all in."

Nic shook his head. "I'm not sure I want the judge to know we're onto him yet. Not until I have a lock on the runner and know who he's working for."

"Because of your daughter?" Andy asked.

Nic nodded.

"But they don't know who she is. You didn't even know who she was."

"No argument there, either."

"Then you need to force their hands, Nic. Get everyone worrying so someone makes a mistake. Especially the judge. The only way to protect your daughter is with a conviction, you know that. The sooner you build your case, the sooner she'll be out of the equation."

"Under any other circumstances I might agree, but

the minute I tip my hand then every one of them will know I've got something. Or in this case *someone*. It won't be any stretch to pinpoint the kid who was in the tattoo parlor that night. They all saw her."

Andy didn't reply, just leaned back in the chair, clearly considering. He finally said, "Listen, Nic, I understand the position you're in. You're worried about your daughter. I got two kids of my own. So trust me when I tell you I understand. I'm still saying bring them in. That's why you're *debating*. You know it's the only thing you've got. Don't drag your heels so these crooks can bury themselves where you can't get to them."

"I hear you."

"You know how best to conduct your investigation. Take my advice and don't let concerns about your daughter cloud your judgment." Andy extended his hand across the table. "But I don't mind saying that this is precisely what we're hoping to accomplish here, as you well know. Good work, Nic."

He shook Andy's hand and accepted the praise graciously. Then he watched Andy gather papers into the folder, still unable to shake the gnawing doubt that too many factors were out of his control. Nic didn't feel as if he was even close to having enough of a handle on this situation.

Andy was right about that much—concerns about Violet were clouding Nic's judgment. No family mess he'd ever cleaned up came even close to this one. As if the stakes were higher than anything he'd ever faced before.

And they were. This was Violet they were talking about.

His daughter.

CHAPTER FIFTEEN

"YEAH, DAD," MEGAN forced the words out. "It's me."

"This is a surprise. Will you get the gate, Meggie?"

Surprise? What had she been thinking?

She hadn't been thinking. That much was obvious. Launching into action, Megan headed for the release that would pull the iron gate open. She could see her mother in the passenger side as her father pulled in the driveway and drove toward the garage around back. Her expression was set in stone. Great.

Megan eased the gate shut slowly, buying herself time as she commanded her pulse to stop racing, willed away all her upset over Violet.

Oh, why had she given in to that frenetic need to move? Why had she wound up here of all places?

But as Megan crossed the few steps toward the smaller gate that accessed the walkway, she understood why her path had led her here.

This was home. Somewhere deep inside her dwelled a girl not much older than Violet, a girl who'd left home one day, never expecting that she wouldn't return.

Wouldn't be welcomed.

A car door slammed, then another, and Megan wondered if her parents would expect her to meet them at the side door on the gallery or if she should wait at the front.

Letting herself in through the gate, she stuck to the

path of least resistance, noticing the yard had been recently mowed. The annuals that had once lined the walkway had been replaced with low-maintenance juniper.

Megan remembered her mother's trellis the last time she'd seen it, almost collapsing beneath the weight of the climbing roses. Her mother always had such a gift with anything that bloomed, but the trellis was gone. Likely hadn't survived Katrina. The gingerbread trim looked freshly painted, though, a bright white that complimented the yellow of the house.

Taking a deep breath, Megan made her way up the steps. She waited, unsure if her parents would come around the gallery to greet her or if they'd already entered the house. She saw the shiny gold doorbell, but didn't ring. She didn't have to. She could hear the sound of the chimes in memory, so vibrant. She'd forgotten until now. They'd been a surprise indulgence by her father for her mother's promotion to dean of her department. Megan had loved them.

Yet she'd forgotten.

She'd been born in this house, had grown up here, had a youth filled with memories.

Now she was a guest, waiting to be let in.

The door opened. Suddenly she faced her mother, dressed in a business suit, which meant they'd likely been at the university.

There was a moment of awkward silence, a moment when neither of them seemed sure of the appropriate greeting—kiss, hug, shake hands?

Megan took the initiative, covered the distance between them and kissed her mother's cheek. "Good to see you, Mom."

"You should have called, Megan. We weren't expecting you."

"I planned to, but…well, here I am." Megan squelched a pang at the omission.

Her mother didn't reply, only stepped aside to allow Megan to enter.

"You look well, Mom."

Which wasn't entirely true. Her mother had always been a beautiful woman, slender and lovely, with a head full of shiny dark hair that Megan had inherited.

Today she looked tired, frail almost, as if her body wasn't quite doing the job of holding up her suit.

Had her mother lost weight?

"Thank you."

Her mother's response was cooler than Megan expected. Or maybe she was projecting her mood. She hadn't been prepared to see her parents, didn't feel ready. Neither were her parents, clearly. She should have called. This was her own stupid fault, and now she'd put them on the spot, too.

Megan glanced around the foyer, recognized the addition of a few new antiques—an unfamiliar mirror, a small Tiffany lamp. Everything perfect to greet guests.

"Meggie, look at you. You're in town," her father said when he appeared.

She expected him to spread his arms for a hug. He'd always been the more demonstrative of her parents, her smiling, laughing, oh, so smart dad. He'd been the one her friends had asked about first, the one who had generally made the impression with his twinkling bright blue eyes.

But he only exchanged a glance with her mother.

It was one of those glances Megan had seen a thousand times in her youth, a look of silent communication between two people who had always seemed able to read each other's minds. There had been a time when Megan had admired their solidarity. But that had been before they'd ganged up on her.

"If now's a bad time," she said, giving them an out, "I can come back. I should have called."

"That would have been nice," her mother said, and there was no missing the stony edge to her voice.

"Come on in, Meggie." Her father slipped an arm around her shoulders. "You're here now. Would you like something to drink? Your mother brewed tea last night."

He led her into the kitchen.

"How are you, Dad?" Maybe if she kept the conversation light, they could segue through the awkwardness and keep dancing around the elephant in the middle of the room.

"Healthy, which is always good."

They stood around the butcher block in the middle of the kitchen, a habit from another lifetime. Without a word her mother went through the motions of placing napkins, spoons, lemons, ice and sweetener in a perfect display. She set the pitcher in the middle and glasses. Perfect.

"Thank you," Megan said. "How are things going at the university? Keeping you busy?"

"We've taken some hits to the faculty because of the economy, I'm afraid," her father explained. "As a result, the rest of us have had to pick up extra classes."

"Any problems with that?"

"Not really. It's always nice to interact with students. Your mother and I have had to cut back on publication, though. And guest lecturing. Not enough hours in the day to do everything."

"Never enough hours in the day," her mother agreed.

"So what brings you into town, Meggie? You haven't been in the States in how long?"

"Over six years." She dropped a slice of lemon in her glass. "Since San Sebastian Mission in Southern California."

"That's right. I remember. And how's Violet?"

Megan hadn't prepared what she wanted to share, didn't intend to explain the details about what had brought them to New Orleans. That much she knew. Determined to keep things cordial, she faced them. They stood together as they'd always done, a team. And she was surprised by how much older they looked than when she'd last seen them. Time marched on. Life, too. Only they hadn't been living it together because the past was in the way.

Megan was so tired of the past.

"Violet's wonderful, thanks." She forced a smile. "She's a loving, smart girl, and she's doing very well in school. I couldn't be more proud."

"Where is she now?" her mother asked.

The moment of truth. "Violet's here in town with me."

"And her father?"

Such a simple question. But there was nothing simple about the answer. The long-ago past, all the uncertainty, all the disapproval, all the disappointment swelled in that one simple, but deceptive question.

"Violet wanted to get to know her father, so here we are. It was time."

Past time, but Megan didn't share that. She set her spoon down on a napkin, took a sip of tea, determined to keep things positive, determined to stay in the moment and let the past remain history.

She didn't know how her parents would react, whether or not they would reject her choice as they had all those years ago, whether they'd stand side by side and tell her she wasn't welcome home with her daughter.

"You're not a teenager anymore, Megan." Her mother frowned, a look of such disapproval that Megan withered a little inside. "So why are you still sneaking around like one? It was unbecoming then. It's unbecoming now."

Megan stood there with the glass in her hand, confused. "I don't understand. You asked me a question. I answered it."

She glanced at her father, saw resignation in his face.

"We know you've been in town for days, Meggie," he said. "You never called to tell us."

"Father Lafevre saw you at the airport with the new *police chief*," her mother added. "He asked about you after mass. Of course, we had no idea you were even in the country."

That came at her sideways. Maybe because she hadn't yet gotten her feet under her after her talk with Violet. Hadn't had a chance to get up before she felt knocked down again. But Megan's chest grew tight, made it impossible to breathe, to do anything beyond the basics of survival.

She'd brought this on herself. *She* was the one who'd shown up uninvited. The one who hadn't called when she'd first gotten to town. How had she not seen Father Lafevre, a fixture in their home parish on the university campus? But Megan already knew that answer—she'd only seen Nic.

She'd never meant to place her parents in an awkward situation, felt guilty because she had. Once again.

But as she struggled to rein in her emotions, tried to drag in an anxious breath, there was a part of her that rejected this entire situation. Not the hurt young girl who'd left home without realizing she wouldn't be invited back, but the grown woman, the single mother, who simply couldn't imagine ever treating her daughter this way. Not for any reason.

She'd always taught Violet that there wasn't anything she could do to make Megan not love her. She'd tried to live an example of unconditional love. Whether her daughter hopped on a plane and took off for a different continent without leaving a note. Whether she lashed out in anger to be hurtful.

"I love you. No matter what." Megan had even made sure Violet understood if anything unexpected should ever happen. "It doesn't matter if the last time we were together you were angry with me or we had an argument. Just remember I knew you loved me no matter what."

No matter what.

Megan had even walked into the DiLeos' home after keeping one very big secret and hadn't been made to feel anything but welcome. Not a one of them had tried to make her feel guilty. Not even Nic, who had every right in the world to resent the way she'd treated him.

But in her home…with parents who were supposed to love her *no matter what*…

Setting down the glass, she took a deep, steadying breath. A small effort, but the vise eased up on her chest.

Shifting her gaze from her mother to her dad, she said, "My apologies for embarrassing you. I'm afraid I had my hands full when I first got into town. It's taken me a few days to get things under control."

Only truth in there.

"You didn't embarrass us, Meggie. We were hurt that you came to town and didn't tell us." And he looked so hurt.

"You involved yourself with that boy again and didn't even bother to tell us," her mother admonished. "How did you expect us to feel? We had to hear about it through the grapevine."

Guilt, guilt and more guilt.

Megan was being crushed beneath the weight.

"Mom, that boy is a man now. And one who has missed out on his daughter's entire life. I was very focused on facilitating a good start to that relationship, and to be truthful, it never occurred to me you'd want to hear what was going on with Nic." There, she'd said his name in front of them.

"Of course, we want to know what's going on in your life, Meggie. Whatever it is."

"Forgive me, Dad, but how was I supposed to know that? The only things you ever ask me about are work and how Violet's doing in school."

Her mother stepped away from the butcher block and went to stand in front of the sink, clearly struggling for control. "You're blaming us?"

"No, Mom. I'm not blaming anyone. But we don't talk all that often. When we do we usually catch up on the big stuff."

"Phone lines work both ways, Megan. Maybe not in the countries you've been living in, but here in New Orleans, it's as easy for us to pick up the phone as it is for you."

It took Megan a moment to get past her surprise. "As

far as I knew you had as much of a relationship with me as you wanted. I didn't realize you were interested in anything more."

"How could you think that? You're our daughter." Her mother turned her back and stared out the window, visibly trembling. Her dad went over and slipped an arm around her waist.

Megan stared at her parents' backs and their show of solidarity, feeling taken aback by all the emotion, feeling ganged up on again, feeling as if she was missing something important.

Her own anger kept getting in the way. "How could I think that? Well, it might have had something to do with you telling me I wasn't welcome home with my daughter."

Her mother flinched, but her dad frowned at her over his shoulder. "Now, Meggie. That was a long time ago. I thought we moved past that."

"How could we move past it, Dad? We've never talked about it. Not once in all these years."

"We only wanted what was best for you."

She shrugged helplessly. "How was telling me I wasn't welcome to come home with Violet the best for me?"

That brought her mother around. "We didn't expect you to run off and replace us. We expected you to come to your senses and come home."

"I don't understand what you're talking about. What do you mean replace you?"

"With the Gleasons, Megan. And now Marie lives with you. How did you expect us to feel?"

"They helped me when I needed help. I'm grateful to them."

"We're your parents. It was our job to help you."

"Then why didn't you?" Megan's voice broke.

Her mother exhaled an exasperated sigh. "We were trying to get you to come to your senses. You were so young. You had your whole life ahead of you, and we didn't want you to ruin it because of one mistake."

"Meggie," her father said, his tone conciliatory, ever the peacemaker. "Please try to understand. You're a parent. You can imagine what we went through. We had no idea you were dating that boy before you told us you were pregnant. We only wanted to help you resolve a difficult situation. You would do the same for Violet."

"I would never abandon my daughter in another country and tell her she wasn't welcome home with a newborn."

Her dad recoiled as if she'd slapped him and her mother intervened. "Megan, you're not thinking clearly. You weren't then. If you'd have come home with a baby, the father would have known. You'd have been committing to a course that would have altered your whole life. What were you going to do? Share custody while you both worked to support her and tried to get through college? Get married and raise her together? Would you have moved in with his family or invited him to live here?" She spread her hands in entreaty. "Don't you see? You were a bright, beautiful young woman and we loved you so much. We wanted so much more than that for you."

For a moment Megan could only stare, trying to register everything, unable. It was too much. Her head wrapped around the only part that made any sense. "You told me I couldn't come home to keep me from Nic?"

"That boy used you," her father bellowed, making Megan jump. All vestiges of the peacemaker were gone. "He had no right to go near you after what he did. I told him to stay away from you or else he'd be answering to the police. You were underage. There are laws."

She shook her head, not sure she was hearing clearly. "You spoke to Nic? When?"

"When he showed up at this house looking for you."

"What did you tell him?"

"That you'd started summer session and he wasn't to see you again or else he'd face the consequences of his actions."

Nic hadn't told her any of this. Not one word. But he'd come here looking for her, never even considering that she'd take off without a word. Knowing Nic, he likely hadn't believed her dad. He'd probably waited for her to contact him. She knew it deep down inside. He would have waited for her to contact him because he'd believed in her. He believed in them.

Suddenly, she could see Nic as he'd once been, the young man she'd fallen in love with, standing on the doorstep of this house, being threatened.

She'd failed so utterly and completely.

"My daughter is not a mistake." Megan's voice broke the quiet. "She never was. She's an incredible, intelligent, funny girl who is everything important in my life. She taught me that nothing else matters but the people who love you. That's all."

She was coming unglued. It was coming on like a wave so she did the only thing she could think to do. "Now, if you'll excuse me. It's best we table this conversation for the time being."

Megan turned and headed down the hallway, didn't look back when her dad called her name. She forced her feet to move quickly, and only as she let herself out the door did the tears finally break through, practically blinding her as she stumbled down the steps.

When she'd left fifteen years ago, it had never occurred to her she wouldn't look at her lifelong home again until now, when the life she'd created for herself and her daughter was over.

Megan circled through the neighborhood toward St. Charles Avenue again, tears still streaming down her face, thoughts racing with memories.

"Healthy," someone said.

And Megan, wasted from fifteen hours of labor, sweaty and feeling half-dead, opened her eyes.

A boy or a girl?

No one was going to tell her. They'd prepared her for this moment, worked her through the issues, helped her reach the decision that giving up this child for adoption was a good thing, in the best interests of all concerned. She'd been at peace with that.

Or thought she had.

Until this very instant, when the most important thing in the world became knowing whether her baby was a boy or a girl, had she realized this wasn't peace at all. No, Megan had simply been disconnected. Pregnancy had been a thing—a mistake—that had been happening to her body, something to endure and take care of so she could put this all behind her and get on with the rest of her life.

But now...

She opened her eyes and found herself looking at the tiniest baby, the sweetest face.

A girl.

She looked like a little pineapple, her hair half plastered crazily against her perfectly round head, her face wrinkled and her eyes still shut tight against life.

Precious and beautiful and vulnerable.

All the pregnancy classes, all the careful preparation from the people at St. Gianna's hadn't come close to making Megan ready for the reality of sitting half-naked on this birthing table, sweaty and drained, gazing at her daughter for the very first time.

Give her away? To strangers?

Megan knew all the arguments, every one of them had been branded into her brain during the long months of the pregnancy.

A responsible person would want the baby to have the kind of life an unwed, teenage mother couldn't provide.

If she cared at all for Nic, she wouldn't want to saddle him with the responsibility of a wife and child, or at the very least eighteen years of child support payments he couldn't afford.

And what about all the married couples who wanted a child and hadn't been blessed to have one of their own?

Megan didn't care. Not about any of it. Not when she looked at that sweet face and her mistake *was suddenly a tiny little person who deserved to be loved.*

Her arms felt like noodles when she reached toward the nurse and said, "Give me my daughter."

Megan's cell phone rang, jerking her to the present. Fumbling to reach into her pocket, she slipped the phone in her hand, glanced at the display and recognized Nic's number. She flipped it open and forced his name through her throat grown rusty with tears.

"I got reservations at Commander's Palace for seven-thirty, but I'm still wrapping things up here. Violet and I won't have time to pick you up. Can you meet us there?"

"Nic." His name came out on a strangled breath. She tried again, a battle of wills. "I hope you won't mind if I bail on you. Give you and Violet a chance to be together. Are you okay with that?"

There was a beat of silence on the other end. "I'm good with it. Violet?"

"Is looking forward to spending time with you."

The situation was really very simple.

She and Nic needed to interact as parents.

Violet needed to establish a relationship with her father.

They were not a family.

Not in any sense that mattered, anyway.

CHAPTER SIXTEEN

THE INTERCOM ON THE PANEL beside the front door buzzed, and Nic crossed the living room and headed straight toward it.

"Hey," he said into the speaker.

"Hey, Nic. It's Megan."

"Come on up." He depressed the button that would unlock the door downstairs.

Then he stood paralyzed like a damned idiot, knowing she still had to wait for the elevator that would bring her to the fourth floor. His heart thumped too hard in his chest.

What in hell was wrong with him? They'd been alone before. At the airport. The notary. So why was he getting worked up now?

Forcing himself away from the door, he walked through the breakfast area and into the living room. He opened the shutters on all the windows overlooking the courtyard as if opening them might ease this strangled feeling, a feeling of being trapped. The sun was setting outside, but the courtyard below was well lit. Didn't matter. Opening the shutters didn't do a damned thing. He practically jumped when the doorbell rang.

He went back to the door. He opened it. And there she was, standing in the hallway, wearing a smile.

"Hello, Nic," she said.

"Megan." He stepped aside and motioned for her to enter. "Come on in."

She passed in front of him and he held his breath to avoid the smell of her shampoo, didn't need any more attacks on his senses no matter how subtle they might be.

"Wow," she said. "Your place is wonderful."

Wide-eyed, she glanced around the spacious living area of his corner condo with fourteen-foot ceilings, exposed masonry and big windows that overlooked the courtyard on one side and the street on the other. It was a good condo as far as condos went, which was why he'd plunked down the money to buy it. The seven-block walk to the French Quarter was a perk.

"Thanks," he said. "Parking garage and a fitness center. Can't beat it. Violet get off okay?"

"Tess and Anthony picked her up when they dropped off the twins with your mother. That was really sweet of them to include her. I don't imagine they get out all that often with the twins being so young."

"It's not as bad as you might think. My mother's always up for babysitting."

"Well, I'm not surprised. She's been great with Violet."

"Can I get you anything?"

"I'm good, thanks."

Nic swept past her and headed into the living room. He sat in a recliner leaving the couch for Megan.

She followed him, but didn't sit. Instead, she strolled to one set of windows then to the other, making him glad he'd opened the shutters. "What a lovely view. How on earth did you luck into a corner unit?"

"Family inheritance, so to speak." Nic studied her. She wore another one of those long, flowy skirts that worked with the crazy spring weather as it swirled around the lines of her legs.

Funny, he wasn't at peace with this woman on too many levels, but he could still remember everything about her legs. Long, lean legs that looked great in shorts, that felt like warm silk wrapped around his.

"By any chance do you remember Anthony's girl-friend from high school?"

She glanced at him and nodded, silhouetted in pro-file. The delicate line of her nose, the full lips, seemed so familiar. God, he was *such* an idiot.

"I do. Very pretty redhead, right?"

"That's her. Well, she's a private investigator nowa-days. She works for the guy who originally bought this warehouse and renovated it into units."

"So you bought it from him?"

"Nope. I bought it from Anthony, who bought it from him. After Anthony and Tess got married, they decided to get something bigger Uptown."

"I'm sure they need it with the twins." She cast one more glance out the window before finally sitting on the couch. "Guess it pays to know the right people."

Nic didn't reply, only watched as she slid the purse from her arm and put it on the floor beside her. After smoothing her skirt over her lap nervously, she finally lifted her gaze. They faced each other across the narrow expanse of table.

"So here we are," she said.

"Here we are."

"Thanks for inviting me over."

He shrugged. "Thought you'd probably want to check out the place since Violet will be staying here, and with her going to the race, it seemed like a good opportunity to talk. I didn't really want to hash through all this stuff in public."

"You've been very decent, Nic," she said in that soft voice he remembered so well, a voice that caressed all kinds of crazy places inside him. "Thank you for that."

He inclined his head. Decent wasn't coming without effort. "So, what are you thinking?"

"I've got some ideas, but I'd rather start with you and work from there, if you don't mind."

He suspected she didn't want to impose, to suggest something that might make him feel obligated. Made sense that she'd want an idea of what might be too much time or too little for him. Then there was the whole money issue. He supposed he should be glad she wanted to accommodate his wants and needs for a change. He couldn't manage it, though. He still struggled with too many conflicting emotions. And the anger, always the anger.

But Nic wanted to keep things productive, didn't want to dwell on the years he missed or the fact she'd thought it was okay for him to miss them. Bottom line was: she was the mother of his child. They needed to put aside everything else and start there. They needed some sort of working relationship otherwise the future wasn't going to be constructive for anyone.

He wished he could have come up with something brilliant, something that solved all their problems. He was supposed to be a problem-solver. That was the whole reason the mayor and the U.S. attorney had wanted him to become chief. But his abilities got real cloudy when it came to Megan because the only solution that made any sense made no sense at all.

"Okay," he finally said. "I've been doing a lot of thinking as I'm sure you have."

She nodded, so serious.

No damn sense at all. He couldn't even believe he was going to suggest it. Ignoring the heartbeat suddenly pounding so hard it echoed in his ears, he forced out the words that would breathe life into the stupidest idea he'd ever had. "I think it would be in everyone's best interests if you accepted the project here in New Orleans."

Megan blinked as if she hadn't heard him correctly. Then she gave a quick little shake of her head. "You do?"

He nodded, giving voice to the problems that had been battering the inside of his skull nonstop. "Think about it, Megan. Violet doesn't know me. I don't know Violet. You live on another continent, which means the only way I'm going to get to know her is on vacations. A week or two here and there isn't going to do the trick. And quite frankly, it's not good enough. Even if you both were willing to commit to summers, it's not as if I can take all that time off, and she has a life. She's not going to want to drop everything for two months and sit around here waiting for me to get off work."

He leaned forward, folded his hands over his knees, his case gaining speed in his mind. "I know how this works. I have divorced friends. It's tough. I don't want to be a father who sits at Starbucks staring at my kid on alternate weekends with nothing to say. I've missed everything already."

He hadn't meant to bash her with reality, but she blanched anyway, her chest rising and falling on a deep breath as she forced herself to keep meeting his gaze.

"If you take the project, you'll relocate here for a year or two, which is what you guys are used to doing anyway. I'll get time with my daughter. She'll get time with my family. You won't have to ship her off alone for crazy periods of time, and we can figure out how to parent together. It'll be the easiest transition all the way around."

Of course, it in no way addressed how he was going to feel about Megan being so close. Especially when anger kept rearing its ugly head, stealing his good sense and reason and making him rehash all the events he'd missed in his daughter's life.

Making him dwell on feeling betrayed.

He shouldn't be reliving all the feelings he'd once had for this woman, a woman who could claim to love him then run away and not look back. A woman who could lie through her teeth.

He shouldn't care at all. The past was fifteen years over, but it didn't feel that way. He was reliving, big-time. The damned confusion he'd felt when she'd dropped off the planet. The shame he'd felt when her father had verbally taken him out, accusing Nic of taking advantage of his daughter, claiming Nic wasn't good enough for her, would never be.

The disbelief. The stupid ass he was had refused to believe Megan wouldn't contact him no matter what her father said.

And he was supposed to understand now? Forgive?

He wished he had a brilliant solution for that one, too, because as he met her blue, blue gaze, Nic realized what was angering him most of all. She'd lied about so many things. How could he believe her claims that she'd ever loved him?

And why in holy hell did it still matter now?

CHAPTER SEVENTEEN

MEGAN KNEW EVERYTHING Nic said made sense, such perfect sense the arrangement seemed divinely inspired. She'd been considering this move for a variety of reasons, debating whether the time had come to finally face this mess she'd made.

Nic. Violet. Her parents.

Such a mess. Every time she confronted an issue, instead of getting better, the situation seemed to get worse. And she totally hadn't counted on the reality of facing Nic again, the reality of sitting here with her heart pounding too hard because he'd asked her to come home.

No part of her thought Nic wanted her here for his own sake. He hadn't forgiven her. He didn't care for her anymore. He only wanted her in New Orleans because her presence made sense in the broader picture. Megan understood that.

But she didn't *feel* it.

No, she comprehended Nic's reasoning. And she appreciated that he wanted what was best for their daughter. But all that knowing didn't stop the crazy expectation that was making it impossible to catch a good breath or the wild fluttering in the pit of her stomach. Reactions she'd felt long ago for this man.

Marie had been right. Time hadn't resolved Megan's feelings for Nic in any way. How could it? She hadn't ever been able to move on. Her ties to him and the past had been alive and well every minute of every day in their daughter.

And she'd dated some very nice men through the years. But Megan had always stopped short when it came to considering rearranging their lives to include someone new, had never loved a man enough to make a special place for him in their family.

No small wonder she'd been a train wreck ever since she'd been offered the Helping Hands project. Her boss had thought he was doing her a favor, offering a welcomed chance to come home. But coming home would mean facing her feelings for Nic, ending their long-ago relationship to begin a new one as single parents who were united in the best interests of their daughter.

Megan watched as Nic went to stand in front of a window, recognized in a rare flash of insight that he was as conflicted as she was. Not because he let her see. No. The Nic of the past hadn't been nearly so guarded or skilled at hiding his feelings as this Nic. No doubt his face wouldn't have revealed a thing. But with his back to her, she could see tension all over him, in his shoulders, the way he held his head, the fingers slightly flexing into fists.

The irony of the situation might have made her laugh, or more likely weep, at the bittersweet truth—after all these years they were united in circumstance and in conflict, but they were more separated than they'd ever been by geography.

Because of her actions.

And Megan knew right then how she would respond, even though she didn't know where she would find the strength to step aside and pretend she didn't still care deeply for this man.

She owed him.

She owed their daughter.

Somehow she would find it within herself to end the past and start the future. She was a strong, independent woman now, not the clueless eighteen-year-old she'd once been.

"You're right, Nic. Accepting the project does make the most sense. Violet and I will come to New Orleans."

His shoulders tensed. She wouldn't have thought that was even possible, but she could see the slight flexing of muscles beneath the Henley shirt he wore. Then he turned toward her, an absurdly slow motion as she braced herself for his reaction.

"You will?" For an unexpected moment, she could see behind the law enforcement mask that hid the man so well. She could see *Nic,* the boy he'd once been, the boy she'd fallen in love with.

But only for an instant.

Then the surprise vanished as suddenly as if a channel had been changed by remote control.

"I think you're right," she said again, amazed by how rational she sounded when there was nothing rational about the way she felt. "We want the transition to be as easy as possible for Violet."

Even though she couldn't think around this man.

Hadn't ever been able to.

But Megan held his gaze steadily, tried to project a confidence she didn't feel in any part of her. Suddenly, she couldn't sit still for another second.

Sliding to her feet, she said, "Do I get a grand tour of the place? I'd love to see it."

Nic looked as relieved as she felt. The poor man.

"Living room." He motioned perfunctorily. "Windows overlooking the courtyard. Windows overlooking the street. You can actually see the bridge from here."

"Really? Bet it's lovely at night."

"Come look." He covered the distance in a few long strides, soft-soled Doc Martens silent on the wood floor.

Opening the shutters, he motioned her to him. Then they were standing shoulder to shoulder, peering out to the city. She forced herself not to notice the warmth radiating from his body. The way the top of her head only reached his chin. She might have been a silly eighteen-year-old again for the way she was aware of everything about him.

She forced herself to look out the window. The city lights were already twinkling in the fading twilight.

"Wow. You can see the bridge. And you're only on the fourth floor. I wouldn't have guessed."

"Higher ground, believe it or not. Who knew we even had higher ground in New Orleans, right?"

"Really," was all she said, because then his hand slipped over her elbow and he led her away.

"Breakfast nook." He motioned to the small area that adjoined the kitchen by a pass-through bar.

He'd chosen a circular table that didn't take up much space but would be perfect for him to sit with the newspaper spread out before him, enjoying the sunrise through the eastern windows, sipping morning coffee. In fact, an espresso machine sat on the bar occupying an esteemed place, the stainless-steel carafe polished to a gleam.

"Hallway with a guest bathroom." He pushed open a door to reveal a small, but nicely decorated bathroom, complete with hand towels and ornamental soap.

"You keep a really neat house, Nic. I'm impressed."

"Don't be." He gave a snort of laughter. "One of Mom's stylists moonlights for a cleaning service. Ever since Vince finished med school, I've been able to afford her. You met her—Corinne. She was at lunch."

"I did." Megan thought so, anyway. There'd been quite a few people there and she hadn't exactly been thinking clearly.

They moved out of the living room.

"My office." Swinging the door wide, he revealed a sparsely furnished room with a neat desk and the requisite computer setup. He narrowed his gaze. "I suppose I can turn this into Violet's room. Do you think she'll want to decorate?"

Megan's heart broke then, into a thousand little pieces. He knew almost nothing about their daughter. Had no clue the amount of effort she spent personalizing her bedrooms every time they relocated. Creating each one as if it was a work of art. Violet's way of empowering herself to feel at home in a new place.

The tribal room in Ghana with the ebony bed frame that Bonsom had carved by hand especially for her.

The Oriental inspired room in Hat Yai with the shoji screen that she simply had to have that cost Megan a small fortune.

Her room in Chile was a hands-on room. She'd been painting a mural on one wall the entire time they'd lived there. And she *still* wasn't finished.

Nic had no clue. Because of Megan.

"She'll want to decorate herself," she said. "She's very into creating the perfect space. I'm thinking her space at Dad's will be the most special yet."

"Okay." He nodded decidedly. "That'll give us something to do. We can shop for her room."

"She'll like that."

He didn't seem to mind giving up his office, but Megan imagined with the nature of his job, he probably did most of his work at the police station.

"Good thing this is a two-bedroom unit," he said. "There are only a few in the building. I just bought it off Anthony. I didn't really care either way. But the corner units are the best in the place."

And if there were only two bedrooms then the next door he opened would be…

"My bedroom."

She leaned in only far enough to see into the masculine personal space. Dark wood. Cherry, she thought. Dresser. Armoire. Bed. Queen, by the looks of it. Comforter and matching shams in a simple pattern of rusts and browns.

There was something about seeing the broad expanse of mattress on the heels of discussing their daughter that made everything feel too raw. For Nic, too, from all appearances. He pulled the door shut with a decided slam and was leading her the way they came, suddenly all brisk business.

In the kitchen he headed straight to a cabinet and pulled open the door.

There was a wine rack inside with a variety of bottles resting neatly on their sides.

"Do you like red?" he asked. "I hope so. I only have red."

"I like red."

"Good." He scanned the rack. "Merlot? Cab?" He slid a bottle out of its slot. "I've got a malbec. From Argentina, I'm afraid. Not Chile."

"I like malbec."

He nodded, and she stood in the entrance of the kitchen, watching a new aspect of Nic revealed. He liked wine. She hadn't known that way back when as they hadn't been of legal age to drink. Reaching into another cabinet, he retrieved a decanter, then went through the practiced motions of opening the bottle and pouring.

"So how does this work, exactly?" he asked.

"What?"

"Do we need to find you a place to live?"

Megan folded her arms over her chest and leaned against the archway. "Usually my firm scouts a few places for us to choose from. Then we decide when we get into town. Doesn't have to work like that, though. Just saves me from making a long trip. We could actually take a look around now since we're here. Violet would probably like that."

Anything that got a smile out of her daughter would be a good thing.

He took two wineglasses from an overhead rack then set them beside the decanter. "Might be a good idea. She was gunning to stay in New Orleans."

"Was she?"

"Hinted around about how I'd get to see her all the time if she lived here."

Megan nodded, forcing back the hurt that nearly stole her breath. She wasn't surprised. No. Not after their interaction the other day. Just hurt that Violet was so eager to leave their life behind, leave Megan. As if all the years hadn't counted for anything. God, Megan knew this feeling all too well.

She reminded herself that she'd reared Violet to be an independent young woman. Independence meant figuring things out for herself and how to cope in constructive ways. For Violet to do that she had to step away from her mom and learn to stand on her own two feet, to trust her decisions.

Megan hadn't anticipated that part.

Or how much it would hurt to let go.

"Violet's working through her feelings about everything and trying to exercise some control." An explanation for Nic. A reminder for herself. "That's a good thing. My job is to have faith in her. If I believe in her, she learns to have confidence in the choices she makes."

Nic stared down at the glasses, seemed to consider that. "She's giving you a hard time?"

"What makes you think that?"

"She's fourteen."

He knew firsthand what raising a teenager was like. Times five. Which was probably why the man was currently single. Had he ever come close to getting married? Any closer than she had?

"She's coming to terms with the fact that her mother isn't perfect." Megan wasn't going *there*. "That's never easy."

"It'll take time for everything to settle in. For all of us."

"It's a big shock."

He slanted his head and met her gaze. "Even for you?"

"Even for me," she admitted, not sure he'd believe her. "Even though I've known all along. Everything's out of my control now. It's scary. I'm not going to lie."

Nic grabbed the decanter and poured a glass. Then he took a long, deep gulp.

Any man who kept wine behind closed doors and knew the difference between Argentinean and Chilean malbec would know one didn't gulp freshly decanted wine. Even she knew that and the extent of her experience was the Food Network and the screw-top Bordeaux she cooked with.

She was driving this man to drink.

Add that to her list of crimes.

"We can do this, Megan. I'm going to stay focused on now, not the past," he said as if trying to convince himself as much as her. "If I start getting hung up on the past, I'll just drag myself back to the present. I can do this. No problem."

Another deep gulp. The glass was nearly empty, and he refilled it then poured another, which he handed to her absently. He gave a short laugh. "Not sure why I even bothered decanting this."

Megan didn't say a word. She brought the glass to her lips, inhaled deeply of the earthy scent and took a small sip.

Nic ran a hand through his hair, an uncharacteristically revealing gesture. The man was clearly unsettled.

Now it was her turn to gulp.

"We're going to handle everything as adults concerned with our daughter's best interests?"

There was a question in there. She nodded, hoping to reassure him. She took another sip.

"All right. Sounds like a plan." Grabbing his glass in one hand and the decanter in the other, he strode toward her. "Come on. Let's go talk money."

Megan didn't get a chance to reply, or to back away from the archway leading into the dining room before he was on top of her. Hanging on to her own glass so she didn't do anything stupid like spill wine all over herself, she glanced up at him, was startled at what she saw in his golden-brown gaze.

Surprise.

It flared in his eyes unmistakably, and with a gasp of premonition, Megan knew what he was going to do even before he took that last step that closed the distance between them.

Before he brought his mouth down on hers.

CHAPTER EIGHTEEN

MEGAN TOLD HERSELF THIS kiss was nothing more than his lips on hers. How could it be anything more? He had a decanter in one hand and a wineglass in the other. He crowded her in a doorway, bent at an odd angle, and she clutched her own glass as if it were a buoy in the middle of an ocean.

But then, this kiss was much, much more.

His mouth slanted over hers as if it belonged there, his lips tasting of malbec and *him*. And she knew him. From somewhere deep in memory, someplace she'd shut down and hidden long ago, Megan remembered him and his kisses.

She might have buried those memories deep, but how could she ever forget this wild expectation snaking its way into every remote part of her.

Reason shrieked wildly that they shouldn't be doing this. Reason warned they would only make a difficult situation even more difficult. Reason urged her to deny this physical reaction that was sucking her under fast, an undertow she wouldn't fight for long. Reason implored her to pretend it wasn't possible to feel this way when so many years and so much had passed between them.

But this was Nic.

And she'd never been able to deny him.

So her lips parted on the edge of a sigh, the most natural response in the world. The only response Megan had to give when he took immediate advantage of her compliance, deepening his kiss, teasing her lips apart, tasting her as if he'd waited forever for the privilege.

Their tongues met, all familiarity and earthy malbec, all warm breath and incredible surprise.

She could taste it on his lips, taste it on his tongue, taste it in every shallow gasp he took. Surprise at so much need between them when years and circumstance should have calmed this storm long ago.

If there had been any question that their desire had been a product of youth and hormones, the way he breathed her name against her mouth, almost a plea, answered any speculation.

They weren't teenagers anymore.

The realization this was Nic—*now*—came at her sideways.

Megan never thought she'd kiss this man again.

That thought sank in with physical force and, suddenly, she couldn't get enough of him. This was her chance to touch him again. Megan couldn't have resisted if she'd wanted to.

She didn't.

She wanted to taste him, to feel the urgency of their desire, to remember him.

And she remembered.

Just how much she'd wanted Nic, wanted him to touch her in ways she'd never been touched before. Just how much she hadn't cared about the consequences, hadn't cared about anything but the feel of his mouth on hers, the feel of his hands everywhere. Just how much she'd never known anything like the way she felt right now, not as a teenager, not in all the years since.

As if *this* was exactly what life was supposed to be

about, savoring the unique magic two special people could make together, only together.

Need swelled inside like a wave, built with such urgency and intensity she could only rise with it, anticipating the inevitable and sweet crash ahead.

She wanted to drink in the taste of him with her mouth. She wanted to touch him, but they had no hands, the glassware an external control that kept them from melting into each other, engaging more than their mouths in this kiss.

A kiss she wanted to last forever.

DESIRE HAD ALWAYS BEEN like this between them. Nic didn't know how it could be this way now. The betrayal, the anger and he'd still lost control. He didn't know how he could lose control, but he had. He'd kissed her.

And didn't want to stop.

Fifteen years of pent-up desire had burst like a dam inside him. He hadn't known it was there, but it was, and he was powerless to hold it back. The striking image of the wine decanter crashing to the floor flashed in his mind. He wanted to free up his hands so he could touch her, *finally* touch her.

This shouldn't be happening. But Nic couldn't think beyond her sighs bursting softly against his mouth, the familiarity of her eagerness. This was Megan, and she wanted him, too. Had always wanted him. That much he did know. *That* and how right she felt with her face tipped up to kiss him, this woman he hadn't known he still wanted.

But he did. Nic knew that now, too.

He hadn't realized that he'd shut down a part of himself all those years ago. Had no damned clue that every woman he'd slept with since hadn't matched up to what was inside his head. Because *this* was the way a kiss should be, all hot want and sweet greed.

They might have been two teenagers again, except that what he felt right now had been years in the making. This wasn't any hormonal excitement by an overeager kid who wanted to see some skin. This was survival.

He'd been denied what he wanted for too long.

Suddenly, he was crowding her against the wall. With his arms outstretched and his mouth on hers, he forced her to yield until she could go no farther, unable to stop himself, needing to press close and feel her against him.

Her glass was the first casualty. It shattered the instant it hit the kitchen tile, but Nic didn't care. All he could think about was that one of them had free hands...

Her arms slipped around him like a silken vise, and they came together as if their bodies were magnetized. He could feel every smooth curve against him, breasts gently crushing his chest, thighs lifting her closer, ever closer. Her hips tipped slightly, enough to cradle what had become a raging erection when he hadn't been paying attention.

How he wanted...

His body's response was electric. Every drop of blood surged through him with such force he groaned. She kissed the sound from his mouth, hot liquid glides of her tongue that somehow echoed the pulse throbbing inside him.

She wasn't tentative or shy, only needy. He could only kiss her back, refusing to let thoughts interfere with the way he felt right now, as if he'd been dead and hadn't known it, until now when he'd come back to life.

"I want you."

"I know." Came her breathless reply.

No pretense. No denial.

Only need.

He broke his mouth from hers with effort. The dining room table was closest, and with his last few working brain cells, he unloaded the decanter and glass, freed his hands.

Then she was all his. He wouldn't let her get away.

Not again.

Those blue, blue eyes were liquid when he turned to face her, her mouth was parted and red from his kisses. She was so beautiful, the real woman so much more than his memory.

For one startling instant, Nic couldn't move, afraid she might disappear before his eyes, vanish as she had before.

Then he stepped close, blocking any escape with his body, pinning her against the wall. Bracing himself with a hand above her head, he stared down into that face, tried to convince himself she was real.

Megan. She was here, and she was his.

For the moment.

The thought spurred him into action. He fully intended to make the most of this moment. With his free hand, he thumbed her lower lip, a slow, sensual motion that made fire flare in her eyes.

"Make love to me." A dare.

Her expression visibly melted, and he recognized what he saw—eagerness, want. For him.

No matter what had passed between them, Nic knew there was no lie in her now. And knowing that she still wanted the way he did punched him low in the gut.

Sliding his fingers down, he traced the curve of her chin, the slim lines of her throat, the feel of her skin so impossibly familiar. He hadn't known he remembered.

But the familiarity was there, proving that he could still feel for her despite every rational objection.

Fingering the top button, he paused to give her a chance to deny him, but there was no denial in her. She slipped her arms around his neck, tipped her face to his and melted into him, moves that gave permission louder than any words ever could.

She wanted. *Him.*

He brought his mouth down on hers again, unable to resist the whisper of her shallow breaths, unable to deny how much he needed to feel her desire right then.

And he felt it, in the way they kissed, as if he hadn't kissed in forever. Fingering the buttons of her blouse, he released each one with precise motions. She arched into his motions as he brushed aside the silky fabric, rested his palm against her chest, warm skin against warm skin.

Such a simple touch.

Suddenly, she was tugging up his shirt, splaying her fingers over his chest. She dragged smooth palms along his skin, reacquainting herself with no hesitation. Her hair tickled his nose when she dropped a kiss onto the exposed throat over his collar, such a sweetly seductive gesture that he could only close his eyes.

The scent of her shampoo—that damned tropical scent—wound its way through his senses, undermining the very last of his control.

Then he was dragging his shirt over his head, tossing it away before making quick work of her blouse. She stood before him, a delectable sight with the swell of her breasts peeking above a lacy bra, the smooth expanse of her stomach exposed above her skirt.

He made quick work of the skirt, too.

With a soft whoosh, the fabric slid over her hips and

down her legs to puddle at her feet. He pushed away from the wall enough to gaze down and enjoy the view.

Sucked in a hard breath at the sight.

Megan, all lean curves and creamy skin, standing before him in nothing more than a lacy bra, barely there panties and peep-toed sandals.

Megan, a vision he'd never allowed himself to remember.

How could he when his hand trembled stupidly while snapping open the clasp of the bra, brushing lace out of his way until her breasts spilled out in a swell of creamy skin. Dragging a thumb across a nipple, he watched as the delicate skin puckered. She gasped, a raw sound in the quiet.

Had anyone ever responded so eagerly to him, so attuned to his slightest touch?

Only Megan.

Their gazes met. Hers dreamy with desire his surely wild with need.

Suddenly, Nic was done playing. Unsure where the shattered glass was and refusing to waste time finding out, he lifted her into his arms. She clung to him, arms slithering around his neck to hang on as if her life depended on it. He wanted her in his bed, naked and stretched out against him.

He headed to his bedroom.

He couldn't risk thinking right now, couldn't do anything but kick open the bedroom door and send it crashing against the wall with a sound that made her start in his arms.

Lowering Megan to her feet, he savored every inch of her as she slid full length against him, warm skin and sleek curves, a drug that kept the buzz going, kept rational thought at bay.

The night had cast the room in darkness, but Nic didn't bother with lights, content with the glow from outside that concealed almost as much as it revealed, illuminated her fair skin until she became his beacon.

He didn't want to see her face right now, didn't want to meet her expression, not with this urgency spurring him to strip off the remainder of his clothes. He just wanted to lose himself in her arms. He didn't want to think about how long it had been since he'd felt alive. Didn't want to question why only she made him feel this way.

He wanted to hear her soft sighs, feel her body unfold beneath his, bridging the distance of the years and proving she felt exactly the same way about him.

Her pale arms beckoned. Nic sank onto the bed and pulled her against him.

And got exactly what he wanted.

CHAPTER NINETEEN

MEGAN AWOKE SOMETIME during the night and stared into the darkness, remembering.

Nic.

He cocooned her with his body, arm draped around her waist keeping her tucked firmly against him, legs tangled with hers so she couldn't get away if she'd wanted. She didn't. Her body curled perfectly within his, fitting everywhere as if they'd been designed exclusively for each other.

Megan lay utterly still, refused to do anything that might bring an end to this moment, to the hot weight of this man wrapped all around her in the dark. She only wanted to memorize the steady rise and fall of his chest, listen to the slight whisper of his each breath against her ear.

She remembered everything about him, yet the Nic who held her now was no longer the young man who'd seduced her with his irresistible kisses so long ago. He was harder, bigger, so much more closed—a grown man who'd spent the years obviously honing his skills at making love.

Her body ached tenderly in places she didn't even know could ache, and she *still* couldn't think straight.

Not that she ever could around him.

They'd never slept together like this before, either, wrapped in each other's arms, passed out from passion.

Not once in all their reckless months together. They'd been so young. They'd had to steal each moment. Her more so than Nic because she couldn't stand up to her parents. Tonight was no less stolen. But rather than the desperate excitement of their youth, tonight was the bittersweet past mixed with a difficult present.

They'd made their situation so much more impossible. Why had they needed to know they could still want each other? That despite everything that had passed between them, all the unresolved feelings, his anger, her guilt, their need to make peace to usher in a new era of parenting their daughter together, why had they needed to know that the passion they'd once shared still smoldered beneath the surface?

Why had Megan needed to know she still could be influenced against her better judgment after convincing herself she was a strong, independent woman?

Because she wasn't as strong as she thought.

Independent, maybe, but not nearly as strong.

She'd wanted Nic, even knowing that giving in would complicate things between them, for both of them. They'd never concluded their relationship, hadn't seen where it would lead, hadn't let it work its way to a natural end.

She'd hadn't given either of them that chance, had run away instead, and avoided him ever since because she'd been in over her head and determined to stand on her own two feet.

She'd done that, hadn't she?

As she stared into the darkness, wrapped tightly in the arms of this man who'd influenced so much of her life, knowingly and unknowingly, Megan realized the truth.

It was very simple.

She'd been honest with Nic, hadn't known if she would have eventually accepted the New Orleans project. It seemed as soon as she convinced herself facing the past was the best for all concerned, she'd talk herself out of that decision.

Back and forth. Day after day.

Now here she was, in the only place in the world she wanted to be, the very place she had no right to be.

Because Violet had made the choice for her.

Because Nic had made the choice for her.

Given her way, Megan would still be in Chile bouncing between accepting or not accepting the project, no closer to a decision as the deadline neared and her anxiety elevated to a feverish pitch.

She'd had no choice but to deal with Violet's rebellion.

Like she'd had no choice but to deal with her parents when they'd driven up yesterday.

But she'd had a choice with Nic tonight, and she'd let desire—hers and his—dissuade her from behaving rationally.

A simple truth. Megan might be independent, but she wasn't strong. She'd only been avoiding the tests.

Tonight had been a test.

As she felt Nic's warm breaths against her hair, felt the solid strength of his body around hers, Megan could only acknowledge…

Epic fail.

So she lay in his arms, memorizing every hard hollow of his body, staring into the darkness… Her gaze caught sight of a dull green glow of a alarm clock on the night table.

Two forty-two.

Oh, no… Megan's heart throbbed dully in her chest, so hard she could barely draw a breath.

Her cell phone was still in her purse in the living room. And Violet would have texted—to let Megan know she'd arrived at Dixie Downs safely, to let Megan know when she'd arrived home safely since her mother wasn't there to greet her.

And of course, the cell phone was the only way to reach Megan if there'd been any sort of problem.

Epic, epic fail.

In one fluid motion, she maneuvered out of Nic's grip and slid off the side of the bed. Her feet didn't make a sound on the carpet, but Nic was awake in an instant.

"Megan—"

"My phone," she whispered. "I left it in my purse on vibrate. I wouldn't hear it if Violet needed me."

She was halfway out the door when he said, "Anthony and Tess know you're with me. They'd have called if—"

Megan was gone. The moonlight through the open shutters cast silver light in the living room to guide her way. She dug through her purse and retrieved the phone, flipped it open and glanced at the display.

Four text messages from Violet, who'd behaved responsibly by keeping Megan in the loop about where she was.

Alive!

Translated meant she'd arrived safely at the track.

Dinner with Tess's uncle. He won first place!

Home. You're not here.

Tired. Going to bed. Hope you're alive.

Megan flipped the phone shut. Some mother she was.

When she returned to the bedroom, she found Nic sitting up in bed, a knee drawn before him, watching her. He'd flipped on a bedside lamp and the soft glow illuminated the room enough to make her feel self-conscious. Why hadn't she thought to pick up her clothes in the dining room?

"Violet okay?" he asked.

"Yes. She went to bed a few hours ago."

Megan couldn't seem to meet his gaze, wasn't sure what was up with that. Maybe she didn't want to let him know how rattled she was right now. Or maybe she didn't want any more tests tonight. He was one big fat test, sitting there in the lamp's golden glow, looking all sleep tousled and sexy, making her body tingle with the memories of what they'd done in this bed.

Spotting her bra clinging to the comforter, she grabbed it, glanced around for her underwear.

On the floor in front of the closet.

One sandal beneath the bed skirt. The other by the nightstand.

All out of place, all strangers in Nic's bedroom.

As she was.

"Megan," he said softly. "We need to talk."

She shook her head, still not ready to meet his gaze, needing to be anywhere in the world but here right now.

"I've got to go."

Setting her sandals on the edge of the bed, she slid her hands through the straps of her bra then dragged them up her arms. She'd feel better if she were dressed. Even a little dressed would be better than nothing right now.

"It's late. Stay."

"I can't tell Violet I spent the night here."

"What will you tell her?"

Megan could feel his gaze on her, made quick work of getting her underwear on. "I don't know. Probably that we were talking about how to work things out and lost track of time."

"Are you going to tell her that you'll accept the project and move here?"

She nodded. "That'll make her happy and distract her from the fact that I haven't responded to her texts."

"You think she's worried?"

Megan dropped her sandals on the floor and stepped into them. "I don't ever ignore her texts."

"Megan."

There was something in his voice that drew her gaze. She finally faced him, recognized the stranger's mask was gone. Maybe sleep had dulled the edges. Or maybe what had passed between them since she'd arrived had changed things. Either way, the intimacy of staring at him across the bed, of seeing the hurt in his eyes, was too much.

"I've got to go."

"You're running again?" There was surprise in his hoarse whisper.

"No. No, I'm not. I'll be at your mom's. I promise." She was struggling to catch a deep breath. "Please don't get up, Nic. I'll let myself out."

She was halfway down the hall, before realizing Nic likely hadn't meant running from New Orleans.

But from him.

Oh, God, please don't have let my skirt been sitting in a puddle of malbec and broken glass all night.

She'd wind up right back in his bedroom again borrowing something to wear, which would, in turn, raise questions about what happened to her clothes if she ran into her daughter.

Luck was with her and, thankfully, the puddle of wine had missed her skirt by mere inches. She could barely make out the mess in the darkness, hated leaving the result of her clumsiness for Nic to deal with.

But as she dragged on her skirt and hastily buttoned her blouse, she talked herself out of cleaning up. If he heard her clanking around in here, looking for paper towels, a broom and the trash, he'd surely come out.

So she grabbed her purse and headed toward the door, half expecting him to show up as she unlocked the dead bolt.

He didn't.

By the time she arrived at the first floor, she could almost breathe again. But she couldn't help glancing up at his windows on the top floor before she got in the Jeep.

He was there in the window.

She wasn't surprised.

He might have respected her wishes and let her leave, but he would never be able to deal with not knowing whether or not she'd gotten safely to the car.

Fifteen years may have passed. He might have grown up, but he was still Nic.

JURADO POPPED HIS HEAD inside Nic's office door and announced, "Chief, they're all here."

"Good," Nic said. "They can see each other?"

"You betcha. The judge is foaming at the mouth. I can tell you that."

"Let him foam. I'll be there. Later rather than sooner."

Jurado grinned. "Better you than me. Promise you I won't be mentioning that to him."

Then he vanished, leaving Nic staring at the closing door. He set the department's monthly budget report on the desk. He hadn't been looking at it anyway. Well, he'd been looking at it, but he'd been thinking about Megan.

How in hell had this happened?

The instant he'd said he was going to get out from under all the responsibilities and start paying attention to what he wanted for a change, the shit had hit the fan, starting with the mayor and this appointment. Then Violet. Now Megan.

What a damned mess.

Now he had Judge Dubos sitting in an interrogation room ready to eat Nic alive for dragging him out of the courtroom to *talk*. Of course, he'd also dragged in Big Mike, who wouldn't be happy to be out of bed so early. The only one who might be remotely okay with him was the massage therapist. She'd feel as if the police were taking her complaint seriously. But her boss wouldn't be so happy—Busybodies's owner would assume they were trying to manufacture evidence for a prostitution charge.

Nic rubbed his temples. Forcing this confrontation had been a last resort, but Andy had been right. Until Nic could ID Great Eye guy, he had nothing. His officers were still combing through every case Judge Dubos had heard for the past year. So far they hadn't been able to make any connections.

With any luck—and Nic wasn't holding his breath on this one—the judge would think the only people he had to worry about were Big Mike and the women from Busybodies. Nic was placing the judge under surveillance.

Then he was going to hope that someone gave him

something to work with here, so he could protect his daughter.

Nic wasn't used to hoping and was *not* a happy camper.

Not at work. Not at home. And that part largely had to do with the woman he'd made love to last night.

They'd picked up right where they'd left off as if the years and the lies had never happened.

What did that mean? That he'd never gotten over her? That the years, the lies, the betrayal all meant nothing?

The thought alone made him scowl. So what if he still had feelings that went beyond this anger simmering in the pit of his stomach. What the hell could he do?

Not a damned thing. Not even if he wanted to. He had no control over Megan and she'd run away from him again.

Pushing away from his desk, Nic got to his feet. He had three people sitting in Operations waiting for him to come vent his frustration.

The judge wasn't the only one foaming at the mouth today.

CHAPTER TWENTY

"WHAT DO YOU MEAN I CAN'T ride with Uncle Damon's students?" Violet wasn't sure she heard her dad right. "But it's the Easter parade, a New Orleans tradition. He invited me."

"I'm sorry. It's not a good idea, Violet. Not this time."

Her dad had come to pick her up from Grandmama's shop. She hadn't seen him all day and had been really excited ever since Mom had given her the news this morning.

They were moving to New Orleans.

Violet thought her dad would be happy. Everyone else seemed happy—well, everyone she'd told, anyway. Grandmama was thrilled. She was going to teach Violet how to cook Italian and do something really cool to her hair.

"But I don't understand why. They've got a float."

"I know. It's a decent one, too. Always wonder whether I should assign extra duty officers. If those karate kids went berserk in the crowd, they could do some damage."

Was he trying to be funny? "Did you want to talk to Uncle Damon?"

"There's no need, Violet. It's not a good time for you to be riding on top of a float."

"But why?"

"Because I said so and I'm the police chief."

Violet almost laughed. The sound was nearly out of her mouth before she saw that he was *for real*. He was staring at her like he didn't even want to be having this conversation but couldn't get out of it.

Wow. Took a minute to wrap her brain around that.

Unfortunately for him, she wasn't some little kid who was okay with following orders. She liked to be part of the process.

It was only fair.

"Is this some sort of police thing or do you have a beef against Uncle Damon?"

Her dad ran his fingers through his hair, making it stand up sort of squirrely. He opened his mouth to answer, but then Grandmama came out of the back room, where she'd been mixing up a bowl of color for a client.

"You need a cut," she told him. "If you hang around for a few minutes, I'll have time while Millie's processing."

"Thanks, not now. I'll come another day."

Grandmama nodded and went about her business. "You know where to find me."

Violet was about to continue the conversation, but his phone vibrated. He frowned apologetically and took the call, leaving her nothing to do but spin in the chair, glancing in the mirror as she went around. How would dreds look with this nose ring? Tribal. Just the thought made her smile. Mom would faint. And Dad... What was up with him today?

She really hoped he wasn't trying to get all parental since they were moving here. She might have to explain how she was always part of the decision-making process. But the usual stuff that worked with Mom wasn't working on him. Mom always listened to reasonable game plans. The more rational she was, the more willing Mom was to negotiate nos into yeses. She always said if they handled situations rationally, they could come up with something to meet both their needs.

Except for the nose ring. Violet had to take matters into her own hands on that one.

But her dad obviously thought she was supposed to accept no for an answer without any explanation. And about something as stupid as riding on a parade float.

Violet wasn't sure what she thought about that. She'd been so hyped about having a dad that she hadn't really thought about what having a *police chief* dad might be like. Who else would have an issue with a parade float?

"Seriously, *padre*." She gave him another shot after he ended the call. Hopefully he only needed some training. He hadn't had any kids before. "What's up with this? Problem with the police? Problem with me? Help me out here."

"Problem with you and the police."

"Oh, Great Eye guy?"

He nodded.

Bummer. She wasn't happy that she hadn't been able to find the guy in all those books. She'd wanted to help her dad before. But now, *not* helping was becoming a problem.

"So, what? Am I in danger or something?"

"No. But it's not the time for you to be parading through the French Quarter on top of a float. Anyone could be in the crowd and see you."

"Damn." A little danger might have been exciting. She could have gone on the run or something. Tweet every time she dodged a bullet. Catching his reflection in the mirror, she recognized the narrowed gaze and made a correction. "Dang."

He eased up. "Are we good?"

Violet had to think about that. All he'd needed to do was explain the problem. No big deal. "We're good."

Wow. The novelty was wearing off faster than she'd have thought.

NIC ARRIVED AT HIS MOTHER'S house early on Saturday. The week might officially be over, but the problems had followed him into the weekend. He heard voices from the direction of the kitchen and hung in the hall, steeling himself to see *her*. Their plan was to spend some time scouting neighborhoods and rental properties from a list a real estate buddy of his had pulled together.

Megan had been dodging him ever since they'd made love. She delivered Violet. She retrieved Violet. She spoke with him on the phone to make arrangements for Violet, but not once had she addressed what had taken place between them. And she dodged his every attempt to talk about it.

He hated not knowing where they stood, needed to get her alone to force the issue and figure out where they were going from here. They still had feelings for each other.

There, he'd admitted it. But that didn't mean he had a damned clue what to do about it, and he hated standing on the edge of an abyss. That's exactly what the future felt like—a huge chasm filled with awkward meetings and unresolved issues and that distant politeness Megan had honed to a science. A future spent trying to interact as involved responsible parents when he could barely look at her without thoughts of kissing her.

Violet needed to be the priority here, and his

relationship with her. They had a lifetime to catch up on, and Megan needed to be a part of that process. Their plan made sense. But when he thought about how they were jumping into parenthood—and into bed—over a gap of fifteen years…*chasm.*

And a mighty big one at that.

Irony at its finest. He meant to move on with his life, and he was. In a direction he'd never once considered. A daughter he hadn't known existed. A woman he couldn't trust.

How was this moving on?

Maybe he was with Violet. Stepping into his role as father, a role he'd spent a lifetime preparing for. But with Megan everything was history. And she was still running. He didn't have a damned clue why.

Because they still had feelings for each other?

That presented a problem, he agreed. They couldn't be together. There were too many years and too many issues between them even though his gut told him it wasn't over. Bouncing back and forth between this gut-wrenching excitement to see her and resentment because the feeling was so out of his control.

God, he hated this. They needed to address the situation and figure out what to do about *them.* Before they wound up in bed again. Once Violet and Megan moved back to New Orleans, she wasn't going to be able to run far.

But he didn't see much hope they could talk today, not while spending the day with Violet.

"She's quite capable of making her own breakfast, Mama," he heard Megan say.

"Come on, Mom." That was Violet. "Grandmama wants to dote on me, and I'm okay with that. We're getting to know each other. You know how much I love French toast, but she doesn't."

Nic made his way into the kitchen, where he found his mother standing over the stove, dressed for work and wearing an apron, a spatula in one hand and a smile on her face.

She was enjoying her houseguests. No real surprise there, but he was glad. She hated knocking around this empty house.

"You're late, Nic," she said when she saw him. "I need to get to the shop soon. I've got a nine o'clock."

"I'm your man then."

"You always are. Hungry?"

"For French toast? Um, yeah."

Violet giggled, and he planted a kiss on the top of her head before heading to the stove and kissing his mother, too.

"Everything okay at the station?" she asked.

"It is, and I've got some good news." He braced himself to face Megan. She stood at the corner of the counter by the back door, nursing a mug of coffee, looking as beautiful as she always did. Except today she seemed more like the Megan of his memory with faded jeans riding low on her hips and the scoop-necked T-shirt clinging to every curve.

Or maybe she looked like the girl he'd fallen in love with because he could picture her naked again.

"We always welcome good news, Nic." She was all smiles, and he couldn't see anything left of the woman who'd fled his apartment in the wee hours and had been dodging him ever since.

"Megan." He strode toward her, close enough to make her tilt her head to meet his gaze, eyes widening uncertainly when he reached above her head to pull open the cabinet and grab a mug. "Excuse me."

She recovered quickly, reaching for the coffeepot and pouring for him.

"Thanks," he said. "Might have made a connection in the case. Keep your fingers crossed that it pans out."

"Great Eye guy?" Violet asked.

"No, I'm afraid not. But something is better than nothing. After we're done, I'll go down to the station and see what they've come up with."

"What is it?" Violet asked. "Can't you tell us?"

"Not yet. It's a police chief thing. But keep your fingers crossed. If it pans out, I can tell you."

Violet raised her hands and crossed her fingers, followed by Megan and his mother.

"Can't lose with luck like that." He smiled.

Nic and Violet made quick work of breakfast, and soon they were on their way to the shop. He didn't open his mouth on the trip, couldn't have gotten a word in with the way Violet and his mother talked nonstop. Megan piped in every so often, too, proving she paid attention to the conversation while she scanned the listings of rental properties. He played chauffeur, amazed by how women could find so much to talk about in the morning.

Surprised by his feeling of *right*.

He'd been tired, no question, ready to take a break from his responsibilities to everyone and everything in his life, but Nic didn't know when those responsibilities had started to feel like burdens. But they had. He knew it now as he squired around these women, *his* women, couldn't imagine anything else he'd rather be doing at the crack of dawn on a Saturday.

That's what they felt like. *His*.

And Violet was. His mother, too.

But not Megan. She was only along for the ride.

He dropped off his mother at the shop, eager to get busy with the house hunting so he could stop thinking.

"Where to, ladies?" he asked.

"Once we figure out what neighborhoods we're interested in, we can drive by these places and make the first round of cuts that way," Megan suggested. "If we see anything we like we can call the agent and ask to see inside. Sound like a plan?"

"Sounds good to me."

"What about schools?" Violet suddenly appeared, blond head practically in the front seat as she strained against the seat belt. "What's the deal? We usually figure out what the best school is and then work from there."

Nic maneuvered into traffic on Magazine Street and headed out of the commercial area. "Okay, define best."

"Like, where all the decent kids go."

He could hear a *duh* in there and, sure enough, one look in the rearview mirror found her glancing askance at Megan as if to question why she'd reproduced with someone so dense.

"Well, we've got Newman, which is a great school. Tuition is steep, but we should be able to swing it. Or Sacred Heart, which is where your mother went. Tuition's more reasonable, but it's all girls. Wasn't sure how you'd feel about that."

Another glance in the rearview mirror where he found horrified blue eyes staring back.

"Okay then, how about De La Salle?" He glanced at Megan. "Didn't they become coed before you left?"

"When I was a sophomore, I think."

"Sound better?" he asked. "What about St. Augustine's? Only boys there."

Violet continued to stare wide-eyed.

"There's St. Mary's and the Ursuline Academy—"

"Don't they have, like, public schools around here?"

"They do. And as a public servant, I should probably recommend our school system. But as your father, I'd be very remiss if I didn't mention that the school situation took a massive hit in Katrina. We lost about a hundred of our hundred and twenty-eight school buildings."

Megan gasped.

Nic nodded. "Yeah. Not pretty. So the legislature stepped in to get the new school system off to a good start." In much the same way the federal government had stepped in with the police department.

"So, now we have charter schools or the recovery school district. They're still working out the bugs on both. I'm thinking Sacred Heart."

"All girls? Ugh. Mom, come on."

"It's a very good school, pup. Why don't we drive by and take a look at the campus. De La Salle isn't far from there, either. We'll keep open minds and do our homework. We have time to make a decision."

Violet didn't look too open-minded from where Nic sat, but Megan seemed to have given the choice to their daughter. He wasn't sure what he thought about that. Okay, he supposed, *if* she made the right choice.

"Why do you like public schools?" he asked.

"Friends."

"They might have friends in private schools."

"Funny." She didn't look as though she appreciated his attempt at humor one bit. "I'm not into snotty rich kids."

A generalization if ever he'd heard one, but Nic didn't

think she'd appreciate him pointing that out. He chose a safer route. "I have a question. With the way you move around, do you ever run into trouble with your classes? You guys live in some out-of-the-way places."

"Never been a problem. I'm always ahead. And if the curriculum is too behind, then I take virtual classes to keep my brain entertained. No big deal."

Nic was impressed. Then again, Megan's parents were both academics. He would expect Megan to place a lot of importance on education. "So you might be interested in dual enrollment. We have some good universities around here that make classes available to the high schools. It's a great opportunity to get some of the general education classes out of the way before college. You could even start college as a sophomore."

"Cool." She strained against the seat belt again, suddenly interested. "What about Grandpa Bell's school, Mom? Do you think they have classes there?"

"We can certainly find out."

"Oh, yeah, man. That'd be cool. I'm going to make the most of the whole family thing while we're here. Just so you know."

Megan glanced over her shoulder, the smile forced. "Now would be the time."

Nic turned west on St. Charles Avenue, and Violet fell silent as the lawns stretched out and the houses grew impressive. He found Violet's heads-up about the Professors Bell interesting. Had the trouble between Megan and her parents started when she decided to keep Violet? He'd had to make more assumptions since Megan hadn't filled in the blanks. He wondered how things would work out once she and Violet came here to live then reminded himself it wasn't his problem.

Pulling up to the curb, he announced, "First stop."

"Wow, it doesn't really look much different," Megan said softly. "This is where I went to school."

Violet pushed open the door and stood so she could check out the grounds behind the majestic gates that displayed the words *Sacre Coeur* in elaborate ironwork. No sooner did she get out when a class filed from a side building into the courtyard.

He heard Violet gasp.

"What do you think?" he asked Megan, who shook her head.

"Not looking promising."

Violet hopped back in the car. "Let's go. I'm thinking my nose ring won't work with those cute little uniforms."

"Might not be a problem," Megan said drily. "Since we haven't actually addressed your nose hardware yet. I was saving that conversation until things settled down a bit."

"What's there to talk about?" Violet feigned innocence, then shifted to evasive maneuvers. "I have a question. If you went to a girls' school, how'd you two meet?"

Nic caught her gaze in the rearview mirror, just to let her know he knew exactly what she was doing. This kid was too slick for her own good. "Your mother was my Spanish tutor."

"Where did you go to school?"

"Public high school not far from here."

"Are we going there, too?"

"We can drive by the vacant lot where it used to be."

"Oh. Bummer." She shifted around to look at Megan. "So how'd you wind up a tutor?"

"Community service," Megan explained. "We needed

volunteer hours like you do. My Spanish teacher knew your dad's teacher and set us up."

"Where did you guys meet to study?"

"The public library."

"Is that still here? Can we go see it?"

"That we can. We can swing by when we head back to look at some properties Uptown. Sound good?"

Slowing, he angled for another spot along the curb so Violet could see the school across the street, supposing it was natural that she'd be interested in how her parents met.

"There's De La Salle," Megan said. "What do you think?"

Violet's seat belt snapped back with a jangle as she shot to the other window. Nic turned off the lock and lowered it so she could see better.

"Not nearly as impressive, is it?" she admitted, eyeing the self-contained building. "Do they wear uniforms? I don't see anyone around."

"We'll probably be able to find out on the website," Megan suggested.

"I'll get right on that as soon as we're home." She scooted across the seat and buckled in again.

Megan just shook her head, and Nic supposed he was getting a much better handle on what *best* meant.

"Oh, Nic." Megan placed a hand on the seat between them suddenly, a casual gesture, so near his thigh that he got the sense that she'd only just stopped herself from touching him. "Let's drive by the universities since we're so close."

"Can do." He checked the side mirror before pulling away.

Keeping course west on St. Charles Avenue, he was glad it was Saturday and traffic wasn't too bad. Except for the guy he was driving behind. Most people recognized the unmarked cruiser and slowed to a crawl. Why? Nic had no clue. He'd never been able to figure out why anyone would want to piss off the cop on their tail by driving *below* the limit.

They reached the campus of Loyola University first, one of the top ten Southern colleges.

"There you go, pup. That's where your grandparents work. And your father went to school here, too."

"You did?" Violet asked, surprised. "With Mom's parents?"

Even Megan turned to face him for that answer. "I didn't actually take classes with them."

Purely by design, but he didn't admit that. Her mother, as dean of Languages and Cultures, hadn't been much of an issue since he'd fulfilled his language requirements, but her father's history classes had popped up all over his schedule.

Neither Megan nor Violet seemed to find that a surprise and Nic wondered how much Megan had shared with their daughter about the past. He'd noticed how she frequently kept her mouth shut to encourage Violet's involvement in all sorts of things and had to wonder if her seemingly liberal parenting style translated into that sort of openness.

God, he hoped not.

They cruised past Tulane University before he U-turned and officially started the search for a place to live.

A top floor of a two-story clapboard with a pool in Marlyville-Fountainebleu.

A cottage in Freret.

Two duplexes Uptown.

"Don't they have any real houses to rent?" Violet

finally asked. "These are all, like, apartments. It's not just us. We need room for GigiMarie, too."

"I'm looking at the square footage," Megan said, "And there are quite a few that are a fairly good size."

Nic agreed. "Most are houses that have been renovated into apartments because they were so big in the first place."

"And there are so many on here." Megan held up the list. "I wasn't sure what to expect after the hurricane."

He only nodded, not needing a reminder of the FEMA trailer days. "Megan, let me see that. Maybe I can help narrow the choices. There have got to be at least fifty listings here."

He pulled over at the stop sign and glanced at the list. "All right, here goes."

There was a single-family Queen Anne that Nic knew by just looking was way the hell out of their price range.

An Uptown bungalow that had a great gallery porch. This one didn't have a rental price, either.

He liked the look of the house that had been split into a duplex on Pitt Street the best, a location so close to the Academy of the Sacred Heart that Violet could easily walk.

His daughter didn't miss a beat, though, and knew exactly what he was doing—trying to keep her close to the schools he considered appropriate. He was actually trying to keep them in the Second District, where he was much more comfortable with the crime rate.

"OMG, is that— Dad, turn right." Violet practically hopped in her seat. "Mom, isn't that your street? Joseph? That's what's on Grandma and Grandpa's Christmas cards."

"Sure is. But I spoke with your grandparents, Violet.

They've had budget cuts at the university. Both of them have taken on extra classes, so they're really busy right now. But they'll invite us over. You can see the house then."

Nic was surprised she didn't suggest a drive-by to at least let Violet see the place. Then it hit him. Saturday. He didn't care how busy her parents were at work. They were professors and probably would be home. Didn't take a rocket scientist to figure out this one.

He was still her dirty little secret.

God, for a brief, shining few hours he'd actually felt good about what lay ahead. But Megan was still playing games.

Only Nic wasn't eighteen anymore. This time he wasn't going to sit back and keep his mouth shut.

CHAPTER TWENTY-ONE

OKAY, VIOLET WAS OFFICIALLY over being bullied by the police chief. She wasn't sure why Mom was letting him dictate where she was allowed to go to school and where they were allowed to live, but Violet wasn't going to put up with this crap anymore. No way.

Besides, what did she have to lose? Mom was probably going to make her take out her nose ring and with this sort of backup, what chance did Violet have of reasoning with her?

Not much. The police chief obviously wasn't big on reasoning. He liked to give orders and have them obeyed.

"Yes, sir, Chief!"

Well, Violet didn't work for the police department, and they needed to get that straight before she moved to town.

She made the mistake of pointing out that all the places they were looking at were in a totally different direction than his place and Grandmama's, which got her treated to a soliloquy about the crime rate in New Orleans.

Then, just to prove he could be flexible, he'd pulled over and started going through the list item by item until she was ready to jump out the window or asphyxiate from exhaust fumes. He did manage to find *two* he considered suitable.

The second floor of a double gallery house on Magazine Street that Violet could tell from one glance would be way too dark for Mom's taste. And a first floor that wasn't far from his condo that looked like a prison with the gate higher than the building and signs everywhere about the property being under video surveillance. *Puhleeze*.

The only thing that even remotely redeemed the day was when they passed a Starbucks and he pulled in, looking like he needed a break as much as she did. Not only did Violet get out of the car, but she soaked him for a venti Frappuccino with three extra shots. He didn't even blink when the barista rang it up.

Mom did though.

"Be right back, Nic," she said while herding Violet toward the bathroom. She shut the door behind them and demanded, "Was that really necessary?"

"He's being a total jerk, Mom. Looking for a place to live is always the fun part. But not with *him*."

"Cut him a break, Violet." Mom sighed. Flipping on the water, she washed her hands. Probably trying to drown out the sounds of their voices in case *he* was listening at the keyhole. "He's trying to make sure we're someplace safe, and he doesn't have a lot of practice dealing with our family unit, as you well know. Not to mention that we're used to doing this. He isn't. Instead of getting frustrated, why don't you help make it fun?"

"I am. Mood elevation through caffeine and sugar."

Mom met her gaze through her reflection in the mirror and frowned. "The only way this is going to work is with some compromise. You have to get to know each other. Being part of a family isn't always easy. You know that."

She did know that, but wasn't about to admit it. Not

when she kept getting annoyed when Mom said things like *you have to get to know each other* and not including herself. It was as if she was abandoning Violet to the police chief when she should have been explaining how things were done in this family.

They made it out of Starbucks alive, and Violet even said "Thanks," for the expensive Frappuccino. The caffeine and sugar helped, too.

Then they found a perfectly perfect cottage with gingerbread trim and lots of character tucked away on a tiny cul-de-sac.

Violet was instantly in love.

Of course, *he* started up about how they were on the fringes of Uptown, but he did call the real estate agent when Mom asked nicely. Then they walked around, checking out the neighborhood while waiting for him to arrive.

The cottage was only a block from St. Charles Avenue, and Violet was certain that no matter what school she got stuck in, it would be in the part of town around her grandparents' university. That seemed to be the only part of town *he* approved.

"I could take the streetcar to school," she said. "Way better than the bus."

Especially if she got stuck in a school with *uniforms*.

Megan nodded. "Much better than walking in Accra."

"Especially during monsoon."

The police chief didn't say a peep, and Violet felt her mood improve a little more. Okay, the street leading to the cul-de-sac wasn't as great as some of the others they'd seen, but it was a perfectly good street with lots of trees and well-kept lawns. There weren't any clunker cars abandoned on the curbs, if that's what he was looking for.

And the cottage was really perfect.

When the agent guy got there, he unlocked the front door and deactivated the alarm while they stood on the front porch.

"Oooh, a security system." That should make the police chief sleep better. "Nice and safe in here."

Mom was staring her down, but then the guy invited them in, and they all filed into the most perfect place Violet had ever seen. Exactly what a deep-South cottage should look like.

Floor-to-ceiling windows and a really high ceiling that Mom would love. Hardwood floors that gleamed. A brick fireplace and a decent size kitchen. A staircase led up to a loft-looking place that Violet hoped was a bedroom. Hers, to be exact.

The agent led them away from the stairs. "Says here there's been an addition to the original."

They all filed through the kitchen, which had been a decent size until cramming four people in it. She stood on one side of the counter as Mom went into the small room with a cool bay window that opened on an over-grown garden.

"Looks like a small suite," the agent said. "I see what the problem is. They can't market it as a mother-in-law apartment because it's open. But it has a bedroom with a full bath and a walk-in closet. This sitting area is adequate."

Mom vanished into the bedroom, and Violet couldn't stand it any longer. She squeezed past her dad and the agent and followed into a bedroom that had windows to the backyard with a patio table and lots of plants that needed trimming.

Violet was completely, totally in love.

"OMG, Mom! This is perfect. GigiMarie will have a place to hide when I have all my friends over."

"That she would."

They exchanged a glance and Violet knew right then they were both thinking the same thing.

Perfect.

She grabbed her mom's hand. "Come on." They scoped out the bathroom, the closet, the little paved area outside the window with a bird bath and yard gnome. Then they headed into the sitting room that connected to the kitchen.

Just enough space for GigiMarie to make a cozy little space with a comfy chair and an ottoman and a lamp brighter than the sun so she could knit.

Perfect.

There was a back door in the kitchen leading to a laundry room that was sort of outside, but still covered by an overhang. Washer and dryer. Yard needed a boat-load of work because everything was growing wild, but Mom said, "It just needs some tender loving care."

Then they headed upstairs to see the loft, which had another small sitting area overlooking the living room.

"You could put a desk for schoolwork here," Mom suggested.

For her notebook computer, thank you. "And some chairs. It'll be like my own living room to hang with my friends."

The bedroom even had a dormer window and a pitched ceiling.

"This is sweet. It'll be my best room yet!"

Mom laughed. "Let's check out the rest of the house. There has to be someplace for me to sleep, too."

There was. Another bedroom on the bottom floor, below the stairs with a full bath and the same floor-to-ceiling windows as the living room, only these opened onto a back balcony.

Violet wedged up against Mom in the doorway and wrapped her arm around her shoulders. Mom rested her head against Violet's and they stood quietly together for a few minutes.

"Are you seeing it?" Mom asked.

"I'm seeing it."

"What about school? We'll keep looking, but you may need to compromise. Think you can handle that?"

She'd be around family without having to abandon Mom—*again*. "I will if I have to. The police chief needs to get with the program. Think it'll take long?"

Mom smiled. "I can't honestly say. I haven't seen him in fifteen years, but he's a smart man. Always was. He seems to genuinely want a good relationship with you, so I'm thinking he'll make the effort to figure it out." She tilted her head until they were forehead to forehead and eye to eye. "*If* you're patient and realistic with your expectations. He is who he is. You need to give him a chance and get to know him, too. Lots of things about you remind me of him."

"Did you love him a lot once upon a time?"

Mom got this stupid grin on her face and gave a funny little sigh. "With my whole heart and soul."

Perfect.

"MAKE MY NIGHT, JURADO," Nic told the deputy chief when he arrived at the station. "Otherwise I'm not going to be happy to be here on a Saturday night."

"Cut me a break, Chief." Jurado scowled. "And on a holiday, too. Only thing making this okay is that I'm going to miss the Easter Vigil. Madeleine isn't happy, but work's work. And Bouyelas isn't on shift, either, you should know. He's in there working his butt off because he likes you."

Nic liked Bouyelas, too. He never needed much of an excuse to make a Starbucks run for his shift.

"Well, then, show me what you got so we can all go home." He glanced at his watch. "But don't talk too fast. If we're out of here before eight-thirty, you'll be on your way to church."

"That is one long mass," Jurado agreed.

They entered the interrogation room the officers had commandeered to spread out and review a year's worth of cases. The sheer number of files almost stopped him. "Damn. Looks like the judge has been earning his salary."

"Hey, Chief." Bouyelas glanced up. "Don't get crazy. We yanked another six months of case files a few hours ago."

"Where's Prescott?"

"Making a dinner run. Want me to call him? We can probably catch him if you're hungry."

"No, thanks. But dinner's on me if you were able to find something."

"If we'd have known that, we'd have sent him into the Quarter for Easter dinner," Jurado said.

"Madeleine will be cooking tomorrow, so don't worry about it." Nic grabbed a chair, spun it around and sat beside Bouyelas. "Show me what you got."

Bouyelas made a neat lineup of case files side by side on the table. "Take a look and see if you notice anything odd."

As Honorable Hugo A. Dubos was chief judge of the parish criminal district court, he tried cases that looked

a lot like the reports during any night shift when Nic
had been on the job as the Eighth District commander.
Crimes, misdemeanors and offenses committed within
the parish that weren't vested in some other court. Nic
scanned docket information and case files, one after
another.

A repeat offender charged with battery with a deadly
weapon out on a five hundred dollar bond?

An ex-felon in possession of a firearm out on even
less?

The list went on.

"These cases are trending with stupidly low or, hell,
even no bail."

"Bingo, Chief." Bouyelas rocked back in his chair
and hooked his hands behind his head. "Here and
there, going back a year and a half so far, but they're
spread apart on the docket so they likely wouldn't be
questioned."

"Bondsmen?"

"You ready?" Bouyelas was grinning like a fool.
"Abram's, E-Z Credit and Surety."

Nic slanted a glance at Jurado and exhaled a surprised breath. "So technically bonds*man*."

Abram's Bonding Agency, E-Z Credit Bonds and
Surety Services were a multigenerational family opera-
tion that had been serving New Orleans for thirty years
that Nic knew of. He'd also believed grandfather, father
and sons had been running reputable businesses.

This was their first real break.

"Good work, gentlemen," Nic said, pleased. He'd
been expecting the surveillance to kick-start the investigation, but this was just as good a place to start.

"Looks like today's your lucky day, Chief." Jurado hailed him with a mock salute. "You get to buy us dinner."

OKAY, MEGAN COULD HANDLE this. All she had to do was take a deep breath. Another. There, that was better. If she kept breathing, she'd be fine. She was only responsible for a few dishes, after all. And she'd already done the bulk of the work last night with Violet's help.

They'd no sooner walked in the door from their house-hunting excursion when Mama DiLeo had informed her that she'd heard Megan liked to cook.

Thank you, Violet.

Would Megan be interested in helping out by cooking some Chilean dishes for Easter Sunday dinner?

Of course, Megan would help out, which meant a breakneck trip to the French Market, where she'd been able to get the ingredients that would make her Chilean dishes successful.

Violet had been helpful in deciding the menu and thrilled with the trip, of course; not so much when Megan had recruited her as *sous chef* upon their return. But they'd accomplished everything they could with prepping, and dessert had been chilling overnight in the fridge.

They'd decided on *arroz con leche,* which was a rice pudding with milk, sugar and cinnamon, and *sémola con leche*, which was a flan with sweet corn flour and caramel. Both would be perfect for the large crowd Mama expected after the parade through downtown and mass at St. Louis Cathedral.

So right now Megan stood over the stove in a moment of blissful quiet before the storm, bringing milk and breadcrumbs for the *marisco* to a slow boil with a steady stirring motion. She wanted everything assembled and ready to pop into the oven before the parade was over.

Violet was still out of sorts with Nic because he'd asked her not to ride on Damon's float. As a consolation prize, though, Nic, along with Tess and Anthony, had taken Violet to the parade. Megan and Mama would catch up with them for the mass.

"Do you have everything you need?" Mama asked, appearing in the kitchen, looking lovely and very put-together in a yellow silk suit that was gorgeous with her olive skin.

"I'm not in your way, am I?"

"No way. I feel like I'm on vacation with all your help." She grinned. "I made up baskets for the grandkid-dies. Wanted everyone to have a little something special today. Thought an egg hunt would be fun, but the twins are too young and Violet too old. She's not too old for a basket, is she?"

"Not if it has candy in it."

"It does, along with a few other things."

Megan didn't ask. She didn't want to know. Mama DiLeo was proving to be a bit more of a character than Megan remembered.

Stepping aside, she allowed Mama to open the oven door and check on the bread dough rising inside.

"Should be done in plenty of time so we can start everything cooking," she announced, lowering the dish towels into place over the dough.

"How does this work, exactly?" Megan was a little unclear on the details since Mama looked as if she'd dressed for church. "We're not catching up with every-one for mass?"

"Of course we are. Write down what goes in the oven on what temperature for how long and Vince will see that everything gets in and out of the oven. He's quite good at that." She laughed fondly. "He's had a lot of practice. He hasn't made a mass with this family since he started medical school. Spreads his schoolbooks out on the table and studies when we're all gone. Claims to like the quiet. Can't imagine who he takes after."

She shut the oven door gently, allowing Megan to move closer to the pot she hadn't stopped stirring. "I'm going to come right out and ask. How are you and Nic doing? Everything working out okay?"

Nic had been trying to talk with her about that night, but Megan didn't share that with Mama. She had an opportunity here and seized it with both hands. "Much better than I had any right to expect. You all have been wonderful. Please know how much it's appreciated."

Mama met her gaze levelly. "You're welcome. Things don't always work out the way we think they should, but they do always work out. You're raising a lovely girl and that didn't happen by accident. I know because I've raised six kids."

"Thank you." Megan had no other words.

"You seem to be willing to play fair now that everything's out on the table. That's really all I'm interested in, Megan. Nic's happiness. He deserves to be happy. He's always the one to count on. He manages to shove past all the nonsense and get to what's important. That's what makes him such a good police chief. It'll make him a good father, too."

"That was never a concern."

Mama smiled as if she knew she was putting Megan on the spot with her candidness. "He's had loads of practice around here. He's responsible to everyone he loves. Except himself. He needs to make more time to live his own life."

"I've dropped more responsibility into his lap."

Mama reached up and patted Megan's cheek. "I think you and Violet are exactly what the doctor ordered."

Then she strolled out of the kitchen again, leaving Megan staring after her, wishing she felt the same way.

It took a lot of emotional energy to deal with this mess. She hadn't intended to add sleeping with Nic to the list. Nor had she intended to find out she was still in over her head with him. She simply couldn't deal with that right now.

Was her whole life about avoidance?

But she'd made some of the decisions that had had the biggest impact on her life in the heat of reacting to Nic.

And right now she needed to reason. Her daughter needed parenting to establish a foundation for a solid, realistic relationship with her father. Nic, too, had recognized the transition would be much easier with Megan around, which equaled an admission on his part that he could use some help getting to know their daughter. Their headstrong daughter who was so very much like him.

Add to that trying to figure out the relationship with her parents, solidifying details for the Helping Hands project and making arrangements for the relocation, and Megan simply couldn't handle any more. And particularly not Nic. Not yet.

They'd slept together. Period. Aside from the fact that they were both a lot older, how was that any different than it had ever been? He'd kiss her. She'd wind up naked. No difference there. The only difference now was complications from all the decisions she'd made. Now Violet was making decisions that impacted all of them. And Nic, too. These were the important things. The things they needed to focus on. They were adults with a responsibility to their daughter. Period.

But as she took the pot from the flame, a nagging voice inside accused Megan of adding fear to her list of sins. Fear that Nic could never overcome their issues. Fear of facing how much she wanted him to.

CHAPTER TWENTY-TWO

MEGAN WAS PRACTICALLY vibrating by the time they arrived back at Mama's house. Mass, which usually left her feeling calm and contemplative, had been of the supersize variety as St. Louis Cathedral was the final stop along the historic parade route. Half of New Orleans had attended.

Still, she was too busy smiling and greeting people when they arrived back at the house where, true to Mama's word, Vince had managed the cooking skillfully. The Chilean dishes seemed to be going over well, vanishing apace of Mama's more traditional Italian fare.

"Is there going to be enough?" she asked Mama at one time when they found themselves together at the kitchen sink.

"Anyone who misses the meal will catch coffee and dessert." She grinned, clearly in her element in a noisy house filled with people. "It's an open house. People come and go. That way I get to see everyone because everyone usually has more than one place to visit on holidays. Anyone who knows me knows if they want food, they'd better arrive at the front end of the festivities."

Megan thought that was a humble way of acknowledging her cooking skills were legendary. Violet certainly seemed to think so because Megan spent much of her time in the kitchen, the self-appointed keeper of the table, so there was no missing how often her daughter appeared there, helping herself.

Violet was the star of today's celebration, and like her Grandmama, reveled in the attention. She seemed to have put aside her mood to allow Nic to introduce her to everyone who walked through the door. People Megan had met or heard about. Even guests she would have *never* expected to run into here.

"Mom, look who it is." Violet appeared in the kitchen again, only this time she'd abandoned her plate and brought along two guests.

"Dad? Mom?" Megan blinked stupidly. It took her a moment before she greeted her parents. "Happy Easter. I'm so happy to see you."

She sounded as shell-shocked as her parents looked, both dressed as if they'd come from mass at their church on the university campus where Father Lafevre was pastor.

Mama was right behind them, carrying a gorgeous bouquet of flowers. "Your parents brought it. Won't it decorate the table perfectly?" she asked Megan, who nodded perfunctorily. "I wanted everyone to have something special today. I didn't think you'd appreciate a basket."

Violet gave a snort of laughter. "I don't know about that. I have to hide the chocolate so she doesn't eat it all."

Mama winked. "Then share some of yours with her, gorgeous. I thought it would be nice for you and Violet to have all your family together since you're in town."

"We appreciate the invitation," her father said. Then he looked at Megan and spread his arms wide in greeting.

She crossed the distance with a welcoming smile, and

his arms came around her, arms that had once been the safest place in her world. "I'm glad you're here."

She wasn't surprised Mama had invited her parents, but she was very surprised her parents had accepted the invitation. Glancing between her parents, she willed them to know how much she appreciated the gesture, how much making this choice meant.

"Go on, dear," Mama said. "Get out of this kitchen and enjoy the day. Get your parents something to eat and eat with them. Don't think I haven't noticed you haven't had a bite."

"Mom and I made some Chilean dishes," Violet said. "You've got to try the *humitas*—they're my favorite."

Megan shook off her shock with effort, recognizing that her parents had taken an enormous step by coming here. She could only assume they wanted to put the past behind them and move their relationship in a new direction. Take a chance that they could do things differently.

Now the responsibility was Megan's to accept the gesture and help them feel welcome in an unfamiliar place among people they once hadn't been interested in knowing. To bridge the gap between the two halves of Violet's family and prepare for the inevitable meeting with Nic.

She followed Mama's advice, leading her parents to the buffet table. Mama set the bouquet in a place of honor where it would be admired, while Megan and Violet told them all about the Chilean dishes they'd prepared.

Megan got the sense they weren't sure how to respond, not because they didn't want to bridge the distance that had grown between them, but because they might not know how.

That had never occurred to her before.

"Phone lines work both ways, Megan," her mother had said.

Could it be that they didn't so much disapprove of this daughter, the one who was living her own life, making her own choices, as simply not know what to do with her? This daughter had grown up to be a stranger, was still growing, an independent single mom trying to figure out how to be stronger.

Maybe they needed reassurance that she was still their daughter, that she hadn't wanted to replace them.

They'd given her a chance today to prove it.

"I'm so glad you're here," she said as they made their way into the living room with plates filled with food. "Violet, do you want to tell your grandparents the good news?"

Violet beamed. "Mom's taking a project here, so we're coming to town. Happy Easter!"

Both parents looked surprised, so Megan stepped into the breach. "We are. I'll be getting Helping Hands up and running. When we return home, I'll wrap things up. Probably take six weeks."

Her parents exchanged a glance. Then her mother met Megan's gaze and said, "I hope we'll get to see you all while you're in town. We can have dinner. And maybe go shopping."

Everyday activities that most families took for granted. The DiLeos certainly did. Activities that brought family members together. Activities that may seem ordinary, but were really very, very special in their way.

"I love to shop, Grandma Bell." Violet took her grandmother's plate courteously, so she could get settled on the couch. "Dad told me they built a mall inside an old brewery."

"They did indeed, and you might like to see the university, too," her mother added. "You'll be looking at colleges soon."

"Can I, Mom?" Violet asked.

"Meggie, you should bring her by. We'll give her a grand tour. Maybe even let her sit in on a lecture."

Violet looked eager, and Megan smiled, feeling something that had nothing at all to do with the past, but everything to do with the future. Something that felt a lot like hope.

"I think that's a great idea."

NIC HADN'T REALIZED until seeing Megan and Violet with the Doctors Bell how much baggage he'd carried from the past into the present. But somehow, seeing them together for the first time… Megan, who was smiling too hard, had her mother's coloring, but actually looked a lot like her father. Violet didn't look like any of them.

The baggage wasn't overt—rather flashes of memory. Scheduling classes during his first semester in the criminal justice program at Loyola and wondering how Megan's father would react to glancing up in the lecture hall to find Nic in his class. His refusal to walk during graduation for either of his degrees though his mother had insisted because she'd wanted to throw parties to celebrate his accomplishments.

Of course he'd never forgotten the one and only time he'd spoken to Megan's father, when Nic had finally grown frustrated enough to knock on Megan's front door, even though he'd never so much as picked her up from her house.

The day he'd found out why.

Nic had seen Megan's mother around campus, had recognized her from faculty photos, but they'd never formally met. And as he strode into the family room where they'd congregated with plates in their laps, politely engaged in conversation with Anthony and Tess, the twins at their feet entertained by Violet, he resisted the urge to introduce himself as Violet's father, police chief of the city they lived in.

Megan looked up and saw him. He recognized the resignation in her face. Nic's heart was thumping dully in his chest as he crossed the room, his best press-conference expression securely in place.

He wasn't going to be her dirty little secret anymore. And definitely not sitting in his mother's living room.

"Doctor Bell, welcome." He extended his hand.

Megan's father stood and they shook. "George, please. It was kind of your mother to include us on your holiday."

"Nic, have you met my mother?" Megan asked.

Before he could reply, her father made the introduction.

"My wife, Helen."

"Pleased to meet you," he said, then wondered what came next. He didn't have a damned clue.

Violet distracted them all when little Rocco made a mad dash toward Anthony's beer, which had been strategically positioned beside the couch to avoid such an occurrence.

"Oh, no, you don't, kid!" She caught him by the ankle.

"Nice save." Nic seized his nephew around the waist and hoisted him into the air. Swinging a rocking chair

JEANIE LONDON   241

around, he sat, positioning his nephew on his lap with an arm locked around the kid's waist like a vise.

"Thanks." Tess held up her fork in a salute of gratitude. "If not for Violet, we'd have missed out on all the goodies. I don't know what this stuff with the shrimp is, Megan, but I'm already working on Anthony's helping. Delicious."

"I wouldn't know." Anthony lifted his plate above her head where she couldn't get to it.

His family was a damned side show, but for once Nic was grateful.

"You've been doing a lot of good work with the NOPD," Megan's father said.

They were nowhere near the first-name stage of the game yet, no matter what *George* said, but Nic inclined his head in acknowledgment of the compliment and resisted a juvenile urge to pound his chest and roar.

"We've got a lot of work to do in the city and inside the department," he said.

"From what we hear on the news, you're getting a fair amount of support."

"We are." He gave his standard the-feds-are-in-town spiel, which invited a few more questions about the various roles of the U.S. attorney, the DEA and the ATF, which Nic answered with his standard what-the-feds-hope-to-accomplish spiel.

The whole exchange was very civilized, and there was no doubt in Nic's mind that each one of them was very aware of their responsibility to the young girl on the floor between them. This conversation was ushering in a new era, and Nic grudgingly gave Megan's parents credit for walking into the lion's den. That couldn't have been easy.

He wasn't the only one who'd been surprised her

parents had been invited today. His mother had probably thought she was doing a good thing, opening her home to Megan's family the way she always did with Tess's. One big happy family.

Nic caught Megan's gaze, and knew it was going to take a lot of work to make a big happy family out of this crew. He'd been angry as hell fifteen years ago when learning that he'd been her dirty little secret. He'd been angry as hell yesterday because Megan was still hiding him. But as he considered her now, it occurred to him for the first time to ask why she might feel as if she had to hide him.

He thought he might be seeing an answer right now. In how difficult this exchange seemed to be for all concerned, particularly Megan. In the way Violet kept jumping into the conversation if it looked like it might lag, creating a bridge between her mother and her grandparents. She had her mother's back, and Nic felt proud about that.

But it made him recall what Megan had shared about her parents not being involved with her decision to keep Violet. The Doctors Bell obviously hadn't had their daughter's back all those years ago, had obviously not inspired the same sort of loyalty Violet demonstrated for Megan right now.

Were they finally trying to heal that breach?

There were still a lot of missing pieces to this puzzle, but he was putting it together, slowly but surely. His own anger was a lot easier to understand.

He'd harbored a lot after being told he hadn't been good enough for Megan, and he suspected that anger had fueled his ambition through the years, a need to prove himself worthy of the girl he'd loved.

The girl he still loved.

No way to deny it. Not when the truth was in the antagonism he felt every time he looked at her father with a ridiculous urge to prove himself. He might not see where they could go from here, but he was certain about how he felt.

His gut told him Megan still had feelings for him. He'd known it when she'd lain in his arms. He knew it now as he watched her play nice with the folks.

But as he bounced his nephew on his knee and listened to his daughter relating an amusing tale of eating soup with her hands in Africa, he realized he would have to find a way to let go of the anger if he wanted even a chance to be with Megan, to convince her to take a chance on him.

He did.

He didn't understand what was holding Megan back, but knew he'd never get his chance unless he figured it out.

His cell phone vibrated. He glanced at the display and recognized Jurado's number as Rocco tried to snatch the phone from his hand.

Snapping it open, he said, "Hang on. I'm here." Then he stood and said to Megan and her folks, "Excuse me. I've got to take this."

Passing Rocco off to Anthony, Nic headed out onto the porch where he could hear.

"What's up?" he asked.

"You're sure popular this week, Chief," Jurado answered. "Your interrogation party finally got a response."

"Yeah, who?"

"Big Mike. He's ready to talk, but only to you."

"I am popular." Finally. Short of a full confession from the judge, which had lower odds than winning the lottery, Big Mike was the best lead Nic had. He'd take it. "When and where?"

"His place. The gay parade's going on so he refuses to shut down the shop. Got all kinds of people dropping in for ink and holes, apparently. He said to blend in with the crowd so no one sees you and use the back door. He'll be waiting for you."

"On my way." Nic glanced at the cars parked in the driveway, the yard, lining both sides of the street. His car was trapped, and he didn't recognize all the cars blocking it.

Slipping the phone into the case at his waist, he headed inside, straight for the living room where he'd find… "Anthony, keys. Won't be long. Work."

Without a word, Anthony stuck a hand into his pocket, produced car keys and tossed them.

Nic caught them. "Thanks."

Anthony tipped the beer bottle in an acknowledgment before Nic said goodbye to Megan, Violet and the Bells. Then he was out the door and speeding down the street in Anthony's antique Firebird. So much for blending in.

In minutes he was searching for a parking space on the street well out of the line of the parade routes. And as former commander of the Eighth District, he knew them all. He finally found a spot a few blocks from Insane, Ink.

Avoiding Iberville, he headed down an alley that brought him behind the shop. Sure enough, he only had to knock once because Big Mike was waiting.

"Happy Easter, Mike." Nic didn't bother looking up, just invited himself inside and squeezed past the big man.

He hadn't gotten fully into the cramped back room

when he saw what sat in a place of honor on a Formica counter.

A pipe bomb.

His phone was in his hand as fast as he might have drawn his service-issue automatic. "Jesus. I didn't get the memo we needed bomb techs—"

"Cut me a goddamned break, Chief. Can you say Vietnam and the Gulf? I know a real bomb when I see it."

Which was saying something as Nic's heart had nearly dropped through the floor.

Big Mike slammed the door shut. If that had been a real pipe bomb, it would have blown right there and taken half the building with it. "Keep your voice down. I got employees and customers up front who aren't supposed to know you're here."

Nic was already inspecting what was one official-looking fake explosive device. Using the antenna of his phone to avoid leaving his prints, he lifted the bottom enough to read the scrap of paper below.

NEXT TIME IT'S REAL.

"Looks like you made a friend." Nic set down the device.

"Already touched it. To make sure I called it right."

If not there would be a crater where Big Mike was standing and Nic would still be at his mother's being treated to stellar conversation with Megan and the folks. "Come on, man. Crime scene 101. You know better than that."

"Excuse the hell out of me, Chief. Some of us are concerned about the welfare of law-abiding citizens around here."

Nic glanced pointedly at the door leading to the front of the shop. "Oh, you must be talking about your customers. Any minors without parents out there today?"

Big Mike scowled harder.

Nic snapped off a few shots of the device with his phone camera. "I assume you're referring to the police."

"They're the ones causing the trouble."

"Why don't you fill me in on what's going on?" Nic suggested, turning his back on the fake bomb. "Unless you called me down here because you wanted to interrupt Sunday dinner."

"You started all this shit. Dragging me down to the station like a criminal. You made sure he saw me."

"Who saw you?"

Big Mike growled. "You know who I'm talking about."

Nic did. And he'd bet money Big Mike thought this fake bomb was a gift from the judge, a warning to keep his mouth shut. But Nic wasn't about to lead the witness. Big Mike had called him down here, so Big Mike could kindly fill in the blanks so his testimony would be admissible in court if he ever consented to make an appearance there. Not likely, but Nic could always hope.

"I'm going to ask you nicely one more time to tell me what you know," he said. "But this is my last offer. I'm tired of asking. So either start talking or I'm out of here."

Big Mike barreled across the room like a bull. He cracked the door to the front of the shop and glanced through as if to reassure himself no one was listening on the other side.

Then he came and stood so close that Nic was

forced to crane his head to meet the man's gaze. An intimidation tactic? Nic didn't think so. Big Mike was worried.

"I saw the kid pass off an envelope to Judge Dubos, but I have never seen the kid before in my life. I can give you a description, but I have no idea who he is. God as my witness."

"So you didn't give him that ink?"

"Shit." Big Mike grunted. "I'm an artist. I don't do movie memorabilia. Check with Sergio or Polack Joe."

Nic believed him.

"But now that you've dragged my ass into the middle of this mess, you damn sure better protect me." He brought a beefy hand down onto the Formica counter hard enough to make the fake bomb jump. "I hope like hell you're as good as everyone thinks you are, *Chief,* because this is exactly why no one ever sees or hears anything around here. They wind up in bloody chunks all over Bourbon Street when they do."

Nic couldn't argue, as the ugly truth of the problems in the NOPD was a matter of public record. But he felt like slamming down his own fist on the counter in growing frustration. He'd gotten Big Mike to talk, all right, but Nic still didn't have an ID on the kid who'd delivered the envelope.

Instead, he had a death threat. He could talk to some other tattoo artists in town, but Nic had already considered that avenue. As Big Mike pointed out, movie memorabilia wasn't exactly original. According to Violet, Great Eye guy wasn't much older than she was. Who was going to admit to inking a minor?

Unless they had proper documentation.

Yeah, right.

"You have my word," Nic said. "Work with us and we'll keep you safe."

Big Mike wasn't the only one Nic needed to keep safe.

CHAPTER TWENTY-THREE

THE UNMARKED CRUISER was waiting for Nic in front of his mother's house when he returned. The party was winding down, too, which would make the patrolmen's jobs easier. Less traffic to keep their eyes on.

Low visibility. High alert.

Nic wanted to know everything happening within a one-block radius. No one got near this house unless the patrolmen knew.

No fake bombs were showing up here. No real ones, either.

He'd no sooner climbed the porch steps when the front door opened. Megan appeared with her parents and Violet behind her.

"Oh, hi, Nic," she said, and the first thing he noticed was the purse over her shoulder and the keys in her hand. "Violet and I are running over to show my parents the house we're looking at renting. We want Mom's opinion on the yard."

He stopped on the top step and acknowledged her parents with a nod. "Reschedule. Now isn't a good time."

He tried to keep eye contact with Megan, but she was still busy making nice with the folks, no less flustered than when he'd left her.

"We won't be long," she said. "We don't want your mother dealing with all the cleanup alone."

"I don't want you leaving the house right now."

"How come?" Violet asked.

Nic didn't answer. Instead, he told Megan's mother, "I'm glad I had the chance to officially meet you." He extended his hand to Megan's father. "Glad you both came. I'm afraid Megan and Violet will need to reschedule this trip."

Her father frowned and Megan glanced up at him, clearly startled. "Nic?"

His mother chose that exact moment to show up and see her guests off. Of course, she didn't miss a beat. Slanting a surprised glance between him and the unmarked cruiser, she asked, "Why do you have a patrol parked in front of the house?"

Naturally, everyone followed her gaze to the street.

Megan paled visibly. "Did something happen, Nic? Violet?"

"Everything's okay. The patrol is a precaution. I want the officers to stick close to you for the time being."

As far as Nic was concerned there wasn't much else to say since he wasn't offering details about the case.

"Are my daughter and granddaughter in some kind of trouble?" Megan's father asked.

One glance at Megan assured him that her parents had no clue about the details of Violet's visit.

More secrets.

"Don't worry. It's a precaution. I'll make sure they're safe. That's all I can say." The standard no-comment spiel.

"Is she free to walk us to our car?" This from Megan's mother.

He didn't miss the sarcasm and nodded.

"Pup, why don't you wait inside?" Megan finally intervened, sounding a lot more collected than she looked.

"I'll see your grandparents off and we'll make plans for another day."

"Got it," she said. "Bye, Grandpa and Grandma. Don't forget the tour. I'm game whenever."

"We're counting on it, young lady," Megan's father said, before thanking their hostess for the invitation and accompanying Megan to their car.

Violet watched them go, and one look assured Nic that his daughter was not happy with this turn of events. He wasn't sure why—that her plans had been derailed or that the situation she'd inadvertently stepped into hadn't simply vanished.

Either way, she shot him a withering glance as she turned on her heel and stalked inside.

His mother met his gaze. "I'll go with her."

Then she disappeared inside the house. Nic waited, watching Megan attempt to reassure her parents before they finally got into their Cadillac and backed out of the driveway.

She returned, looking somber, and he held the door for her. She paused before going through.

"Are you going to tell me what's going on?"

"Someone screwed up and someone started talking."

She nodded, but didn't say another word, obviously convinced he was doing everything he could to protect their daughter.

Nic was the one having a problem with that. He didn't like working at a snail's pace when people started making threats.

"I'm going to get a start on the kitchen," Megan said before vanishing down the hall.

She was upset. He wished he had something reassuring to offer. He didn't. If it had been easy to get a judge off the bench, someone would have removed this one long ago. Everything began and ended with Nic's department providing admissible evidence. That was on him.

Making his way into the living room, he found family and friends still clustered around, chatting, eating and enjoying the day together. He wished he felt like celebrating.

Violet caught up with him in the dining room. "Dude, FYI," she said under her breath. "Mom's on overload already. Keep backing her into corners like that and you stress her out more."

Nic opened his mouth to reply, but Damon, the only one sitting at the table, laughed.

"Good luck with that, niece girl."

Violet ignored him and looked at Nic, annoyance firing up those bright blue eyes. "I know you haven't seen her in a long time. That's why I'm telling you."

He still hadn't wrapped his brain around her point, but he did know this had nothing to do with him. This was all about protecting her mother. *From* him.

"Violet, explain to me how I backed her into a corner. I don't understand."

"The grandparents came here. Didn't you see how stressed everyone was? Come on, they were dripping polite." She rolled her eyes and pulled a face. "Instead of helping, you start ordering Mom around."

Another laugh from Damon.

This time Nic glared at him, silently warning him to disappear before there was trouble.

Nic was *not* in the mood.

"You can't go all police chief over her. Didn't you see how you were freaking her out?"

He had seen. No denying that. "Please define what *going all police chief* means."

She gave a huff and shook her head as if she couldn't believe he was even asking the question.

"The same thing you did yesterday. You start giving orders and expecting everyone to hop to it and say, 'Yes, sir, Chief.'" She snapped a sharp salute to make her point.

Okay. He still didn't understand much more than she was growing more frustrated with him. God, this day was just getting better and better. Bad enough he was dealing with fake bombs. Now he felt stupid to boot. "What did I order you to do?"

"Go to private school. Then you started up on the house we like. You didn't listen to a thing Mom or I said."

"I was listening. I didn't agree. I prefer a location farther Uptown."

"But you won't be living there."

He didn't have a defense because she was right. He was only a peripheral part of the family.

"Mom said that we all had to compromise and get to know each other to make this work. And she's right. So you can't walk around bullying everyone. We don't work like that." Tipping her chin proudly, she met his gaze straight on. "I thought you should know."

Nic stared into that face so like his and didn't have a clue what to say.

"I *really* wish you luck with this, niece girl." Damon stood and tossed napkins on his empty plate. "Maybe you'll get through to the chief here. He sure doesn't hear anyone around here when we tell him what an overbearing asshole he is."

Damon didn't wait for a reply. He winked at Violet

and strolled from the room. She swallowed a gasp that was a strangled mixture of half shock, half laughter, clearly deciding it wasn't in her best interests to react.

Not to his face, at least.

"I'm glad you shared what you were feeling." Nic sounded so calm even he was impressed. Not too many choices here. Act like an adult in front of his daughter or act like the overbearing asshole his brother had accused him of being.

Violet looked relieved. "I hope I didn't hurt your feelings. I really thought you should know."

He nodded.

Then she bolted into the kitchen, probably posting herself as Megan's bodyguard in case he went all *police chief* again. Nic headed in the opposite direction. Now was not the time to attempt polite conversation, not when the top of his head felt as if it might blow and take the roof off.

Luck wasn't with him. He ran into Damon, who was heading out the front door, making a break for it before Nic got a hold of him.

He didn't think. He reacted, and suddenly his fist was wrapped in Damon's ponytail, and he was shoving his little brother through the open door.

"What in hell is wrong with you?" he demanded, kicking the door shut behind them, not caring who heard them.

Sensei Damon disentangled himself in one slick move. He might hold black belts in four disciplines and be well on his way to a fifth, but Nic didn't care. He'd had it. He would kick his brother's ass if he were freaking Bruce Lee. Nic was the oldest and that meant size and strength made no difference whatsoever. Seniority and anger gave him superpowers.

"What the hell is *your* problem, man?" Damon took a gratifying step backward.

"If you ever open your mouth and undermine any conversation I have with my daughter again, your mother will be down a son for good. Do you hear me?"

"Oh, I hear you. Now you listen to me, *Chief.*" Damon ground out the words. "You are out of control, and this whole family is sick of it, and sick of you. The only thing saving your ass right now is that kid in there. Everyone knows you've been blindsided and is cutting you slack. But I'm damned tired of being your punching bag. Find someone else."

Punching bag? Nic would give this idiot punching bag. "Grow the hell up, Damon. Stop torturing everyone with your ridiculous affairs and your never-ending money grief and the rest of your pathetic bullshit. All everyone ever does is worry about you. It's time you started pulling your weight with this family."

"Who the hell are you to tell me what to do?"

"I am the one trying to keep this family on track." It always came back to him. Always had.

"No one asked you to play God, Nic. No one wants you—"

Exactly the wrong thing to say. Damon's defiance pitched Nic right over the edge. Before he knew what he was doing, he'd advanced on his brother and was shoving him backward. They were going to have this out here and now.

"Don't push me or I will take you down." Damon extricated himself with another move, a defensive one this time, but he didn't engage. That only made Nic angrier.

"Chief, everything okay?"

Damn it. He'd forgotten the cops in the yard.

Chest heaving, he fought for control as he turned to Officer Derouchey. "Everything's okay. Thanks."

The officer nodded and slanted a glance at his partner and the two of them crossed the lawn back to their cruiser.

Great. Just what his men needed to see.

Damon didn't get a chance to open his mouth again because suddenly the front door opened and his mother was storming out.

"Knock it off, you two. You will not behave this way in my house. Do you hear me?"

The fierceness… Another rite of passage. Didn't matter that Nic was a foot taller and outweighed his mother by a hundred pounds. She would take him down. Damon, too. That's the way it worked.

"Damon, you get about your business. Nic and I need to talk."

Scowling, Damon took off.

She didn't say another word. She didn't accuse him of chasing his brother off from her celebration. She only went to the swing Marc had installed as a surprise while rebuilding the front porch after Katrina. She'd always wanted one.

Patting the seat beside her, she motioned him to sit. Then she started rocking the swing back and forth, an easy motion, as if she had nothing better to do with her day than sit here and wait for him to start talking.

Nic stonewalled. Anger had started the adrenaline pumping. He didn't know who, if anyone, had sent her outside. Anthony, maybe, who'd had a front-row seat in the living room. If, as Damon said, everyone was cutting him slack because of Violet's sudden appearance, then Anthony wouldn't have stepped out that door unless he'd wanted to get sucked into the fight.

He'd have called in the big guns.

This was all Damon's fault for opening his damned mouth, but their mother wouldn't want to hear that. She was only interested in him right now, which brought him right back to… "Am I really an overbearing asshole?"

She arched a quizzical eyebrow. "Do you really have to ask?"

"I'm serious."

"You don't think I am?"

God, what did he even say to that? His knee-jerk reaction was denial, but this wasn't the first time today he was hearing commentary about his domineering personality.

"Violet accused me of going *police chief* all over Megan."

"That would be one way to put it."

"You know what she's talking about then?"

"She's your daughter, Nic. Doesn't really matter what I think I know. What do you think?"

Nic considered that. He thought about the young girl who'd crossed continents to meet him. About her eagerness to spend time together, her efforts to convince her mother to take a project in town, and her worry about hurting his feelings.

She'd confronted him anyway.

"I think I don't like the reaction I'm getting lately. Probably means something needs attention."

"Usually does," his mother agreed.

"I'm tired. Every time I think I'm finally off duty around here something or someone else comes up. It never felt like a burden before. It does now."

"Why do you think that is?"

He shrugged, didn't have an answer.

"You've got such a good heart, Nic. That's one of the

things I love best about you. Your brothers and sister…
well, depends on who you're bossing around. This month
it's Damon."

"Damon's an idiot."

Her turn to shrug. "Sometimes he is. I could argue
that the more you clean up his messes the longer it's
going to take him to figure things out for himself, which
is what you should be doing. If you were, you wouldn't
be noticing what he's doing."

"I told you every time I try to back off around here
something comes up and gets in my way."

"Something's always going to come up, Nic. That's
life. You know that better than anyone. You can't control
that. You can control letting it get in your way."

"How do you do that? I've been helping out around
here for almost as long as I remember. How do I stop
caring?"

She frowned. "You don't. Just because you're not
running interference for everyone, or contributing fi-
nancially or bossing people around doesn't mean you
don't care anymore."

Twisting around, she motioned to the house. "Violet's
a perfect example. You didn't know that child existed
until last week. You haven't had a thing to do with her
upbringing since she was conceived, yet she walks into
your life and you care."

Nic did care. Before the shock had worn off, he'd
looked at Violet and seen another responsibility. But
that wasn't how he felt. He did care. About his daughter.
And her mother.

"It's all about balance, Nic. You can't protect everyone you care about. Not from life. Not from themselves."
No doubt she was referring to Damon. "It's part of your
big heart that you want to, and that's a good thing. As

long as you realize that caring doesn't mean controlling. You've got to let everyone live life. And you've got to live yours."

She smiled thoughtfully. "That's what I'm going to let you do now. Figure it out for yourself. But I do want you to know something. You've been a special blessing to me all these years. Helping me keep your brothers from running wild after your father died. You've helped me make things possible for this family that otherwise wouldn't have happened even if I'd have worked around the clock. I love you for that, and I admire you for it. So does everyone else, even if they're not inclined to admit it yet." She was talking about Damon again. "But if I'd have thought for one second that you would lose *you* along the way, I'd have kicked your butt right out the door."

He gave a short laugh, almost felt amused.

She smiled. "Just think about what I've said. Think about what your daughter said. You're a smart man and it's not all that hard. Decide what you want in your life and don't let anything get in your way. Not us. Not you."

Reaching up, she ruffled his hair fondly. "You need a haircut. Make time to get into the shop. Soon." Then she got up and went back inside with a breezy, "I love you."

Nic didn't follow her, just sat there staring into the yard, outside while everyone else was inside having fun. Apart.

Was he getting in his own way?

He glanced at the unmarked cruiser and remembered the Cadillac that had pulled out not long ago. He'd meant to ask his mother why she'd invited Megan's parents without consulting anyone, but realized he already had the answer.

This was his mother's house and her party. She could invite whomever she liked. And she'd already told Nic she thought he had a second chance for a life with his family. She didn't go all *police chief* over everyone. She didn't force her opinion down anyone's throat. She welcomed Megan and the Bells into her home, did what she could to help. His mother had his back, much in the way Megan had Violet's back and Violet had Megan's.

"Instead of helping, you started ordering Mom around," Violet had accused him. "We don't work like that."

She'd been talking about bullying, about making a situation worse instead of better.

She's on overload already. Keep backing her into corners like that and you stress her out more.

Which is exactly what he'd done. Violet had pointed it out to him because in her infinite fourteen-year-old wisdom, she'd recognized what Nic had not.

He wasn't looking at anyone's perspective but his own.

True, he'd been trying to place his daughter in the best school and his family in a safe neighborhood. But Violet was completely right. He hadn't heard a word anyone had said. It had been all about what *he* thought was best, what *he* thought was safe. He'd dismissed what everyone else wanted.

"You are out of control," Damon had said.

Nic sat on the swing, listening to the sounds of muffled laughter coming from inside the house, family and friends enjoying the day. Life happening. When had he assumed so much responsibility for everyone that he'd taken everything onto his shoulders and eliminated them from the equation?

No wonder life had been feeling like a burden.

He'd always assumed responsibility so easily. Like his mother had said, that could be a good thing and had been after his father had died. But like anything else in life, being responsible could have a downside.

Nic was living it.

And considering that, he had to ask, what would the effect be on someone who wasn't as used to shouldering responsibility?

He remembered what Megan had told him at the airport, about how long it had taken her to learn to stand on her own, about how she hadn't been prepared to become a parent because her parents had always made the decisions for her.

He hadn't understood why she'd run away all those years ago. He couldn't believe she had run the other night when it was so obvious they still had feelings for each other.

But when he thought about the way her parents had tried to force her into giving up Violet for adoption, when he thought about the way he'd assumed the responsibility for his family from the minute he'd realized he'd had one, deciding everything from where they were going to stay while they were in town, to what they would drive, to where they could live, Nic thought he was beginning to understand.

And he absolutely knew what he wanted in his life.

CHAPTER TWENTY-FOUR

"It looks like a normal school," Violet said when Mom stopped the Jeep in front of the charter high school.

"Much bigger than I thought. When I heard charter school I thought small. Definitely not the case." She watched the unmarked police cruiser pull up behind them and a tiny frown creased between her eyebrows.

"We'll be perfectly fine, Mom. We have our own personal security. What's going to happen?"

"I know we'll be fine. But I'm not entirely sure why this trip couldn't have waited."

"Are you kidding me?" Violet stared. "Because we needed to get out of the house. We're, like, in prison. Visiting a school was the only way *he* was going to let us go anywhere."

"That's overstating the case a little, don't you think? We hung around the house with your grandmother for one day. I hardly think that's prison. Besides, I thought you enjoyed all the home movies and pictures."

"I did. This family is nuts."

"No argument there. I always liked them."

Violet looked at her mom and the fond smile on her face and decided to go for it. "Way different than your family. Think Grandpa and Grandma Bell can handle it?"

"Looks like they're going to try, and that's all we can ask of anyone."

She recognized another "pearl of wisdom" as Mom

always called them. Today, Violet had one of her own to add. "And then we have to let it be enough."

Mom's smile widened. "That's exactly right. When did you get so wise?"

"Had a good teacher." She scowled. "Now don't go getting all mushy or I wouldn't have said anything. But I wanted you to know I'm glad you took the project here even though I might get stuck wearing a uniform."

There was no missing that weepy look in Mom's eyes, but she battled the mush. With effort.

"Everything will work out the way it's supposed to. Always does," she said.

"Remember that, will you?"

"Regarding what, specifically?"

Violet shrugged. "About Dad mostly. Grandmama's right. He needs us. Dude doesn't have much of a life from what I can tell. We need to show him how to have some fun."

"Well, I won't argue that, pup. But he's a grown man. I'm sure he's happy with the way he's living or he wouldn't be living that way."

"You don't sound so sure."

Mom bit back a grin. "Are you a mind reader now?"

"Um, don't need to be."

"Okay, I won't deny it. I have no answers. I haven't seen the man in fifteen years."

They could talk. Violet liked that. Not all her friends' moms were like that. Even though Mom was too stressed out and overprotective… Correction. Mom wasn't really all *that* bad compared to the police chief. Violet couldn't forget she had two parents now.

"BTW, I'm sorry I took off the way I did."

Mom cocked her head to the side and looked at Violet

as if she could see inside her head. Or wished she could. "Apology accepted. But I'm not sure if I should be worried. Seriously."

"Don't be. Everything's under control." She reached for the door handle. "Come on. I want to catch at least a class or two before the police chief calls off parole."

Now Mom totally knew something was up. The *look* was all over her. She was trying to figure it out, but Violet knew she wouldn't even come close.

"Don't be paranoid." The least she could do was try and reassure Mom. "You said we should do our research, and I'm not getting stuck in a uniform without checking out all my options. The recovery school district is on spring break this week, but the charter schools started back today. It was totally meant to be."

That part was true. Of course, it wasn't the whole truth, but Mom didn't need to know the rest. Not yet, anyway. Not until Violet worked things out so this stupid mess would finally be over. *Finally.*

She hopped out of the Jeep and the door beeped behind her as Mom locked the car. She motioned to the officers in the unmarked car that they were heading inside.

"The website said they have early college credit classes with the university." Violet glanced up and down the street as they crossed. "And I don't think Dad will be able to complain about the neighborhood."

"He's the police chief, Violet. He deals with things that most people try to avoid dealing with, so it gives him a different perspective. That can also be good."

Yeah, right. "Is that why he doesn't have a sense of humor? I think Grandmama's right. He needs to get a life."

And Violet knew exactly who she wanted her dad

to get a life with. Something else Mom didn't need to know right now.

"I'm still surprised your father was okay with us coming here. I'm not sure exactly what our escort could do to rescue us sitting outside this big place."

"*Puh-leeze.* Dad's being an overprotective freak and he knows it. He flat-out said he didn't think there was any way the old pervert could identify me."

"He cares, and that's a good thing."

Yeah, yeah, yeah. Violet didn't mind the caring, but the rest of this crap had to stop. Pronto. She was over it.

They went straight to the main office where a whole bunch of helpful people helped them.

"We're assigning you someone to shadow," the admissions secretary said. "We have a list of teaching assistants who are familiar with getting prospective students around to get a feel for the place."

Hopefully this TA would be helpful in tracking down her reason for coming on campus today.

Great Eye guy.

Violet was done with the *Criminal Minds* crap. If the police chief couldn't close the case, then she was going to help because she was *not* moving to New Orleans with him acting all jerky and bossy because he was worried about her safety.

So one Great Eye guy coming up.

Mom went to sit in the media center and work while she waited—one of Dad's requirements—and the TA turned out to be a junior named Monica who was toying with International Studies for college and fascinated by all the places Violet had lived.

School was school. Really didn't matter what country she was in. The buildings changed—sometimes a lot, depending on where they were. But basically kids were kids. And now that they had Facebook it was easy to make connections and stay in touch. So Violet played up the cultural differences and it didn't take long to get Monica's help.

NIC DECIDED TO SEND HIS officers to dinner in the Quarter for their work on the Dubos case as he tossed another file onto the desk, adding yet another low-bond case as evidence.

His cell vibrated. Grabbing it before it skittered off his desk and landed on the floor, he glanced at the display.

"Hello, Violet. Everything okay?" She usually texted.

"Swell, Dad, swell."

Every red flag in Nic snapped to attention. He could hear that DiLeo pride loud and clear in her voice, and he braced himself.

"This charter school isn't half-bad, for the record, and you'll *never* guess who I ran into here."

Probably not, and he wasn't in the guessing mood. "Who?"

"Great Eye guy."

Nic could smell the setup from here, knew he and Megan had been had without question. He didn't know how, but he knew it to the bone.

"Dad, you there?"

"I'm here. Well, what a coincidence." He couldn't keep out the sarcasm no matter how hard he tried.

"I know. That's exactly what I thought." She laughed. "I only know the kid's first name, so I'm thinking if you want to talk to him, you'll probably want to get down here pretty quick. He just went into guitar class. They're on a block schedule here so the classes are really long. You can catch him if you hurry."

He was already through the door. "On my way."

With the light and siren, Nic made it to the campus in decent time. He pulled in one of the patrol officers who was parked in the street and had him run interference with administration. Once he had a name, he wanted the parents down here fast so he could talk with the kid. He accompanied the principal and a dean of students to the class, where he found Violet hanging out in the hallway.

"Hey...*Chief.*" She eyed the administrators uncertainly, obviously not sure whether or not they should know about the familial connection. "He's still in there."

Nic stepped aside to allow the principal to enter the class and call out the kid.

Jon Romo.

Finally.

But damned if the idiot kid didn't try to make a break for it. He got into the hallway, took one look at Nic in his dress blues then took off down the hall, sneakers squeaking on the linoleum. The principal let out a loud yell and the dean of students took off after him.

Violet said, "Whoa!"

But Nic was already on the horn, calling Officer Daigneault, who he'd left in the cruiser on the street. He caught the kid as he burst through the front doors of the school and had him up against the cruiser by the time they got outside.

"Well, Jon, you just earned yourself a ride to the station," Nic told Great Eye guy before turning to the principal. "I'd hoped to talk to this student in your office with his parents, but unfortunately I don't always get what I want." He handed the principal his business card. "I'll need the emergency card and parents' information."

Then he shook the man's hand, thanked him for his time and told Officer Daigneault, "He's yours."

The kid went white as the officer put a hand on his head and herded him into the cruiser. Nic tapped the roof and the lights started flashing, a full show for this minifelon.

"We'll collect this girl's mother and be on our way."

The principal escorted him and Violet to the media center, where they found Megan seated at a table working on her laptop. She glanced up and did a double take.

"Nic, what are you doing here? Is everything all right?"

Nic looked toward at his daughter. He'd hoped she had the grace to 'fess up, but he could tell she was stubbornly sticking with her coincidence story. "You want to do the honors?"

She shrugged. "You'll never guess who I ran into. Monica and I were leaving AP Lang and he was standing at the lockers."

"Who?" Megan asked.

"Great Eye guy." Violet didn't give her a chance to react before launching into evasive maneuvers. "Do you want to know why his tattoo is in that weird spot? Monica knows someone who's a friend of his. It's so his parents don't see it."

"Shame you couldn't do that with your nose ring," Nic said with a straight face.

"Damn shame," Violet agreed, earning a scowl from Megan. "But, I mean, what luck, huh? I recognized the guy as soon as I saw him and wasn't letting him out of my sight."

Nic wasn't surprised. After all, she'd tailed him through the French Quarter. But Megan clearly hadn't decided what to make of this turn of events yet, so he bought her some more time. "How long until you called me?"

"Not long. I followed him to class, so I knew he'd stay put for a while."

"And he never noticed you?"

She beamed. "I have a gift."

"Like your Uncle Marc, the bounty hunter. He can tail anyone. You should consider law enforcement as a career."

"Or crime." She fingered her nose ring.

"You are out of control, young lady." Megan got to her feet slowly, decision obviously made. "Do not stand there and pretend this was all a coincidence. I am not buying that for one second. You knew that boy would be here today."

"How would I know that?"

"Violet," Megan said in a tone Nic had never heard before.

His daughter obviously had.

She huffed in disgust. "This is retarded, Mom. He was taking forever. I was totally over it."

"You knew your father was worried about your safety yet you maneuvered me—*us*—into letting you check out this school."

"I needed to find the guy."

"You lied to me."

Violet shook her head vehemently. "No, I didn't. You know we wanted to check out the schools around here and I told you I wanted to get us out of the house. All true."

"If you were able to find this boy, why didn't you simply tell your father?"

Violet spread her hands in entreaty. "I only found out his name when I got to talking to some of the kids here."

Nic had to give her credit. For a teenager she was incredibly people savvy. She walked into a new school in a new city and started working the crowd.

"So, we ready to go?" Violet bent over to retrieve Megan's laptop bag. "Can't keep our bodyguards sitting outside all day, and these media center people probably don't want us having this conversation here. It's a library."

Nic wasn't going to open his big, bullying mouth and shove anyone into a corner. But he could back up Megan. "'Fess up now, delinquent, or I'm taking you down to the station."

Violet narrowed her gaze and glared at him. "It wasn't like it was all that hard. He has to be on Facebook or MySpace."

Nic's jaw dropped. Literally. "You tracked down that kid on MySpace?"

"Facebook."

"How exactly?"

"Uh, friends." There was definitely a *duh* in there. "I looked up the high schools. He's got that cool tattoo so someone was going to know who he was. Once I knew what school he went to, I only needed to get here. I knew I'd recognize him."

Megan started packing her laptop, winding the cord around her hand, stuffing it inside the case. "We won't be waiting to have this conversation, Violet, so pencil it in for as soon as we get back to your grandmother's. You can explain to me why you think this behavior is acceptable."

Nic squelched the impulse to weigh in with his opinion. His efforts would be better spent interrogating Great Eye guy. Megan had this part under control.

And as he escorted Megan and Violet from the media center, Megan's shampoo wafting through his senses, making him forget everything but how she would feel in his arms, Violet slanting rebellious glances his way, Nic knew there were things in life that were much, *much* more important.

CHAPTER TWENTY-FIVE

MEGAN JUST NEEDED TO WALK, to be out of the house and moving to shake off the residual effects of a difficult conversation with Violet. She'd come away understanding much more than her daughter had revealed—thankfully—and she needed time to figure out what came next.

This was always a challenge. Particularly when she had to get past her own emotions first because all too often worry and fear and indecision could get in the way.

Megan supposed she shouldn't be surprised when Nic's cruiser stopped as she cleared the front yard. She definitely wasn't surprised by the way her heart started to pound a heavy, slow beat when the driver's door swung wide and he stepped out, looking more devastatingly handsome than he ever did.

The years looked so good on him.

He propped an elbow on the roof. "Where you headed?"

"Just needed to walk."

"Mind if I join you?"

"Please do."

He wasn't dressed to walk, but he gamely tugged off his tie and tossed it in the backseat. Then he walked toward her, unbuttoning his collar and rolling up his sleeves.

"How'd it go with Great Eye guy?" she asked, matching his pace as they headed toward St. Charles Avenue.

She didn't look his way, not until she could control the crazy sensation swelling inside, a feeling of being alive, a feeling she hadn't felt in so long. No man she'd ever dated had been able to make her forget she was a mom. Not the way Nic did. Not even close.

"I learned who the kid was working for, which means I can start unraveling this mess. Nasty business. We appear to have a judge on the take from a prominent bail bondsman."

"Will you need Violet's testimony?"

"Can't imagine why," he said with certainty, and Megan heaved a mental sigh of relief, felt as if such a weight had been lifted.

"Thank you for taking such good care of our daughter."

"Thank you," he repeated, and she glanced at him then, breath hitching when she met his gaze, recognized the melting expression she saw there.

"For what?"

"For taking such good care of our daughter."

Megan looked at the sidewalk ahead through suddenly misty eyes, her throat tight, her focus on keeping one foot in front of the other. She didn't know what to say.

There wasn't anything to say.

She knew. Nic knew.

That was enough.

"So how'd the conversation with our daughter go?" he finally asked.

"She's got a lot going on inside. I'm trying to keep up with what she isn't telling me."

"That's always the trick."

"She's got a life lesson happening right now, so I'm trying not to say too much. Whenever I open my mouth, she automatically doesn't see anything I point out. It's a knee-jerk reaction."

"Like you said, she's got a lot going on inside."

That made Megan smile. "She got what she wanted— you. And a family. But she's realizing she can't control or anticipate everything. She always thought she had the most overprotective mother in the world. She didn't count on you being worse."

Nic chuckled, and Megan found that she liked sharing her thoughts about Violet. She'd been blessed with some wonderful friends through the years, Marie at the top of the list, and she'd valued discussing kids and parenting. But Nic was Violet's father. Turned out that was entirely different.

The buck didn't stop with her any longer. All those fears, natural fears that accompanied parenting, didn't feel quite so overwhelming. If something should happen to Megan, Violet wouldn't be alone. She had a family to be a part of, a father who was getting to know her.

Who already loved her.

Megan didn't need to ask about that. Everything Nic had done revealed how much he cared. Someday Violet would look back and realize how fast he'd stepped up to the plate when she'd dropped out of nowhere into his life. Not because he was honorable, but because he cared. Violet would recognize that and appreciate that. The way Megan did. Because when she got right down to it, regardless of absolutely everything else, Violet began with two high school seniors who'd met and fallen in love.

"To be honest, Violet's emotionally all over the place

right now," Megan admitted. "It was bad before she left. It's worse with everything going on. She's so excited about you and having a family—a big Italian family. It's like her dream come true. She's got to figure out what to make of all this, and she hasn't had the chance yet. I think that's what today was all about. She's been frustrated because you have different expectations than she's used to."

"Yeah, she mentioned that."

"She did?"

Nic nodded.

Megan wasn't really surprised, though. "She isn't usually one to sugarcoat things. I kind of like that about her, but I hope she wasn't too brutal."

"Oh, she's got a streak all right. She gets it from her uncle Damon." Nic scowled.

Megan wanted to ask, but that scowl said everything. "Well, thank God for small favors then. My takeaway is that she was annoyed because the investigation was curtailing what she considers to be her basic human right—independence. My fault entirely, I admit. So not only did she think she'd help you along, but she wanted to impress her dad with how smart and capable she is."

"Mission accomplished. I'm going to get her to teach me how to work those social networks. Sounds like a new investigative technique."

"That should feed nicely into her little diva ego."

Nic didn't reply, just strode along beside her, kicking a soccer ball back into someone's yard, taking her elbow and guiding her around a car whose rear was sticking out of the driveway and blocking the sidewalk.

"So how are you handling all this with her?" Nic eventually asked. "I should probably know."

"Well, I helped her recognize how she was responsible for this whole situation in the first place. If she didn't want her independence curtailed, then she probably shouldn't have made choices that placed her in danger. Then we discussed process. How no one can ever anticipate all the angles, so it's her responsibility to weigh options and decide whether or not she's willing to risk the potential consequences. If she's not, then she needs to make different choices."

Nic seemed to approve. "That's a hugely important lesson. Especially at her age. She's coming up on the big stuff. Alcohol. Drugs. Sex."

Just the mention of sex brought the conversation to a screeching halt. Neither of them needed reminders about how out of control teenage sex could get.

When they got to the end of the block Megan turned left, intending to cut down the street behind his mother's house. As much as she wanted to walk, she kept eyeing his spit-polished dress shoes that couldn't be all that comfortable to walk in.

"What do you think, Nic? You've been curiously silent."

"I have, haven't I? That's because I've been listening."

She couldn't miss the *something* in his voice and glanced up. "You're proud of yourself. For listening?"

He inclined his head with a look of such solemnity that Megan couldn't take her eyes off him and wound up tripping over an elevation in the sidewalk, where a tree root was trying to break through.

He steadied her with another light touch on her elbow. "Can't listen if I'm doing all the talking, can I?"

"Guess not."

"But I do want to talk, Megan. Now. About us. About the other night."

What could she say about the other night? She couldn't deny how she felt. He already knew.

"I don't know where we can go from here," she admitted.

"That's why I want to talk, to figure it out together. There's been a lot of alone happening. Too much, I think."

"That's a pretty way to phrase it."

"I'm trying to help make situations better, not worse."

Something about that sounded scripted, and she wasn't sure if there was an epiphany in there. She didn't ask because they turned the corner to his mother's street and he seemed to recognize where they were.

"We won't be able to talk if we go inside. Do you want to go somewhere?"

She opened her mouth to reply, but then he grinned, that sexy half smile that had always managed to get her out of her clothes. His handsome face seemed so animated in that moment, so alive. Exactly how she felt. "I know where we can go."

Megan knew where he was taking her even before he led her to the end of the driveway and unlatched the gate.

They made their way quietly around to the rear of the house, to the staircase leading to the apartment above the garage.

The very place Violet had been conceived.

Megan felt as if they were stepping into the past. Into memories of their stolen moments. He'd kissed her for the first time on these very steps.

The sun was on the verge of paling into twilight, that

split second where it hung in the sky before beginning to descend. Birds were singing in the trees almost urgently, as if sensing the night would come and silence them.

The man walking beside her, so much older now after a lifetime apart—their daughter's lifetime, in fact—yet a presence still so familiar, so reassuring.

The tread of his steps echoed on the wooden stairs as they climbed, and Megan couldn't shake off the surreal sensation as she took a seat on the top step beside him, somehow knowing they wouldn't go inside that apartment, the memories inside would be too emotionally charged, too much.

This top step was perfect, the moment all about promise. About first kisses. About making the choice to give in to the way they'd felt for each other, to fall in love. A reminder of the way they'd flirted during tutoring sessions. They'd gotten to know each other during long walks home.

For a long time they sat there, staring into the silence as the day predictably faded. Megan wondered if Nic was remembering, too, thought he might be. She could feel the warmth of his body, though he was careful not to touch her, and she was reminded of a newer memory, of the night in his condo, of how his mouth felt on hers, how right. Even after all this time. Even after all that had passed between them.

"I'm realizing that I need balance in my life," he finally said, his voice low, hushed in the fading quiet. "I want a life that involves more than work, more than worrying about all the people I shouldn't be worrying about anymore. It's time to let go of some things to make room for new things."

"Violet?"

"And you."

Megan's eyes fluttered shut, and everything went still. She didn't breathe, couldn't sense her pulse. The moment was utter stillness as she savored the impact of knowing he wanted her.

The way she wanted him.

"We've been given a second chance," he said softly.

She could barely push the words out, resisted reality intruding on the way she felt right now, knowing he wanted her, acknowledging how much she still wanted him. She'd never resolved her feelings for him. She'd run away, dealt with the consequences of their choices, but she'd given her heart to Nic and had never taken it back.

But Megan chose the honorable path this time when she recognized and understood the choices before her. There was no need to tell him how she felt. He already knew.

That much didn't need to be spoken.

"What about the past? The choices I've made?"

"I don't have all the answers, Megan. But I do know that I've never stopped loving you. I want you in my life. We can work through the rest of it. I mean, hell, we're already living with the results, and I don't want to waste any more time. Not with Violet, and not with you."

"You think you can learn to trust me again?"

"If you can trust me not to go *police chief* all over you."

Megan knew exactly where that had come from. "And you don't think she can compete with Damon yet?"

He shook his head. "*Police chief* isn't in the same league as *overbearing asshole*."

"Guess not."

"I need you and Violet to keep me in line. I've got

a long history of bossing people around. Just ask my family."

What Megan found most endearing, loving, *humbling,* was the way he twisted everything around to take the responsibility on himself. He may have done it consciously for once, but he was still Nic, responsible, protective, caring, wonderful Nic.

The years hadn't changed the man she'd fallen in love with.

And if he was willing to take a chance on her, on *them,* to forgive and work through the past and give them the chance for a *now,* then shouldn't she be willing to do the same?

There was only one answer.

Tonight was another first, the first kiss of their future. Only this time, she was the one who wrapped her arms around him, who pressed her mouth to his with seduction on her mind….

And loving him with everything she had to give.

CHAPTER TWENTY-SIX

"Who are you spying on, gorgeous?"

Violet jumped at the sound of Grandmama's voice. The blinds snapped into place with an accusing rattle and she spun to find her grandmother framed in the bedroom doorway.

She considered making up some excuse, but decided not to bother. This was Grandmama—she didn't miss a thing that went on around here. Took one to know one. Violet didn't miss a thing, either.

"Mom and Dad," she admitted. "They're outside."

"What are they doing?"

"They were talking." She grinned. "Now they're kissing."

Grandmama grinned back. "About time, don't you think?"

"I think."

Grandmama sat on the bed and patted the place beside her. Violet went to sit next to her, thinking about Camille or Esperanza and the way they could spend hours in bed talking about everything while they lurked on Facebook. Her grandmother was that *cool,* like a friend.

"Okay, so you're moving to town for at least a year, and your Mom and Dad are kissing. What comes next?"

Violet considered that. "Well, it'll probably be more like two years no matter what Mom says."

"That's even better. Your mom told me she'll be starting work here in around six weeks. Two months max. How does that work? When will you actually move?"

"We'll go back to Chile." Now that she knew they were definitely coming, she didn't have to worry about staying here with Dad. She had to go home and say goodbye to her friends. There'd be going-away parties and presents… "Mom will wrap up the project. We'll take the house apart, grab GigiMarie and come back here."

Grandmama considered that. "You know, I've never been to Chile."

"You haven't?" Violet acted surprised. "Got a passport?"

"I do. Got it to take a seniors' trip last year."

"Then you're all set. Did you know there's everything there? Mountains, desert, even penguins."

"Penguins, really? I had no idea."

Violet whipped out her phone and scrolled through her pictures. "No lie."

Grandmama took the phone and positioned the display in the light so she could see without her reading glasses. "Well, would you look at that? Penguins. I'd like to see one. A real one, I mean. Not like those in the zoo."

"They're really cute."

She handed the phone back. "I'm thinking your father could use a vacation, too. I can't remember the last time he went anywhere that wasn't for work. Do you think he'd come with me if I asked him?"

"Do police chiefs get to take vacations?"

Grandmama rolled her eyes and made Violet laugh.

"I think this police chief has so much unused vacation time, he could take a couple of years off."

"Then you should totally come down. If he gives you any grief, tell him you're scared to fly alone. He won't be able to tell you no."

"Ooh, I like that. Clever girl."

A matter of survival. Had to know how to work the old folks. "But you have to come right before we leave. Mom always takes off the week before we move so we can go around and see anything we've missed."

"What a fun thing to do."

"Mom's pretty big on having fun."

Wrapping an arm around Violet's shoulder, Grand-mama gave a squeeze. "I'm so glad you're here. Have I told you that lately?"

"Every day since I got here." Resting her head on Grandmama's shoulder, Violet admitted, "I don't think I'll get tired of hearing it."

"Good." She pressed a kiss on the top of Violet's head. "Will we all get to fly back together?"

"Yep." She lifted her head, met Grandmama's gaze and told her, "Then I'll have a year or two to figure out how to convince Mom that she wants to stay here for good."

Grandmama laughed. Then she hopped off the bed and went to the window. Lifting a slat, she peered through. "Still kissing. My guess is you won't have to do a thing, gorgeous. Looks like your dad will take it from here."

Violet was counting on it.

COMING NEXT MONTH

Available May 10, 2011

You can find more information on upcoming
Harlequin® titles, free excerpts and more at
www.HarlequinInsideRomance.com.

HSRCNM0411

*With an evil force hell-bent on destruction,
two enemies must unite to find a truth that turns
all-too-personal when passions collide.*

*Enjoy a sneak peek in Jenna Kernan's next installment
in her original* TRACKER *series, GHOST STALKER,
available in May, only from Harlequin Nocturne.*

"Who are you?" he snarled.

Jessie lifted her chin. "Your better."

His smile was cold. "Such arrogance could only come from a Niyanoka."

She nodded. "Why are you here?"

"I don't know." He glanced about her room. "I asked the birds to take me to a healer."

"And they have done so. Is that *all* you asked?"

"No. To lead them away from my friends." His eyes fluttered and she saw them roll over white.

Jessie straightened, preparing to flee, but he roused himself and mastered the momentary weakness. His eyes snapped open, locking on her.

Her heart hammered as she inched back.

"Lead who away?" she whispered, suddenly afraid of the answer.

"The ghosts. Nagi sent them to attack me so I would bring them to her."

The wolf must be deranged because Nagi did not send ghosts to attack living creatures. He captured the evil ones after their death if they refused to walk the Way of Souls, forcing them to face judgment.

"Her? The healer you seek is also female?"

"Michaela. She's Niyanoka, like you. The last Seer of Souls and Nagi wants her dead."

Jessie fell back to her seat on the carpet as the possibility of this ricocheted in her brain. Could it be true?

"Why should I believe you?" But she knew why. His black aura, the part that said he had been touched by death. Only a ghost could do that. But it made no sense.

Why would Nagi hunt one of her people and why would a Skinwalker want to protect her? She had been trained from birth to hate the Skinwalkers, to consider them a threat.

His intent blue eyes pinned her. Jessie felt her mouth go dry as she considered the impossible. Could the trickster be speaking the truth? Great Mystery, what evil was this?

She stared in astonishment. There was only one way to find her answers. But she had never even met a Skinwalker before and so did not even know if they dreamed.

But if he dreamed, she would have her chance to learn the truth.

Look for GHOST STALKER by Jenna Kernan, available May only from Harlequin Nocturne, wherever books and ebooks are sold.

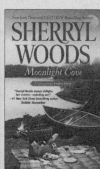
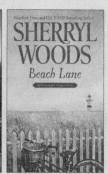